# Spinster's Folly

## Book 3: The Owen Family Saga

# Also by Marsha Ward

*That Tender Light*
*Gone for a Soldier*
*Spinster's Folly*
*Ride to Raton*
*Trail of Storms*

*Mended by Moonlight*

*The Zion Trail*

# Spinster's Folly

## Book 3: The Owen Family Saga

Marsha Ward

WestWard Books
෨◆ೲ
Payson, Arizona

**WestWard Books**
**P. O. Box 53**
**Payson, Arizona**
**www.westwardbooks.com**

Publisher's Note: This is a work of fiction. Names, characters, places, and incidents are either the product of the author's imagination, or are used fictitiously. Locales and public names are sometimes used for atmospheric purposes. Any resemblance to actual people, living or dead, or to businesses, companies, events, institutions, or locales is completely coincidental.

Cover Design: SelfPubBookCovers.com/INeedABookCover
Interior Design by Linda Boulanger/Tell~Tale Book Covers
And Marianna Robb/WW Design

**Spinster's Folly/ Marsha Ward**
ISBN 13: 978-0-9883810-0-1

# Dedication

To all the writers groups and associations that have helped me develop the craft of writing, from Mesa Writers Club to American Night Writers Association, and each one in between.

# Acknowledgments and Notes

*Spinster's Folly* would not have been possible without the powerful brainstorming efforts of Connie Wolfe and Kristie Clement Stevenson. These two good friends picked my ideas apart, tossed me new ones, and helped me come up with plot points that sparkle. I offer them my grateful thanks, along with members of American Night Writers Association who acted as early readers of parts of the manuscript; my community writers' group, Rim Country Writers, for their assistance in finding the places that didn't make sense to them; test readers Anna Arnett, Debra Erfert, Penny Freeman, Susan Haws, Margaret Turley, Kari Pike, Wendy Jorgensen and Carol LaValley (some of whom had never read a Western before), for their valuable insights; esteemed colleagues Johnny Boggs, Irene Bennett Brown, C.K. Crigger, L. J. Martin, and Rod Miller from Western Writers of America, for their generous endorsements of *Spinster's Folly*; numerous prior readers of my books, and fans from Facebook and my religious community, whose begging for a new book kept me motivated to write; and especially Kathy Van Horn, whose friendship and encouragement lights a glow in my heart.

Thank you to Janette and Guy Rallison for their winning bid in a charitable auction that allowed me to hang their names on a couple of my characters. "Any resemblance to actual persons," etc.

The terms "making love to" and "lover" had a different meaning in the 1860s than they do today. They equate to "wooing" and "suitor," so don't let your imagination run away.

# Chapter 1

Marie Owen pressed forward through the crowd that surrounded her brother Carl and his new bride. She pushed her way across the patch of trampled grass in the Colorado meadow, trying to get closer to the bridal pair. She could barely see Ma hugging on Ellen. Mrs. Bates dabbed at her eyes. Mr. Bates stood alongside them, looking stern. Pa stood back a bit, looking pleased with himself.

Someone in a great hurry to leave the site of the makeshift altar bumped Marie's shoulder hard, and a flailing hand knocked her bonnet askew. She cried out, "Have a care!" as she turned to see who had been so heedless, then shook her head as she realized it was only her next older brother, James, fleeing from Carl's triumphant grin.

"You behave, James," she muttered, loosening the strings beneath her chin so she could straighten her headgear. When she was satisfied that it was once again firmly in place, she returned to her purpose of reaching her best friend.

Her youngest brother, Albert, was her last obstacle. He had wormed his way to the front of the crowd, and was enthusiastically engaged in kissing Ellen's cheek. Marie elbowed the youth aside, reached her friend, and threw her arms around her.

"Lawsy," Marie whispered in Ellen's ear as she hugged her tight. "I'd begun to fear this day was never comin'. Now you're truly my sister!"

Ellen pushed back from the embrace slightly, her green eyes shining like dewdrops above her freckled cheeks. "It was so sudden. I didn't figure Pa would bring the priest with him." Her voice quivered. "Who would have thought . . ." She scanned the meadow, craning her neck as she looked back and forth. "Where is James?"

Marie squeezed Ellen's arm. "Now don't you fret about him on your weddin' day. He'll get over his disappointment."

"I want to tell him I am sorry."

"Don't you bother. He's been acting like such a ninny. It was plain as the nose on your face that you loved Carl and not him."

Ellen ducked her head, but when she raised it a moment later, her radiant smile bespoke her happiness.

Marie couldn't help kissing her cheek. "I'm thrilled for you," she murmured, and gave Ellen another hug.

"I cannot believe this happened so fast," Ellen whispered. She took a deep breath, then turned to look at Carl, who was sitting himself down on a chair, his face white.

Ellen's smile disappeared, and she turned back to Marie as people shoved against them. "Carl's bleedin'. I must get him to the cabin." She gripped Marie's shoulder. "You'll be next to marry," she said in a rush. "I see the way Bill Henry looks at you."

"What?" Marie protested, but Ellen had slipped away, entreating Rulon and Clay Owen to haul up the chair and carry Carl to the house.

Marie stood rooted in place by her friend's astonishing words. She watched a crimson stain spread across the hip of Carl's trousers, and a shiver of fear coursed down her spine. Carl had been wounded in a shootout with kidnappers. Surely he wouldn't bleed to death because he got out of bed to marry. Ellen was as good a nurse as anyone hereabouts. She would take ample care of Carl and pull him through this bad spell.

"James!" Ma's sharp call cut through the babble of voices.

Marie turned to see what had alarmed her mother, and saw James loping into the forest. She breathed out in exasperation. He had been so temperamental lately, stumping around like a bear with a hangnail.

"Rod, go see—"

Marie went to her mother's side. "He's fine, Ma. Give him a fortnight to clear his mind, and he'll be the light of your eyes again."

Ma grasped Marie's wrist without looking at her. She spoke

low. "Daughter, he's not fine. Make your pa go after him." She glanced down at her clenched hand, opened it, and let Marie go free. "Tell your pa—"

"James is man-grown, Ma."

Her mother seemed not to hear her. "Good, Rod is going." She called out, "Bring him back," sighed, gave herself a shake, then turned her attention to the departing newlyweds.

Marie shrugged her shoulders and followed her mother's gaze. Ellen walked beside Carl, fussing a little, patting his hand. His brothers carried his chair toward the little log house Carl had built with his own hands to receive his bride. No matter that his wife wasn't the one Pa had intended for him. It seemed such an age since Pa had connived to arrange marriages for two of his sons before they'd all fled the ruins of the Shenandoah Valley and headed out here to Colorado Territory. Carl's betrothed, Ida Hilbrands, was long gone.

"Good riddance," Marie said aloud.

"Good riddance to what?" a young female voice asked behind her.

Marie jumped and whirled to face her younger sister. "Julianna! Don't creep up on me like that. It's not ladylike."

"What do you know about being a lady? More like a spinster, if you ask me."

"Spinster? Don't you call me names!"

"I will if I want to. You're gettin' awful long in the tooth, Marie. You've got no beaus in sight, but I do. I'll be married soon."

"You're lyin' to make me feel bad. You're only thirteen!"

"I'll be fourteen soon," she simpered. "Mama wasn't much older'n that when she and Papa wed."

"You're ridiculous, Jule. Nobody marries so young anymore."

"And you're an old maid, 'cause you're overripe. Papa surely wasn't thinking when he left you off his marryin' list." She swished her skirt with both hands and stuck out her tongue.

Marie felt warm blood rising into her neck and face at her sister's insolence. "Leave Pa out of this," she barked. "You see how well his plans turned out." She gestured toward the departing couple. "True affection conquered his meddlesome—" She

3

fumbled for a word, then spat out, "meddling. Ellen is happy, and so am I."

Julianna smirked, pointing toward the forest. "James ain't happy. He stomped off. Papa went after him, glowerin' almost as much as James."

Marie balled her fists, glaring at her sister. "Thank you for telling me something I already know, Miss Snippety Nose. James'll mend, given enough time."

"But in no time at all, Papa will have to put you on the shelf. Nobody will even look at you by Christmas, old maid!"

∞

Marie turned and stalked off toward the plank tables set out under the oak trees nearby. When Ma had found out Carl was rising from his bed to get married, she had bustled about—with the aid of Rulon's Mary—and put together a special wedding dinner. Well, special, if you count honey drizzled on corn cakes as special. Add the meat pulled from the bones of a few roasted chickens, gallons of milk, cold from sitting in stone crocks in the spring, and the meal could pass as special.

No matter what irritating things Julianna may say, Marie couldn't take the time to tussle with her. There was aplenty of work to do today. Even so, she felt burgeoning anger consuming her good sense as she eyed a washtub full of tableware sitting on the grass beside the table. Which of her brothers had left the dishes on the ground instead of putting them on the table? *Inconsiderate clod!* She bent over, pulled a stack of tin plates from the tub, and slammed them onto the table. Her ears rang with the cacophonous sound. She retrieved a second bunch of plates, dropped them onto the first pile, then grabbed a double handful of tin cups, which she banged down on the planks, not caring if she dented them.

After a few moments of rebellion, reveling in the clinks and clanks of the tinware, she straightened up, put her hands at her waist and stretched her back. Then she blew an escaping lock of hair out of her eyes and twisted the kinks out of her neck. Remembering that—despite Carl and Ellen's hasty withdrawal—

4

there were still plenty of folks to feed, served to pull her out of her misery and helped her transform back into sensible, responsible Marie.

The Spanish priest robed in brown was the first to enter the shade under the oak trees, wiping sweat from his forehead with his sleeve. The Texas cowboys followed, discussing the possibility of a shiveree that night. Mr. and Mrs. Bates came along with Ma. Pa was nowhere to be seen, but the rest of the family pressed forward, intent upon taking nourishment after the arduous work of getting Carl wed.

Marie hurried to get behind the food-laden table to serve as her younger brothers pushed and shoved to position themselves at the head of the line in order to grab generous portions. Marie smacked the backs of their hands with the bowl of the honey spoon.

"Ow!" howled Albert. "There's no call to beat me."

"Guests first," she replied, pointing with the spoon. "Get yourselves to the back of the line."

Clay licked honey off the back of his hand and glared at Marie, but obeyed without a word.

Mr. Bates escorted the priest to the head of the now-orderly line, accompanied by many polite gestures on the part of both men. Marie smiled at the priest, racking her brain for something to say, then, as she heaped his plate, remembered a Spanish word she'd heard recently. "*Señor,*" she said, and made a bobbing sort of curtsey.

"*Muchas gracias, muy amable,*" he said, smiling back at her and making little crosses in the air over the food table.

"Muchas grachius," she parroted back, wondering what she'd just said as the priest moved on.

By and by, everyone who had crowded around the table had their plates full, and all were engaged in seeking places to sit to devour the comestibles. After consolidating the leftovers, Marie picked up a plate and fork.

Just then, an excited voice called from the woods, "Hey, James is riding the mustang!" The Owen brothers and the cowboys abandoned their plates and cups on the grass and hurried off to see the spectacle.

Marie watched them go, then forked up a bit of chicken, put a corn cake on her plate, and drenched it with honey. She found a place to sit by herself on the grass, and bit into the sweetened breadstuff. The bland corn cake reminded her of all such dry mouthfuls she'd endured in the years since Lincoln's Northern soldiers had come marching into Virginia. As she chewed, she wished she'd thought to get a cupful of milk. Eventually, the honey helped ease the ground corn down her throat. She dearly hoped Pa would trade a beef cow or two for part of Mr. Bates's wheat crop after harvest time. Wheat bread would be such a welcome change.

Young Roddy, Rulon's boy, came galloping under the oaks astride a stick Pa had fitted with a stuffed horse head made of burlap. "The horsie bucked," he announced in a high, shrill voice. "Unca James fell off." He pranced around his mother. "Mama, he said bad words."

Marie didn't fight the chortle the boy's comment brought upon her. *I reckon he did*, she thought, covering her mouth. *James don't like blemishes on his reputation as a horseman.* She watched Mary bend over and exhort her son about sticking close to her. *That baby's growin' up. Good thing Mary's got a new wee one to dote on.*

Her good humor faded as her heart constricted. She had empty arms and no prospects for a man to help her fill them with a babe of her own. She wondered if Julianna's words about her being an old maid had any truth. She was eighteen years old, after all. She closed her eyes and felt a chill move up her spine.

Rulon had taken Mary to wife years ago, just before he went to the war. Roddy had come along in the due course of time. Now Carl had wed Ellen. When was her time to marry and have a family? Had it passed her by when Virginia got tangled up in that cursed fight? Marie shivered as the chill enveloped the rest of her body. So many young men had gone for soldiers. So many hadn't returned home once the fighting was done. Now she was way out here in Colorado Territory. Her chances for finding a suitor weren't showing any more promise than they had during the Unpleasantness.

Marie opened her eyes as she heard a murmur of male voices

and a few laughs. Evidently the show at the corral was over. The cowboys drifted back to the serving table and piled their plates a second time.

She shook off her somber thoughts and wondered if she should take Carl and Ellen a bite of dinner. Surely, with Carl so sorely wounded, the two of them wouldn't be in a romantic frame of mind.

But what if they were? She wouldn't dare interrupt their honeymoon.

"Oh claptrap," she muttered. "If Carl's hungry, Ellen will fetch something to feed him."

"I reckon that's so," a male voice said. "May I refill your plate, Miss Marie?"

Drawing in a gasp of air and jerking to attention, Marie almost spilled the food remaining on her plate to the ground. *Bill Henry!*

It took her a moment to recover from her surprise at his overture, but she eventually replied, "I . . . reckon I have plenty to eat here, thank you, Mr. Henry. You're most obliging to ask."

"Not even a cup of milk?"

"No. No, I'm real content." She smoothed her woolen skirt, brushing at a wrinkle.

"Well then, would it be amiss if I joined you here while I ate?"

"Ma might need me," she said, trying unsuccessfully to figure out how to get to her feet in a ladylike manner.

"I reckon she's otherwise occupied, bidding folks good-bye," Mr. Henry said, looking in Mrs. Owen's direction. She stood near a cluster of horses, talking to Mrs. Bates.

"Suit yourself," Marie murmured, wishing she didn't feel so flustered. Bill Henry was a mighty good-looking man, with those deep blue eyes sparkling in his broad, tanned face. But if he had courtship in mind, he was wasting his time talking her. Pa wasn't likely to give his consent to a match of his daughter with a cowhand. *Except it's very likely Pa hasn't given me much thought at all. He has always worried first about setting his boys up in life.* Be that as it may, all the world knew that sooner or later, Mr. Henry was heading back to Texas. Marie's stomach began to ache.

Now he sat beside her in one smooth movement and tucked

into his food. After chewing up a bite of dark chicken meat, he swallowed and looked at her. "Surprising doin's today." He gestured in the direction of Carl's cabin. "Your brother's got pluck to stand up on that leg and get married."

"There's no shortness of pluck amongst my brothers, Mr. Henry," Marie said, measuring her words. "Every single one of them is stuffed full of it. You'd think it would run out their ears, they're so plucky." The last word almost exploded from her lips. Exasperation unexpectedly rose up like gall in her throat. "Pa built it into them from the time they were in short pants."

"Whoa there." Mr. Henry held up his hands. "What did I say to cause you hurt, miss?"

She picked at a stem of grass beside her skirt, pulling it to pieces, playing for time to settle her voice into more suitable tones. She glanced up, saw that the Bates family was riding off with the Spanish preacher in tow. "Nothing, sir," she finally said after taking a deep breath. "I'm right pleased to see my brother wed. Nothing gives me more joy than the happiness of Miss Ellen, my good friend." She knew she was enunciating her words carefully, but she couldn't help the brusque note that had crept into her voice. Somehow, it went well with her stomachache.

"Is it your brothers' pluck or your pa's heavy-handedness that has you in a dither, miss?" Mr. Henry softened his critical words with a quick smile that briefly lifted the corners of his moustache.

"My pa? Heavy-handed? Oh, yes," she said, her voice sounding sarcastic to her ears. She gave a little shudder, and tried to remember herself, tried to beat back the great ache cramping her midsection. She finally managed a more moderate tone, saying, "I'm speaking out of turn, Mr. Henry. My pa is an honorable man."

"He is that," he agreed. "He's also a commandin' figure of a man who wants every soul to do his will."

She didn't reply. There was nothing to debate in his words.

"Aside from that," he said, a muffled snort escaping his throat, "he's my boss, so I reckon *I'm* speakin' out of turn, as well." He lifted his hat and smoothed back his light brown hair before he carefully replaced the hat. "Beggin' your pardon, miss, I'd best get back to my work."

Marie looked around. The cowboys had drifted away and the glade was empty of guests. Only Albert remained, still stuffing food into his apparently bottomless maw. "It appears our weddin' party has come to an end," she said, rearranging the utensils on her plate. "I reckon it's time for me to gather the dishes and such."

He helped her to her feet without further comment, and walked her over to the tables. "I'm grateful for our talk, Miss Marie, even if I am a fair lummox at conversatin'."

"You have no fault in speaking," she said, a bit too forcefully. She looked downward. "I must beg your pardon for putting you ill at ease. I haven't been the best company." She looked up again, right into soft blue eyes that seemed to see into her soul. "I fear I've been a bit, um, cranky."

He bent his head, accepting her apology. "Next time, I'll not come up and surprise you, miss."

She nodded, and he went away, leaving his plate behind on the table. She picked it up and ran her fingers slowly around the smooth rim as she watched him go, her attention fixed on the power in his easy stride. When she realized what her fingers were doing, she hastily set down the plate, pulled her attention back to her chore and made piles of the remains of the meal. Her thoughts buzzed in disarray, crossing one upon the other as she worked.

*That Bill Henry! Is he toying with me? Jule thinks I'm ugly. Am I, truly? All the county boys said I was pretty. Why didn't Pa set me up with a husband when he arranged matches for the boys? I was plenty old enough to get wed. There's hardly anybody out here. Why did Mr. Henry come to sit with me? He is surely going back to Texas. Is Jule right and I'm ripe for the shelf? Why did the county boys go to war? They left me behind to wither away. What does a handsome devil like Mr. Henry want with a homely spinster? He likely left a sweetheart waiting for him. Who is there left to hold his nose and marry me? A Mexican? Tom Morgan? He never played up to me. Tom always hankered after Ellen more than James did. I'll wager Bill kissed a pretty young thing farewell when Pa hired him on. Why didn't Pa think of me?*

Afraid she might dissolve into tears and betray her fragile state of mind to her brother, Marie dumped the dirty dishes into the washtub and fled with it toward the house.

ॐ

Pa burst into the cabin, flinging the door open so hard that it banged against the wall. Marie, placing a stack of washed plates on the shelf beside the fireplace, felt the shaved boards vibrate from the concussion.

"Pa!" She let go of the plates and steadied the pair of kerosene lamps teetering on the shelf. "Mind the lamps."

"He's left! He didn't even come say goodbye to his ma."

"What do you mean? Who's left?" Marie went to close the door, a sick premonition washing through her.

"Your brother. He has no more sense than a beetle, pining over a girl who doesn't care for him." He paced around the room, angrily pounding a fist into his open hand.

She crossed the distance between them and laid her fingers on her father's arm. The queasiness settled in her stomach. "James? Where's he gone to?"

"North. He has an idea of working your uncle's mine. Darn fool boy." He left Marie's grasp and sank into his chair. "He wouldn't even take my coin."

She hesitated, but couldn't keep her question back. "Did you tell Ma? She'll be heartsick."

"Don't I know it!" He shook his head. "She wasn't in sight. I figured she was here in the house."

"She's around back washing the stew kettle. I'll go fetch her." She started towards the door.

"Missy Marie?" Pa's voice sounded worn out, but he got to his feet as she turned around. "I'll do it. You go find the family. Bring 'em all," he said, then paused, gently probing the healing furrow on his scalp where a bullet had grazed him recently, as though it would aid his thought process. "No, leave Carl be. We'll tell him later."

She stood in the open doorway gazing at her father. "Pa," she started, then stopped, uncertainty flooding over her. Her throat tightened, but she finally croaked, "How did James look?"

He snorted. "Full of ire and pride. I reckon he won't be back for a spell."

ɞ

Marie shuddered as she left the cabin. She'd surely misjudged James's hurt. Her thoughts raced, full of foreboding at James's lonely flight. *What if he never comes back? What if a mineshaft falls in on him? What if a mountain lion eats him? What if he falls off a cliff? What if a lowlife sticks a knife in him? What if he dies alone in the mountains?* She looked around the compound as though unsure where to start her search, then set off on her task. Where were her brothers? Where was that scamp, Jule?

She found Albert feeding the horses, and told him to get home as soon as he had finished. Clay labored in the shade of the oaks, taking apart the tables and bundling the planks together so he could cart them to the shed.

"Pa wants us at home," she said. "Soon as you can get there. Have you seen Jule?"

Clay glanced up, blowing a lock of his hair out of an eye. "Can't say that I have. Tell Pa I'll be there when I can." He looked hard at Marie. "Something's amiss?"

She bit her lip. "That's for Pa to recount. Hurry."

When Clay nodded, she turned away, thinking about where her sister could have taken herself. Then she remembered the girl's preoccupation with marriage and ran toward Carl's cabin tucked into the woods.

As she rounded the final bend in the path, she was horrified to see her sister with her back pressed against the log wall of the cabin, listening at the window. Marie darted forward, grabbed her wrist, and hauled her away from the cabin.

"Leave me be!" Julianna shrieked. "Turn me loose!"

Ellen put her head out of the window, a startled look on her face, and pulled the shutters closed.

"See there, now I won't hear anything," the younger girl ranted, struggling against Marie's restraining hand. "You're so mean."

11

"What a despicable thing to do, spying on the newlyweds like that. For shame!" Marie said, tightening her hold and wrapping her other arm around Julianna in a further effort to get her away from the scene. "Whatever possessed you?"

"I need to know about things," Julianna shouted, wriggling in Marie's embrace. "Ma won't tell me what folks do when they're married. I've got to know."

"It's none of your business. You're not married, and won't be for a long spell." Since they were now a suitable distance from the cabin, Marie stopped dragging Julianna away, and stood blocking the path so she couldn't return.

The girl shrugged off Marie's arms and spat out, "I'll be wed before you. Parley Morgan's sweet on me. I wager we'll get married by next spring."

"Parley? That's preposterous! He's ages older than you! Get to the house." Marie pointed to the cabin and shook her finger in emphasis.

Julianna stood upright, thin chest thrust forward, arms akimbo, and spewed out venomous words. "You're jealous. You don't have a beau. You won't ever have a beau. You're too old to catch one!"

Marie felt her cheeks burn. Her hand swung in a short arc and caught Julianna on *her* cheek. "You little vixen," she yelled. "You mind your tongue. Ma's going to hear of this, but not today. She's got enough grief to bear. Get home!"

Julianna turned and stormed off down the path toward the main cabin, muttering imprecations beneath her breath. Marie followed, trying to calm down. It infuriated her that Jule had such power over her. In a few words, she'd managed to throw Marie's world into a blazing, furious uproar, and she didn't like the feeling.

Ma would be beside herself when she learned James took off. She'd only recently got over a measure of her grief from losing Peter, then Ben in the fighting. How could she stand the thought of losing another son to anger? "Pa won't be much use to comfort her," she mumbled out loud in the direction of Jule's retreating back. "He's madder'n a cat caught in a rain barrel."

ʚɞ

Marie shooed Jule into the cabin, and saw that someone had informed Rulon and Mary of the family meeting. They must barely have arrived ahead of herself and her sister. They still huddled together on the periphery of the family gathered around the table.

Rulon had a protective arm around his wife's shoulders as she bounced their infant daughter in her arms. Roddy, still riding his stick horse, galloped around the room. Marie wondered which of her younger brothers would remember to be a gentleman and allow Mary to sit in his chair.

Ma sat in a chair at the head of the table, her face pinched and white as though she knew something horrible was in the air. Pa stood behind her, his forehead drawn into severe lines above his gray eyes. He waved Marie and Julianna into the room, then waited silently while they approached the table.

Clay remembered his manners, quit his chair, drew up a bench, and shoved Albert's shoulder so he would give up his seat. Rulon helped Mary into the chair Albert had abandoned, and Marie perched on the other. The three younger siblings arranged themselves on the bench and fell silent.

Pa took one deep breath, then another. His inhalations and exhalations filled the quiet in the cabin. Marie held her own breath while her father spoke.

"I have hard news. Your brother has taken it into his head that he's not welcome here, so he rode out. He said he'd try his hand at mining. Mining! He's not cut out for going into a hole in the ground." He punctuated his words by smacking his fist into his open hand. In the stillness, the act made a surprising amount of noise.

As Pa's voice died away, a hush moved in to replace it, lasting for perhaps three seconds, stretching and pulling the air until it seemed thin and suffocating. No one moved. Then Rulon leaned forward and said, "You can't be serious, Pa. I reckon he'll ride around a while and come back home, leaving his troubles in the wind."

At the same time, Albert asked, "Can I have his cabin?" at

which Clay cuffed him on the side of the head, yelling, "You ornery son of a—" then bit his lip before he got his own cuffing from Pa for swearing.

Julianna had burst into tears when Rulon spoke. She cried out, "That's not fair! James said he'd take me rabbit hunting."

"Hush, Jule!" Ma said sharply, then dissolved into tears herself, throwing her apron over her head, which served to muffle her sobs a bit.

Albert threw his own punch, then launched himself at Clay, at which the bench went over backwards. Julianna screamed, rubbing her head where it had hit the floor.

Marie finally exhaled, then repeatedly tried to draw air into her protesting lungs, listening to the hubbub without adding more than her gasps to it as she clenched her hands into balls in her lap.

Pa bent over Ma, awkwardly patting her shoulder and making shushing sounds. He looked up and glared at Albert and Clay, who were rolling on the floor, trading blows. Then he included Julianna in his entreaties, trying to quiet her sobs.

Marie hid her face in her hands, overcome with the selfishness of her younger siblings . . . and herself. *Oh James*, she thought, *will I ever see you again? It was wrong of me to think only of Ellen's happiness and not see your side of the hill. I didn't know you cared so much.*

Then Pa cleared his throat and Marie spread her fingers so she could look at him. He drew himself up to his full height. Marie saw a change in his aspect that meant he had gone from comforter to patriarch. "Silence!" he shouted into the noise.

The family members slowly lapsed into silence, Clay and Albert sprawled on the floor, giving each other hard looks. Rulon leaned down, extended a hand to each boy, and hauled them to their feet, giving them quiet words of brotherly admonition.

Pa's brow remained crinkled, and Marie wondered if his worried countenance reflected concern for his son or astonishment that James had defied his father's will.

When he spoke, Pa's tone was commanding. "James is still part of this family, no matter how long he's gone, so we will not be parceling off his belongings just yet. If he's gone more than a year, we'll think about what that means at that time."

Ma let out a moan at Pa's words, and he patted her shoulder again, but followed up the action with a crisper note in his voice. "There now, Julie, don't borrow trouble. He's going to find himself by and by and return home a wiser man."

Ma grabbed Pa's hand and said, "Oh Rod," in a mournful tone.

Marie couldn't look at the naked grief in her mother's face any longer, and turned her eyes away. *Godspeed, James*, she thought. *Come back soon.*

"But Pa," Albert said, "if James don't come back in a hurry, we'll lose his homestead. I reckon I should prove up what he's started."

"You're not old enough," Clay said with a glare at his younger brother. "If anyone can do it, I can."

"You're not old enough, either," Rulon put in. He stroked his chin, then looked at his fingers and rubbed them together. "What if Marie takes the cabin? She's nearly of age."

"It hardly matters if she's of age or not," Pa said. "We bore arms against the Union. None of us can expect to hold our homestead claims, if any should want them."

Rulon's face went white. "We're squatters? I didn't know that."

"I didn't see fit to tell you, once I learned the way of the homestead law. When the time comes to apply for the land rights, we're God-fearing Yankees from West Virginia, you hear?"

Ma was no longer crying. She looked at Pa, her mouth working for a moment before any words came out. "You wouldn't say that." Her tone was low and her words clipped.

"I would say I was a black-skinned slave man if it would get us title to the land!"

"I didn't bear arms," Marie cut in, as she stood up and planted her hands, palms down, on the table. "I can get land on my own, and it will be done honestly." She raised her chin, knowing her defiant words would hurt her father. What did that matter? He had hurt her, putting her welfare last on his list. She looked over at Rulon, whose face was now pinched with worry. "Rule, I would not be a squatter. I can file for your land and sell it to you in exchange for a," she paused and thought, then continued, "a cow."

"There'll be no more talk of this sort," Pa declared, his face working as though he were suffering a fit. "No one is going to do us out of the land. We'll get title to it one way or another. We're here, and it's ours." He brought his fist down on the table, and Marie knew the discussion of James's departure and the status of their homesteads was over. She let out a breath. *Be safe, James, wherever you go.*

# Chapter 2

*He's gone and done it*, Bill Henry thought as he saddled a horse the next morning. *Defied his pa and gone off. He's got more gumption than I thought he did.*

Bill swung into the saddle, gathered the reins, and clucked to his mount, a frisky dun mustang, one of the horses Mr. Owen had bought in Texas. The animal frog-jumped and bucked for a few minutes, but Bill stuck tight and waited out the horse's temper tantrum. The dun would settle down soon and carry him through the morning without further complaint.

Yes, James Owen had sand, he had to give him that. Who else around here was willing to go toe-to-toe and have it out with the fearsome Rod Owen? Nobody else he could name, including himself.

The dun gave a final crow-hop, then stood quiet, waiting for guidance. Bill crossed his wrists, rested them on the saddle horn, and gave himself up to a moment of reverie.

He was no coward, but he had no reason to butt heads with the Old Man, because he didn't hanker to leave Colorado Territory at this time. He'd given his word that he'd teach the Owen men the cattle business. Even though he was without kin in this place, it suited him fine to light here a while, there being no work for him in Texas.

*Besides, if I head back now, I'll never see Miss Marie again.*

There it was, finally, the hitherto unspoken reason for staying. He smoothed his moustache as he contemplated his situation. The Owen boys had caught on to every cattle-handling trick he'd taught them much faster than he'd supposed they would. Nothing kept him here beyond that obligation. Except . . . *I don't want to leave her.*

Bill exhaled. Now the big bear had been flushed into the open, so to speak, and he had to face it or turn tail and run. He'd not ever admitted to himself that in the few short weeks since he'd arrived in Colorado Territory, he had grown mighty fond of the pretty, dark-haired daughter of his boss. Now he let himself acknowledge that he had grown serious feelings for the sprightly miss. Truth was, he'd taken to being on hand when she rode out each morning to exercise her horse. That way he had a glimpse of her to carry in his thoughts throughout the long hours he spent dealing with slab-sided cattle.

No point in avoiding reality. Marie Owen was the reason he was willing to stay on in this unnaturally green land beneath the mountain.

He whispered her name and smiled so broadly that his moustache tickled his cheeks. The very sound, Marie, had a sort of music in it.

Finally realizing that daylight was a-burning, Bill clucked and put his heels into the dun's flanks, turning it toward the uphill path.

He wondered if there was any chance he could woo Miss Marie, any chance of persuading her to marry him. She was prettier than any girl he'd seen before. Feeling as he did about her, he had to try. She was worth every effort to win her.

How could he forget the day he'd met the girl? He'd ramrodded Old Man Owen's cattle drive from Texas. As he, his cowhands, and the Owen men drove the livestock up this same mountain, they encountered the little sister, half paralyzed with fear. She'd barely missed being taken off by an outlaw band. She was safe, but the varmints had kidnapped Marie and the Bates girl.

The whole bunch of them left the beeves behind and tracked the outlaws to a cave, where they managed to recover the girls. That victory came at great cost. His own cousin had paid the ultimate price.

For a moment, Bill let the barely abated grief of losing Bob wash over him, but his cheerful mood didn't want to go toward darkness just now. He shook it off and went back to more pleasant memories of that day.

On the way down the mountain after the shooting affair, they'd stumbled across a deep pool of water surrounded by protective boulders, and so shaded by trees that the water appeared black. Rulon Owen called a brief halt to better bind up Carl's wounds so he wouldn't expire from loss of blood.

Marie rested beside the pool, clearly anxious over Carl's dire condition and desirous of reaching the safety of home. He gave her a tin cup to dip into the water. She looked up at him, gratitude in her eyes as she thanked him for being in the rescue party.

That was the moment she had captured his interest. Even bedraggled as she was, with her shoulders and sleeves covered with dirt and her hair tangled and bedecked with twigs and leaves, she was the most beautiful creature he had ever seen.

Since that day, he had thought of the pool as *their* special spot. Not that they'd ever been back to it, but they would, someday. Maybe when he asked—

The sound of rapid hoof beats brought him out of his reverie. Who was riding a horse hard this early in the morning? Was James Owen coming back?

He looked around for the horse. When he located it, he saw a skirt billowing behind and knew it was Marie. Irritation washed over him. She knew better than to treat horseflesh so harshly. Then concern for her welfare crowded out the negative thought. Had the horse run away with her? Was someone chasing her? He didn't know the state of affairs with the Indian tribes in the area. Maybe she'd had a run in with a party of hostiles.

Bill rode toward the girl, gigging the dun into a gallop, his heart beating as fast as the hooves on the earth. Then he was choking, trying to swallow his fear as he saw her terrified face. Something was horribly wrong.

When he came near, he swung his horse around and caught up to hers. She held only one rein. The other hung loose, dragging on the ground. He leaned over and tried to grab it. She resisted, fending off his hand, shoving it away.

He called out sharply to her, "Don't run the horse," then wished he'd kept his mouth shut. For one thing, it filled with dust, and for another, she looked sideways at him with such wide eyes and such a grimness on her face that she looked as though he'd slapped her.

"Foolish," he muttered, half under his breath.

He chased Marie back to the stable, wishing he'd let her run the horse towards him in the first place. He berated himself the whole time until he pulled up his mount, kicked free of the stirrups, and launched himself out of the saddle.

By this time, Marie's horse had stopped in front of the stable, sides heaving and lathered. The girl slipped off and would have collapsed in a heap if Bill hadn't caught her. She breathed in concert with the laboring horse for a moment, then drew herself up and stepped out of Bill's arms.

"Don't touch me, Mr. Henry," she snapped, and the coldness of her tone brought Bill up short, rocking back on his heels as though *she* had slapped *him*.

"What happened?" he asked. His voice sounded harsh in his ears.

"What does it matter? I'm not foolish."

Bill inhaled sharply. She must have thought his muttered, self-deprecating remark had been aimed at her.

"I didn't mean you." The explanation came too late. Marie's scathing gaze lingered on him for a moment, then she stalked off, jerking on the reins to pull her horse along behind her into the stable.

"Henry." He turned and met the stern eyes of the Old Man. "Get about your work," he commanded, motioning with his head toward the mountain.

Bill nodded and remounted, regret flooding his thoughts. *Not a good start to the day.*

෨෨

*What power on earth or heaven gives him the right to speak to me like that?* Marie fumed as she tromped into the stable. *What an inconsiderate clod, thinking I was foolish to run the horse.* She shook herself, her body still encased in the terror she'd felt as her mount shied to get away from the striking snake and then ran away with her. She'd lost the reins and the stirrups, and almost fell off when the animal had begun to race back toward home.

She'd finally calmed down enough to get her feet back in the stirrups and one rein in her hand when Mr. Heroic Henry had caught up to her. But when he'd leaned over to grab the trailing rein and she'd felt the horse gathering itself to jump away, her sheer terror had returned. Hadn't he seen her predicament? Didn't he care that she was about to be thrown off? What a lout he must be, uncaring and thoughtless of her well-being! Why did men always want to be the heroes?

Marie slid the saddle off the horse and, despite its sidestepping, managed to remove the bit and bridle. Thank goodness she had been riding astride a Western-style saddle with an upright horn. Otherwise she would've had nothing to hang onto. *What if I'd been riding sidesaddle?*

As Marie brushed down her horse, her opinion of Mr. Henry did not improve. *Selfish oaf!* Her brushing increased in both speed and depth.

"Daughter, the horse won't have any coat if you don't lighten your touch."

Marie turned at her father's voice, and almost flung the brush at him. "Imagine that," she said in a strident tone. "You care more for your animals than you do for me." She threw the brush into the corner and flounced toward the door.

"Hold up, there!" Pa said, catching her by the shoulders and turning her to face him. "What's distressin' you? Did that Texas cowhand give you an insult? I'll whip his hide back to the Staked Plains if he did."

Marie held herself stiff against her father's hands. "Pa." Her words were clipped. "It's not him. No. You might say it's him. No. It's mainly you. You don't care a fig for me." She ducked her head, gulped air, then raised her chin, and her words flowed more freely. "You're worked up at James and his leaving. It hardly matters to you that I've got no prospects, no future here."

"Now girl, that's not so." Pa's face burned red. "You've got everything to look forward to. A nice house by and by, plenty of chickens, a kitchen garden. This land will grow a passel of greens, I'll wager."

"Greens!" Marie endeavored to lean away from him, feeling trapped within his confining grip. "You think this is about gardens and eggs and livin' out my life in a fine house with you and Ma? You're wrong." She paused and drew a deep breath, then spit out her words. "I'm upset because there's no one hereabouts for me to marry. No one to cherish me and care about my dreams and wishes."

He dropped his hold on Marie and stood bolt upright, looking like he'd been whacked upside the head with a cast iron skillet.

She continued, feeling as though her insides were squeezed together from the anger that ballooned against her ribs. "You didn't think of that, did you?" Her voice rose. "You were so set on fixin' things up with the neighbors and arrangin' marriages for the boys." She was shouting now. "You didn't give me a single thought."

He seemed to recover himself, then said, "You have it wrong, daughter. I've had it in mind for you and Tom Morgan to wed bye and bye. You're both a bit young yet."

"Young!" Marie almost stamped her foot, but instead brought her bunched fists up to her chin. "Pa, how old do you figure I am? How old do you reckon he is?"

He scratched his head. "Ain't you about fifteen? Tom needs to get set up, grow his crops and sell them, build you a house. There's plenty of time."

Marie felt her heart shrivel in her chest. This was worse than she'd thought. "I'm eighteen," she whispered, her words measured. "Tom is twenty." Her voice rose again. "We're not babies, but at this rate, I won't ever *have* any of those."

He narrowed his eyes. "Eighteen? When did you get to be that age?"

She looked at the floor, anger shaking her body, then looked at her father. Her emotion drained away as she watched his shoulders slump. "How old are you, Pa? Didn't you gain any years while you were away fighting a war?"

He let out his breath in a great gusty sigh. After a few moments of silence, he spoke in a voice tinged with regret. "I didn't do right by you, daughter. I should have been thinkin' that you were growin' up alongside your brothers. I reckon I thought you'd always be my little girl."

Marie's anger boiled anew. She snapped, "I'm not so little now, Pa. I've grown old and lonely on account of the Unpleasantness. Where's my chance for happiness?" She gestured out the door. "This place is nothing but a nice-lookin' graveyard for me."

"That's not so, girl. The countryside is full of young men. Why, there's . . ." He scratched his head again. "Tom, of course, and well, Parley—"

"Who's younger'n me," she interrupted.

"How about one of those young boys I brought back from Texas? That Henry fellow's not so bad, I reckon."

"You were going to whip his hide back to where he came from."

"He's a stout lad, and he knows his business."

"He's bound to go home soon." Marie swallowed hard. "Probably left a girl behind he's anxious to wed." She kicked at a clump of straw, gathering courage to make an outrageous suggestion. "I suppose the Dominguez boys are out of the question?"

Pa looked startled. "They're Mexicans, girl."

"They've been in this territory longer'n we have." Marie twitched her skirt. "They're citizens now. And landowners. Land owners. That's more than we can say."

"But they're not our kind." He brushed the back of his fist across his chin.

Her eyes closed. "Of course. So I have few choices for suitors and little time to marry before I'm truly an old maid, as Jule claims." She opened her eyes, turned away and headed for the door.

He called out before she could leave the stable, "Daughter. Chester Bates says he'll have done harvesting his wheat in a few weeks. I plan to drive a few head of beef steers down to trade for grain. Why don't you come along?"

He paused, and she looked back to see if he expected an answer.

Pa continued, "I'll take a look at Tom and see if he's ready to make a match." He was silent for a moment, then frowned and said, "We'll go on Thursday. Mr. Bates will be good for the wheat after harvest."

Marie didn't reply aloud. She swept a trailing lock of hair from her forehead and thought as she turned away, *At least Pa's finally thinkin' about me. I only hope Tom's ready to settle down.*

&

As he rode toward the group of cowboys gathered at the foot of the trail, Bill wondered if his job was in jeopardy. Mr. Owen hadn't been pleased when he'd caught Bill loitering around the stable talking to his daughter.

*I wasn't harming her, even if she tells her pappy what a dunderhead I am,* he thought. *My lands, she's pretty when her eyes snap fire!*

Bill arrived at the trailhead where the cowboys awaited him, and one of them, Chico Henderson, laughed.

He said, "You got you a woebegone visage, Henry. What's eatin' you?" The cowhand circled his horse around Bill, then drew up in front of him and laughed again. "Saw the daughter out early. Did she waylay you? Is that why you're late?"

"Cut out the palaver, Chico. There's work to be done." Bill pulled the dun's head to the side so he could pass his fellow Texan, and kicked it into motion.

"Don't put your eggs in that basket," Chico said, then laughed a third time.

Bill gritted his teeth. He already felt discombobulated from his encounter with Miss Marie. Tangling with Chico would only put his mood more off-kilter, so he gigged his horse up the trail toward the herd.

Maybe Chico was right. Maybe he shouldn't set his sights on a dubious dream. Mr. Owen would never let his daughter marry the likes of him—a dusty cowhand with nothing to his name but a horse, a saddle, and a lariat. Well, there was the ranch down in Texas, if it hadn't already been claimed by one mangy, tweed-backed carpetbagger or another for taxes due. He'd better keep his dreams within reason. He could never take Old Man Owen's pride and joy a thousand miles away to live.

*Humph! It would serve the Old Man right if Miss Marie left hearth and home and went off to live her own life, far away from pappy. Wouldn't he rant and rave if his daughter showed her own mind and joined her brother in setting him back on his heels?* Bill grinned.

The grin dropped to the ground in the next moment, when he remembered the state Miss Marie had been in when he'd taken his leave of her. Not only was it a poor bet that he could go home with a bride, the chance that he'd have a job much longer was between slim and none.

"I didn't mean no disrespect," he muttered aloud.

"Who you been disrespectin'?" came a voice from a foot or so behind him. "Not the beauteous Miss Owen?"

*Chico again!* "Mind your business, Henderson," Bill snapped. "We got steers to brand."

"I don't use my mouth to brand. It's free to speak my mind." Chico rode up even with Bill, wearing a wide grin.

"You're useless," Bill said.

"I'm your conscience. I keep you from flyin' off to the moon when you should be ropin' a yearling calf."

"You're imagining things. I'm levelheaded and lucid."

"Not lately. I reckon you're in luuuv." Chico drew out the vowel, letting his bottom lip hang away from his mouth. "You're so in luuuv you can't see a painter creepin' up on you in broad daylight. You're so in luuuv—"

Bill shoved hard against Chico's shoulder, and the cowboy winced. "Hey! Leave off, Henry. That wound ain't healed up yet."

"You're a fraud. You got shot in the left side. Don't carry on about your right wing, or I'll shoot you again myself."

"Ah, you wouldn't do that. I'm too good a roper, even with a bad arm."

"You can be replaced with a Mexican," Bill growled. "They're all better ropers than you."

The old trail cook, Sourdough, doubling as a cowhand these days, called out, "Boss a-comin'. Mind your tongues."

Bill glanced over his shoulder. Old Man Owen and his sons were indeed approaching, and he had a serious set to his face. *Uh oh*, he thought. *I reckon I'm in trouble.*

He pulled up his horse, letting the others get ahead of him while he waited at the side of the trail. Mr. Owen waved his sons ahead and stopped to confer with Bill.

"Leave off branding and cut out a dozen steers for sale. I'm takin' 'em down to the Cuchara."

"Want branded stock?"

"Not especially. They're goin' to be butchered soon. It don't matter what the hides say."

"How many hands you want to go with you?"

"Just my boys. They're plenty and to spare to handle that small a herd. The rest of you can get on with the branding once you get the dozen separated out."

"Yes, sir. How soon you need them?"

"We'll head out on Thursday morning," he said. "Bring them down to the lower corral Wednesday night."

Bill agreed, relieved that he yet had a job, and even more elated that he would have an opportunity to seek out Marie in her father's absence.

The Old Man cleared his throat, then spoke again. "I'm takin' my daughter with me, Henry. You won't make free with her feelin's again." He clucked to his horse and moved away.

*He saw right through me. My poker face needs work.* Bill's disappointment stung, but the girl would be back soon.

Rod Owen turned his horse and tossed Bill a bit more news. "I'm matchin' my girl up with a Virginia boy. Tom Morgan is known blood."

Bill caught himself in mid-nod. Strong chills washed over him as though he'd been caught in a freezing rain. *Tom Morgan? The corn farmer's son?*

&

Marie headed toward the creek, intent on dipping up a handful of water to cool her face. Her cheeks still burned from the encounter with her pa, and she didn't want Ma asking uncomfortable questions.

"Drat Pa anyway," she muttered, head down as she tromped along the bank to her favorite place. "Why does he meddle so?"

She started to gather her skirts to kneel in the grass.

"Marie. Good morning to you."

Marie dropped the fabric and looked around for the origin of the familiar voice. It was Ellen, as she had supposed, coming toward her from the opposite side of the creek. What was she doing here? She should be in her cabin, tending to Carl.

"I—" She brushed at one cheek, feeling for heat, hoping Ellen hadn't noticed her discomposure. Perhaps her flush had faded. "I've been out riding," she said, in case it hadn't. "I thought you'd be up yonder." She gestured toward the forested bench where Carl had built his new home.

Ellen's chuckle surprised Marie, but she tried to hide her expression by rubbing her forehead.

"I can't be there all day and all night. We needed water, and besides, I wanted to take the air." She lowered a bucket to the grass.

"Ain't newlyweds supposed to stay indoors? Most all the ones I've known went away and I didn't see them for a long time after the weddin'."

"It's a tiny mite different when the groom is laid up with a horrible wound," Ellen, said, but there was no hint of self pity in her tone.

In fact, Marie detected laughter underneath the grim words. "What's funny?" she demanded to know. "You're all sunshiny for a bride in such a circumstance."

Ellen laughed out loud. "I like being married," she said, once she had regained composure. "I like bein' Carl's wife. He's cheerful, despite bein' laid up, and he's funny, and he loves me to pieces." She wrapped her arms around herself, smiling.

Marie frowned, and thought, *Will Tom Morgan ever make me feel that way?* A shiver ran through her body, top to toe. *Not if he's still mooning after Ellen, he won't.* She hugged herself then, feeling alienated from her friend by her discouragement.

Ellen noticed Marie's movement and laughed again. "Look at us," she said, "a pair of sillies a-huggin' on ourselves." She broke her stance and shook her finger in Marie's direction. "Marie? Something's amiss. You're off woolgatherin' in a dark place."

Marie bent her head forward, hiding her face with her hands, ashamed of the tears gathering behind her eyelids.

"Oh no!" Ellen cried out, and jumped across the water. "There is somethin' wrong." She put her arms around Marie's shoulders and rocked slightly. "You let yourself have a good cry, then you can tell me all about it."

Marie sank against Ellen and surprised herself by bursting into tears. They spilled from between her closed lids, hot and stinging, accompanied by sobs that shook her shoulders and tore at her throat. Shame suffused her body, shame at losing control of her emotions, shame at caring so deeply about her father's ongoing slight, shame at her actions toward Bill Henry, who had only been trying to help her, after all.

She sobbed on, despite Ellen's comforting embrace, despite her father's claim that he would see to her wants and needs, knowing that marriage to a reluctant Tom would never bring her the happiness Ellen enjoyed. Then she sobbed because she was a hypocrite, begrudging Ellen her joy because she herself was miserable.

Finally, she sobbed because James was gone. James had left them, and she didn't know if she would ever see him again. Her last exchange with him had been to belittle his pain, to berate him for his heedless flight from grief. She had not said goodbye.

After a bit, Marie's sobs abated enough that she realized Ellen was rocking her, crooning soothing sounds into her ear, stroking her hair with gentle hands. Ellen's hands. James could never again clasp them in his, nor ever again tuck one into the crook of his arm, even though she had been betrothed to him. Ellen was married. James was gone. She took a long, shuddering breath and let it out slowly. Ellen did not know of his departure.

Marie opened her eyes. Ellen's stared back at her, warm with concern and regard.

"He's gone," Marie said in a high, tight voice.

"Who?"

"James. He's left us."

Ellen inhaled sharply. "Ah!" She let Marie go and put a hand to her mouth. "I drove him away!"

"No. No!" Marie said. "He and Pa had words." She put a hand on Ellen's hair. It was her turn to comfort. "If anybody drove him away, it was Pa."

"I knew I was too happy by half."

"You can't say that. James is prideful. He can't abide losing. Not after. . . . Never mind that. I didn't tell you he'd gone to heap blame on you, or on Carl. James'll work it out. He'll come back."

"You're talkin' about him losing Jessie? Leaving her behind?" At Marie's nod, Ellen spoke hesitantly. "At first, bein' betrothed to me was a heavy cross for him to bear." She began to shake her head. "After he resigned himself to the match your pa made, and knowin' Jessie was lost to him, he worked so hard . . . so hard to accept me, to acknowledge me." Her eyes darted around, unfocused, and when she spoke again, her voice was husky with emotion. "But I couldn't love him, Marie. I couldn't come to care for him. Carl was always the one I loved."

"There, there."

The girls clung together in mutual pain, until Ellen said softly, "Carl needs to know about his brother leavin'. I have to tell him."

"Yes." Marie sniffed and swiped the back of her hand across her eyes. "I reckon you should. Now I've got to be doing my chores." She gave Ellen another squeeze and turned away.

৪১

Feeling the overwhelming fatigue brought on by two days of mourning, Julia Owen only half listened to her husband tell her his plan to leave early Thursday morning on a three-day journey to sell beeves. Getting to sleep was of higher importance to her than staying awake until Rod ran out of steam, turned on his side, and began to snore.

She hoped this was not a night when he felt amorous. She had barely been able to go through the motions of her chores today, and had no strength left to spare for her husband's needs.

Then a question worked its way into the forefront of her mind. She opened one eye, waited for Rod to take a breath, and asked, "Why are you herding cows down to Chester Bates this week? I recall his letter made an offer to trade them for part of his wheat crop. He won't be harvestin' yet."

29

"Steers. I'm taking steers."

She refused to be distracted. "They're all cows to me. Why are you going before harvest?"

"I have a pressing matter to take up in that country. I reckon it won't wait until then." He scratched his chest above the neck of his nightshirt. "I figure I may as well make one trip as two. Chester will bring us the wheat."

She whispered, "If you're goin' after James, that's entirely the wrong direction." Pain at the unexpected loss of her son made her body quiver.

"I know that, woman." His voice had taken on the soft gruff tone he used in tender moments when he felt vulnerable.

Annoyance that he hadn't expanded his answer sufficiently to tell her his business drove Julia to shift her weight, rise on her elbow, and open both eyes to stare down at him. "What airn't you tellin' me?"

After a long moment, he turned his own eyes away and said, "I have an errand."

"Roderick Owen, don't you be speakin' nonsense to me. What errand takes you away from chores at this season?"

When his hand flew to his head, she barked at him, "Don't be a-worryin' that scab or it won't never heal. What's the truth?"

"It's a little errand for Marie," he admitted, tucking his hand under the covers.

"Marie?" Surprised, she almost missed his failure to explain himself further. When she had gathered her wits sufficiently to notice his silence, she poked him in the ribs. "What business does the girl have in the Cuchara country?"

He sighed. "She accused me of neglecting her welfare. She wants a husband."

"No!" Julia sat up.

"She made it plain she's woman-grown and expects me to get her one."

She looked at him. "You're not—"

He cut her off. "She said young Tom Morgan is twenty. I had no notion he'd got to that age."

She shook her head and sighed in turn. "Your matchmaking has an ill reputation." She sank back onto the bed. "Does she have her cap set for Tom?"

He shifted one of his legs. "I've had him in mind for years."

"I asked does Marie want him."

He shifted the other leg. "She didn't say me nay." After another long pause, he continued, "I'll know more when I get the two in the same room."

"What?" She sat up again, her back stiff.

"Julie, shh."

"You're takin' my daughter down country with a passel of cows?"

"Shh. I can best see if Tom is willin' to step up to the mark when he encounters the girl face to face."

"Well, which of the hands will you take to drive the wagon? You dassn't let Albert have the lines when he's got his sister in his care. He's too reckless."

He shifted his leg. "There's no need of a wagon, nor of a crew. Marie rides well, and the boys can handle twelve beeves."

She recognized his blustery tone.

"You're justifyin' using my daughter as a cattle drover because she sits a horse well?"

"No. No. She'll be along for the journey, not driving steers. She'll take charge of the camp chores."

"She'll drive cattle and then cook for you all, besides?"

"Julie, lie back and go to sleep." He sat up and pressed her shoulders backward with gentle hands. "Marie agreed to go along. I reckon she's eager to make a match."

"Humph," she snorted, but she allowed him to make a fuss for a few moments until she let her body relax and her eyes close again.

Although she knew she appeared at rest, her mind zipped to and fro with anxiety. What was the world coming to? Girls chasing around the country looking for husbands? That was not the way things had been done in her youth. No indeed. A proper courtship took time, and wooing, and discreet meetings at county gatherings. She exhaled. The Unpleasantness had changed the world for Marie. That was mighty clear.

# Chapter 3

The night before Pa trailed his beef cows to the Cuchara, Marie tossed and turned. Jule elbowed her once, then went back into slumberland, but Marie's mind seemed to bubble with imaginings like a pot boiling over on a too-hot stove. It wouldn't allow her the relief of sleep.

She wondered whether she dreaded or anticipated the next few days. If Pa liked Tom's prospects and proposed to add him to the family, the young man's reaction would play a big part in Marie's future. He might have given up thinking about Ellen by now. He might accept Pa's suggestion with enthusiasm. He might jump into making and carrying out plans for a wedding and a life together. On the other hand, he might have no notion of marrying her, and his disinclination could doom her to spinsterhood.

Who else was there for her to marry? She lay very still, searching every nook and cranny of her brain for prospects. She'd seen the Dominguez brothers several times when they stopped by to water their horses on their way to Pueblo Town or back. Patricio and Enrique Dominguez cut blazingly romantic figures, with their wide-brimmed hats and differently-styled clothes, their teeth-flashing smiles and flirtatious comments. She thought the pair of them was tremendously exciting. Given the chance, which one would she choose to wed?

After thinking on the exotic brothers for a time, she sighed and discarded the wild idea of being courted by such a man, knowing Pa was dead set against any marriage in that direction. That left her with a suitor pool made up of Tom Morgan, grubby freighters from Pueblo Town, hardrock miners from the north and the west, or her father's cowhands.

Tom had his distinctions. Despite being a farmer, he washed

his hands before eating and wore fresh clothing to social events. He kept his medium brown hair trimmed above his collar, and it was never greasy. He had his moments of merriment, but he'd always treated her with respect. Or maybe it was diffidence.

Marie turned on her side, and let her mind examine that topic. Tom had never sought her out as an object of courtship, although she now suspected his pa and her own had intended for some years for them to marry one day. She and Tom, though, had never discussed marrying. Never once.

During their journey to the West, Tom had acted the same way toward her as he had towards Carl's then-fiancée, Ida Hilbrands, or to Ida's younger sisters. He had turned on the charm with Ellen, but she had given him little chance to make inroads into her heart. Marie alone had known of Ellen's secret yearning for Carl, although she was betrothed to James. Yes, Tom could be witty, but he could be mighty boring, as well.

Patricio Dominguez would never be boring. She didn't know how much English he spoke or understood, but it would certainly be interesting, no, it would be tremendously exciting, to live in his house, learning a new language, having servants, being married. . . .

She inhaled sharply and pulled the quilt over her head. What was she thinking? She was as bad as Jule, trying to picture what goes on behind a couple's closed door. She'd seen horses mating, and a human encounter must involve the same elements. That wasn't her business yet. She'd learn all about it first hand, once she married Bill.

*Bill?* The hot flush of burning cheeks drove her out from under the covers. *I don't mean Bill. I mean Tom. Lawsy! What am I thinking?* She squeezed her eyes tight, trying to banish the errant image that persisted in her brain of Bill Henry's contrite face when she'd lashed out at him in anger the morning her horse had bolted.

The image lingered, however. She could not banish it in favor of Tom's bland visage. Then a series of Bills lined up before her inner eye: Bill, looking stricken as she berated him, the color of his eyes deepening almost to black, as though he willed them to shelter his soul. Bill, saying, "I didn't mean you." Bill, his moustache twitching on the left side of his mouth as she turned away from him.

Marie shook her head, trying to drive the specters away. Bill Henry should not be in her mind when she was, in all likelihood, going to end up in Tom Morgan's marriage bed.

೩

When Pa called Marie to rise, she opened her eyes, surprised that she had, at last, slept. Her last memory was of Bill Henry's face, and her cheeks flushed again as she flipped the quilt aside, swung her legs out of the bed, and drew her nightgown down over her knees.

Jule lay still, her breath rattling a bit in her nose.

*Disgusting!* Marie thought. *She's snoring. Thinks she's so high and mighty.*

After feeling her way to the clothes she'd laid out the previous night, she dressed in the dark. Dawn hadn't broken yet; it wasn't due for another hour. She yawned, shivered a bit, then fastened her shoes. She didn't want to take the trouble or the time to dress her hair in the dark, so she threw it back over her shoulders as she climbed down the ladder from the loft.

Pa had left a lantern on the floor beside the outside door. Marie picked it up, opened the door, and hurried through the dooryard.

As she arrived at the stable, Marie saw that Albert held three saddled horses just past the corner of the building. Pa had already mounted his horse, a crow-hopping dun mustang she remembered from the day her horse ran away. Her face warmed. Bill Henry had been in the mustang's saddle that day. *Is he coming with us?* she wondered, looking around to see if the Texan was hiding outside the reach of her light. *Evidently not.* Her disappointment surprised her.

"There you are," Pa said, catching sight of Marie as the nervous horse turned him around. He sounded impatient.

"I came straight away," she said, lifting her chin.

"Well, find your horse. We must get on the trail." He clicked his tongue at the mustang and moved off into the darkness.

35

Rulon approached and took the lantern from Marie. He hung it on a peg driven into the wall of the stable, then boosted her into the saddle cinched onto the back of a docile brown mare she hadn't ridden before. "Take heart, sis," he said, making a rueful face she could barely see in the lamplight. "He's always grouchy when his horse won't obey, but that one settles down, and Pa will, too."

Marie made her own face back, and adjusted her seat in the saddle. This animal was the one usually ridden by Jule, and she wasn't sure if it would keep up with the others.

As though reading her mind, Rulon patted the horse's neck. "Bess is a traveler," he said. "Good tempered she may be, but she's got heart, as well, and a good gait. You'll like the ride."

"Did you pick her out for me?"

Rulon's smile crinkled the corners of his eyes. "Nope. Pa did that." He nodded in the direction their father had gone. "We'll have a long day's journey, and he looked to your comfort."

Just then, Albert blew out the lamp, and Marie was grateful for the darkness that rushed in to replace the light. She was glad Rulon couldn't see what she felt: her cheeks were burning as they colored. She listened to the twin creaks of leather as her brothers swung onto their horses. Rulon said "Hiyah!" and slapped the free ends of his reins against his horse's side to get it underway. The tinkle of spurs told her Albert used his heels. She clucked Bess into motion to follow them. The warmth of her cheeks spread into her bosom. Her pa did take notice of her well-being.

☙

As the first suggestions of light brightened the eastern sky, Marie let her horse follow Rulon's toward the corral. They drew up in a bunch behind Pa on the side of the trail.

The cowboys had driven the chosen longhorn steers down from the mountain the previous afternoon. Now they bawled and moved around in the enclosure, as Clay went to unlatch the gate and let them out. The moment he swung the gate open, a fat steer burst through the hole, and Albert, on one side, and Pa, on the other, headed the animal toward the trail south. The other eleven

36

steers followed.

Clay mounted his horse and caught up to Albert, while Marie let Rulon follow their father. She lagged to the rear, as she had been told to do the previous day. She didn't expect to do any work, but found that she occasionally needed to urge a steer forward. Bess seemed to know what to do, so she eased up on the reins and let the horse have its head. Marie merely hung on for the ride.

After a while, Marie began to enjoy chasing the errant steers. One took off to the left, and Marie leaned forward in the saddle, put her heels into Bess's sides and yelled "Hi there!" The horse jumped forward and set out after the steer. With Marie's vocal encouragement, Bess drove the animal back to the little herd.

Pa looked around, and rode back to where Marie followed the herd. "I don't mean for you to work the cattle, daughter. Follow along, and if a steer escapes, call out for one of your brothers."

"I can do the job," she answered back.

He scowled. "You mind. Those horns can catch you quick as a wink."

"I'm watching out for them." She raised her chin a bit, but kept her face smooth, expecting a dressing-down.

He gave her a disapproving look, but said nothing else before returning to his position at the side of the herd.

"Hmm," Marie said. "He's going to allow it." She didn't dare give vent to the yell she wanted to launch. Instead, she whispered, "Yippee."

After a while, the steers behaved better, docilely following the lead steer down the trail. Marie, left to her own devices, found herself enjoying the view. Although it wasn't as green as Virginia, the undulating nature of the mostly bare landscape, coupled with occasional buttes poking up like thumbs, intrigued her. At a distance of several miles, she saw a few buildings built in the shade of trees along a watercourse, and others against a hilly upcropping. Where did the Dominguez family live? Was that their homestead tucked beneath one of those worn earthen hills?

She mused on her own wonderings. Pa's stand against her offhand suggestion of a match with a Mexican had left no question in her mind that no such marriage would take place while Roderick Owen lived. She shrugged. She had only tossed the notion into their altercation as a challenge to his authority. She had been angry, true enough. No one likes to feel they've been ignored, or even worse, slighted on purpose. The gentle gait of her horse, Bess, was a testament that Pa did care about her, or at the very least, he was thinking about her now.

Her mind leaped to her uncertainty about Tom. He'd run with a bunch of the county boys who were a tad younger than Carl, always around since she could remember. Yes, he'd gone away when he'd been called up to the infantry, but had managed to come through all the fighting without any major wounds. When he returned, she heard his intention was to go halves with his father on the farm. But the fields had been burned—scorched black—by Sheridan's army, and the ground had not recovered. Mr. Morgan had jumped at Pa's offer to bring them west, and that had been that.

Marie wondered why Pa hadn't arranged a marriage for her with Tom from the outset. Hadn't he seen that she was woman-grown? If they'd been promised, he wouldn't have chased after Ellen.

Not wanting to fall back into her former despair, Marie shook back her wind-whipped hair and started looking around at the countryside again. Far to the south, two mounded peaks thrust up from the prairie, a pair of mountains that looked like, well, very like her own bosom. She blushed at the thought. Ma would be mortified to know her daughter was thinking about body parts. That was unseemly.

She focused again on the steers slowly moving forward before her. Albert and Clay had switched places, and her youngest brother was off chasing a critter. He whooped with great gusto, his high yells filling the air. She thought of telling him to be quiet, that he was scaring the poor animal, but what did she know about how steers reacted to noise? Maybe they liked being chased and harassed by young boys.

*I don't think I would like it*, she thought. *Bertie can be an awful pest. He would drive me wild, if I was a steer, chasin' me and yellupin' that way.*

A steer bawled to her left, running toward a scrubby cedar

tree, and after no one dropped back to head it off, Marie went after it.

Wishing she had a rope like her brothers, she yelled at the animal. Bess got to the far side of the steer and moved to block its progress.

"Get over there," Marie whooped, "scat, go on!" She waved her free arm and the steer turned, showed the whites of its wild eyes, and ran back to the rest of the herd.

*Ha!* she thought. *I'm just as good a cow driver as Bertie.*

Marie looked up to see Rulon riding back toward her. She steeled herself for a confrontation, but saw he was grinning at her.

"Well done, sis," he said.

"I thought Pa sent you to scold me."

Rulon chuckled. "That he did. That he did. You don't have to tell him I reckon you're doing a fine job of work." He winked at her, then raised his voice. "What do you think you're doin', girl?"

Marie put on a contrite face in case Pa was watching, and bowed her head in submission, but she could scarcely keep her giggles in check. Rulon shook his finger in her face for good measure, then winked again, turned his horse around, and rode away. Knowing Pa could see her if he took a notion, Marie compressed her lips to stifle a smile or a laugh, then rode back to the rear of the cavalcade.

The day grew warmer as the sun rose higher in the slate blue sky. Dust arose in abundance behind the steers, hanging in the air in their wake. A swarm of flies happened by, attacking the steers, who switched their tails to drive off the pests.

Marie batted away a few of the biting flies, and wished she had a canteen filled with water to sooth her dry throat. Or maybe, since they were moving through land that had been settled by Mexican folks, she should carry the kind of skin bottle she had seen the Dominguez brothers filling up at Pa's creek. Lacking either one, she'd have to ask one of her brothers for a drink.

Clay was closest to her, so she hurried Bess in his direction. When she caught up to him, she asked for his canteen.

"Where's yours, sis?"

"I don't own a canteen. I'm thirsty, so I'm asking you for water."

Clay held his up. "This is Carl's. He don't need it these days." He held it beside his ear and shook it.

"Clay!" Marie held out her hand so Clay would give her the water container.

He handed it over, and watched as Marie tipped it up and greedily slaked her thirst.

"Huh! I thought girls drank a mite more dainty-like," Clay said.

She swallowed again, then lowered the canteen. "Maybe I would if I wasn't doin' a boy's job. It's dusty back there." She handed it back, then flipped her hair forward over her shoulders, and beat some of the dirt out of it.

Clay shook the canteen, anxiety clouding his countenance. "Sounds like you drank it dry, sister."

Marie lifted her hair in both hands and shook it. "I left you at least one swallow."

"Barely that," Clay protested.

"It's nearly noontime. Pa should call a halt for dinner soon. You can fill it then." She reined Bess around and rode away.

∽

As Marie drove the steers closer to the Southerners' settlement on the Cuchara River, her good humor abandoned her. Nervous foreboding rushed in to take its place.

Bess must have sensed her unease, for she stopped moving forward, turned her head, and looked inquiringly at Marie. Marie looked back at the mare, her stomach flip-flopping with anxiety. Bess shook her head and whinnied. The herd disappeared into a draw, tails flicking the flies away. Marie sighed.

"Let's keep up, good horse," she said, reaching forward to pat the animal on the neck. "I'm nervy enough without getting left behind." She bumped her heels on Bess's flanks, and finally persuaded her to move forward after the steers again.

Rulon's head came up out of the draw, followed by his body, then his mount. When the entirety of him came into view, Marie could see the relief spreading over his tanned face. He waved, and beckoned to her in a "come along" gesture. She waved back, and urged Bess into a lope.

"Trouble?" Rulon asked once they were riding together down the slope of the draw.

"No. Bess took a notion that I needed a rest." She laughed, then reflected on the thinness of the sound. It would not convince a careful listener that she had merriment in her soul. "No matter," she added.

Rulon glanced over at her, studied her face for a moment. "You do look a mite peaked, sis, not to mention sunburnt." He cocked an eyebrow. "Pa says by and by we'll be nooning for a bite to eat and a rest." He nodded at her then. "You keep up, you hear?"

When she nodded in reply, he clucked to his horse, and it jumped forward across the bottom of the draw and up the other side.

The noon stop couldn't come fast enough to suit her. It would be a welcome relief from the sun and the dust and the flies. Marie wiped her sweaty, dusty forehead with the back of her hand, then realized her face was tender to the touch. *Sunburnt indeed*, she thought. *That's my own folly.* She sent Bess into a bit more speed to rejoin the herd, wishing she'd thought to borrow a hat, or at least, to bring her sunbonnet.

An hour later, Pa did call a halt for dinner when the company came upon a stream with a pebbled bottom. After the boys watered the steers in the stream, they drove them up the southern bank and onto a grassy area. Then they watered all the horses and picketed them nearby on the grass.

Marie opened the saddlebags, spread a cloth on the bank, and put out tin plates and cups for her father, her brothers, and herself. She unwrapped the cornbread and beef she and Ma had prepared and put a portion of each on the plates. Then she went to the creek, upstream from the place they'd crossed, and dipped a bucket into the water.

She had almost carried it back to the eating area when Albert swooped in, snatched the bucket, and poured the water over himself.

As he wiped the water from his eyes, Marie cried out, "You oaf! That's drinkin' water!"

"Works just as well to cool me off," he said in a sneering tone, shaking himself like a dog to make Marie wet.

"Bertie, I'll get you," she cried, and picked up the bucket to hurl at him.

Rulon restrained her arm, and thrust the container into Albert's stomach. "Fetch clean water," he barked. "Now."

"Ah, you're no fun." Albert rubbed his abused belly. "You sound just like Pa, orderin' me about."

"That's enough," Pa said, coming onto the scene. "Do as your brother says. Fetch fresh water."

Albert scowled and muttered, but did as he was bidden, stalking to the creek and back with ill humor.

Marie's hand trembled as she ate her meal. Although she was in good health, the sun, wind, dust, and insects all had combined to sap her strength during the morning's drive. Her muscles ached from unfamiliar use. She wondered how she would fare for the rest of the day, and the morrow's trek, as well. *However did I forget to bring my bonnet?* She regretted that she'd been in so great a haste to leave this morning that she gave no thought to effects of the sun.

She scratched surreptitiously at a fly bite on her neck. Her cheeks burned from sun exposure, and her throat was dry and scratchy, no matter how much water she drank. She raked her fingers through her tangled hair, with little success at smoothing it. Then she sighed.

*I'm surely going to make an impression on Tom Morgan, and not for the better!*

∞

When Pa called, "Mount up," at the end of their noon rest, Marie hauled herself up into the saddle with shaky arms. The noon break hadn't been long enough to restore the strength she'd lost as the morning waned. How she would keep up with the steers for the rest of the day was uncertain to her mind, but she surely wasn't going to voice her doubts in this company.

Fortunately, Pa's next words were to Albert. "You take drag this afternoon. Marie can ride in your place."

Mentally thanking her father, Marie rode to where the steers had been grazing as she rested. *How do I get them started?* she wondered, but Clay came along and answered that question by riding up to the rump of the nearest animal and prodding it into motion with his foot. "Get 'em movin'. You don't have a rope, so twist a stick off a tree to poke 'em with, or use your foot. They'll follow this critter, once he's going down the trail."

"Is he the leader? The spotted one?" She gestured toward Clay's steer.

"Yep." Satisfied with his efforts with the first steer, he started in the direction of another, then wheeled his mount and returned to Marie's side. "Do you want me to get you a stick?"

"Might as well," she answered, heading toward a brown animal. "Could be my feet won't work as well, bein' smaller'n yours, by far."

Clay twisted a branch off a nearby willow and stripped off the leaves with his pocket knife. He brought it over to her, and gave it to her with a smirk. "It's going to bend a bit, but should serve the purpose."

"You think this will serve?" she exclaimed, bowing the branch nearly double.

"Whip 'em on the rear, if they won't get movin' fast enough," he said, laughing.

"Oh bother," she said, and shrugged her shoulders. "Men and boys will be the ruination of me yet!"

"We're meant to torment the female of the species," Clay said, and rode off to his position.

"You do a right good job of it," she mumbled, and used the willow slip to good effect.

After what seemed to be hours of riding along the road, they approached another creek, and Pa called out, "We'll stop here for the night. Water 'em and bed 'em down, boys. Daughter, get supper ready."

Marie blew out a breath of air and climbed off Bess. Rulon came and got the mare while Marie set about getting the evening meal together.

After she had eaten and cleaned up, Marie prepared her bed at the foot of a tree, and then sat on her quilt for a while, her back against the trunk. Rulon strolled over and squatted beside her.

"You all set here?" He picked at his teeth with a flayed willow twig.

"Yes sir. Almost as comfy as my bed at home." She hugged herself. "I reckon I'll sleep after a bit, but I can't bring myself to close my eyes yet."

"It's a pretty night," he said, looking at the stars. When he looked at her again, he tilted his head to one side. "Are you sore, sis? You've been in the saddle for a long stretch, and you're not used to the sort of work you've been doin' today."

She smiled wryly. "You caught me out, didn't you? I'm also burned and windblown and fly-bitten. I'll make a handsome prize for Tom Morgan."

"No, sis," Rulon said, drawing out the initial vowel as he shook his head. "You're a beauty despite a tad bit of sunburn. Tom Morgan's a fool if he don't see that tomorrow."

She rolled her eyes. "Big brothers always say such dainty things."

"The truth ain't a dainty thing." Rulon smiled. "Granted, I'm your big brother, and I may be a tad bit partial to you, but there's no denyin' you're a comely woman. You stand the competition on their noses."

Marie couldn't help but laugh.

"There now." He patted her hand. "That's what I like to hear."

"Rulon, who do you reckon is my competition?"

"Just a figure of speech, sis. There is no competition that stands up to you."

"There is no competition at all. I'm the only girl left single hereabouts." She ducked her head so Rulon wouldn't see hopelessness in her eyes.

He put two fingers under her chin, raised her face, and looked at her for a long time. "That is an unfortunate circumstance. You are worth more than any three girls back home. Don't forget that. Not ever."

She hoped the deepening darkness prevented Rulon from seeing the tears that suddenly caused her vision to swim. "That's sweet of you to say," she whispered, catching his hand. "No wonder Mary thinks the sun rises and sets on you."

Now Rulon ducked his head. "Go on!"

"I reckon I think that, too, big brother." She pushed him on the shoulder. "I'm sleepy now. You needn't watch over me tonight."

He touched her on the tip of her nose. "That's what big brothers are for." He got to his feet. "Good night, sis."

"Good night, Rulon."

# Chapter 4

Although Chester Bates was obviously surprised to see a dozen steers being driven into his door yard several weeks before he'd planned for them to arrive, Marie thought he masked it well when he greeted Pa the next day.

"They look hale and hearty," Mr. Bates said, gesturing to the cattle.

"The pick of the lot."

"You're early."

"I need to see Ed Morgan right away. No sense makin' two trips when one will do."

Mr. Bates nodded slowly. "You may as well alight, then. Rest your bones. Let your boys drive the beeves into the pen." He counted the crew members with a glance, his eyes widening when he saw Marie. "You brought the girl?"

"I have business that concerns her." Pa dismounted.

Mr. Bates's brow creased. "Are you brokering another marriage?"

Marie thought she would die as her father nodded. She hoped he would not begin to talk about her while she was still in earshot. She slipped off Bess and led her toward a tie post.

Mrs. Bates came from the house to join her, beaming as Marie looped the reins around the post. "Marie Owen! It is a blessed day when I get a caller." She hugged her, then, beckoning to a brown-skinned lad who was working nearby, called out in Spanish. "Ven aqui, joven."

The boy dropped his pitchfork and came running to see what Mrs. Bates needed.

"Quida al caballo," she said, giving the lad a few more

instructions as to the comfort of the mare.

Marie marveled at the woman's command of the foreign language as the boy left with Bess in tow. "I didn't know you spoke Spanish, ma'am."

Laughing, Mrs. Bates drew her toward the house. "Why girl, a body has to know how to speak it hereabouts if you want to get the work done. It's a pretty tongue." Patting Marie's tangled hair, she said, "Now, we'll just take a brush to that mess of locks, and put buttermilk on your face to take the sting out of the sunburn."

In no more than five minutes, Marie sat on a chair in the kitchen, holding a buttermilk-soaked cloth to her face. She felt the heat lifting from her skin.

Mrs. Bates ran the brush through Marie's hair, stroke after stroke, patiently working out the knots. "Tell me the news, girl. How is your ma? Is Ellen well? How is that husband of hers? Is he on the mend?"

Marie spoke through the wet cloth. "Ma is doin' as well as a body might expect. Carl is still mostly down in bed, but Ellen says he's making progress." She paused to remove the cloth and turn it over to the cool side. "Ellen is well, and she is happy. I ain't never seen a body so content."

"That's right gratifying to hear." Mrs. Bates worked at a particularly stubborn tangle for a moment, then asked, "Did your brother come back yet? Mr. Bates said your pa was right vexed that he left."

"No," Marie mumbled. "He's still gone. Ma grieves."

"I imagine so," Mrs. Bates said. "I imagine so." She lapsed into silence as she tackled another matted spot in Marie's hair.

Marie squeaked as the hairbrush pulled tight against her tender scalp.

"Oh, oh, oh, I'm sorry, girl," Mrs. Bates crooned. "Let me finger comb through that one." She put down the brush and used her fingers to coax the hair to separate. "You didn't bring any pins to put up your hair?"

"No. Pa was in such a hurry to leave, and I didn't have time to dress my hair. I didn't think to bring my bonnet, either. I'm paying the price now." She sighed.

"Let me wet that cloth again. I have plenty of buttermilk

today." Mrs. Bates took the cloth from her, dipped it in a bowl, and wrung out the excess. "The butter specks look like yellow freckles, but I reckon they'll wash off." She gave the cloth back, and started in on the last tangle. "I don't have no spare hairpins. I can try something new, though, a little trick I learned from Paco's mama. She's the one teachin' me the Spanish tongue," she continued. "She helps out here and there when I need her."

Once Marie's hair flowed freely down her back, Mrs. Bates went to a box shelf hanging next to the bed in the corner. She ran her fingers along the tops of the items stored there, then picked something up. She brought back a rectangle of embossed leather and showed it to Marie.

"Oh my, that's pretty," she said, fingering the design in the leather and the carving on a wooden pin that ran through a hole punched in one end and out a corresponding hole in the other. "What's it for?"

"You'll see," Mrs. Bates said, taking the item back and setting it on the table. She twisted Marie's hair into a bunch at the back of her head. "This won't hurt a bit," she murmured, as she fitted the leather piece to curve over the top of the hair. She thrust the wooden spike into one hole, worked it gently through Marie's hair, then poked it out the other. "There now," she said, making sure the clasp was secure. "That's right pretty, and will keep the tangles away, for sure." She handed Marie a bit of mirror. "If you don't like this, I can braid your hair."

Marie caught her breath at the tidy reflection. "I never thought of braids, being so old and all."

"Old!" Mrs. Bates laughed. "When did you get to be old? You're just now at your best, girl."

"My sister tells me I'm old."

"Julianna? That girl has no sense. Get the notion of being old out of your head. It will only give you the vapors. You're as lovely as can be, and don't you forget it."

Pa swung open the door and poked his head into the kitchen. "Time to leave, daughter."

"I'm comin'," she said, and removed the cloth from her face as he pulled his head back through the opening and shut the door. "I thank you for the buttermilk cure, Mrs. Bates, and for pulling

49

the snarls out of my hair." She touched the leather clasp. "May I use this while I'm down hereabouts? I reckon Pa will let me bring it to you when we come back through on the way home."

"You keep it, girl. I'll have Mr. Bates make me another."

"Thank you, ma'am!" Marie almost squealed in her delight.

Mrs. Bates poured the buttermilk from the bowl into a small crockery container. "You take this crock of buttermilk, now. Keep putting it on your face when you get a moment. It will help that burn heal up."

"You're so kind, ma'am."

"Now girl, don't you be 'ma'aming' me any more. You'll be a married lady one of these days. You need to get used to namin' me 'Muriel'."

"Oh, no, ma'am, I couldn't. It wouldn't be fittin'."

Mrs. Bates put the crock and the cloth into Marie's hands. "Nonsense. You'll be a-callin' me 'Muriel' before you know it."

"Perhaps, once I've wed. I'll try it on for size when that time comes."

Mrs. Bates hugged her and started to see her to the door. She stopped and said, "Hold on now. I have something else you can use." She went to a trunk and raised the lid. Rummaging around among the clothes inside, she lifted out a yellow sunbonnet. She dropped the lid, brought the bonnet to Marie, and tied it on her. "There now. That's Ellen's. When you get home, return it to her."

"Thank you, ma'am," Marie said on a gusty sigh. "That will be a relief to my woes."

Even though she looked and felt more presentable now, Marie climbed on Bess's back with dread beginning to curdle her stomach. Inside of a few miles, all the Owens would get off their horses at the Morgan homestead, and Marie would face her future.

80

Without any steers to chase, Marie rode beside Rulon along the bank of the Cuchara River. Clay and Albert loped their horses in the distance, and Pa's dust lingered in the air ahead.

"Calm yourself, sis," he said.

"I'm trying to. Truly I am." She felt like a baby kitten, too weak to open its eyes or walk proper.

"Mrs. Bates did a fine job of fixing you up right nice," he said as he appraised her. "A fine job."

"She has a kind heart," she said, then put her hand to her face. "Did I wipe off all the yellow specks? I don't want to look like a bowl of buttermilk."

He laughed and inspected her closely. "Yep, you're free of specks. You'll pass Mrs. Morgan's muster."

"I can only hope for such good fortune." She rode in silence for a hundred yards, then said, her voice shaking, "Rulon, I'm scared."

"What's got you in a dither, sis?"

"Tom."

"Tom?"

"He's never made any fuss over me. What's to change that now?"

Rulon held his peace for a long time. "There's nothing about you to dislike," he finally said, his voice rumbling, seeming to come from his chest. "Everybody who knows you values your good sense. You're a hard worker. You're a fine looking girl. Once Tom sees his future clear, he's bound to strive to make a good life for you. If he doesn't. . . ." He let his voice trail off.

"If he doesn't, what could you do, Rulon?"

He thought for a moment. "If Tom mistreated you, Pa would have the first right to act, but if he didn't, I would come and fetch you back home."

"Ah," she cried out. "That would be worse than being on the shelf. I'd be the pity of the neighborhood, a rejected wife!"

"There now. I didn't mean to send you off into a state. There now, Marie. That's not so. We'd be . . . We would . . ." He lapsed into silence.

Marie sniffed several times.

"Don't you go to cryin'! You'll make streaks down your face," Rulon said, clearly alarmed.

"Well, we can't have that," she said, and sniffed again, swiping her eyes with her sleeve. "Are we close to the place?"

"I see a barn ahead, a half mile or so off."

"I can't—"

"Yes you can. Raise up your chin, sis. You're an Owen, and no better stock is to be found hereabouts."

"Stock!" she exclaimed. "Yes, as good as any Owen heifer," but she gave herself a little shake and sat upright in the saddle.

The pair rode on without a word until they reached the Morgan farm, when Rulon caught hold of Bess's bridle and murmured to Marie, "Remember, sis, chin up. Tom's a fool if he don't come to care for you."

*More fool me if he doesn't,* she thought, but gave her brother a ghost of a smile.

∞

Rod encountered Edward Morgan in his corn field, where he was engaged in chopping weeds. "Rough work on a warm day," he said.

Ed looked up, straightened his back until it creaked, then leaned on the hoe, pursing his lips before he spoke. "Yep."

"You're lookin' a mite down in the mouth. What's ailin' you?"

The farmer rubbed his upper lip with a knuckle, then dropped his hand and rubbed his thigh.

At length he said, "It's the missus," and shook his head. "She's bothered, so she shares with me."

"Humph," Rod commiserated. "Womenfolk." He doffed his hat and began to feel along the scab above his ear, then let his own hand descend as he re-seated his hat. "What's she bothered about?"

"Lizzie don't much like it out here. She says it's too dusty. Then the wind comes up, blows the dust away, and she complains it's too windy."

"What are you doing about it?"

Ed humphed on his own accord. "Mostly staying out of her way! She'll hunt me down, though, time to time. I got cornered last week, and ended up promisin' to dig her a well." He flung his hand outward. "She's got a perfectly good river just yards away, and she wants a well!"

Rod tugged on his earlobe. "That does make a man weary.

You've got a fair piece of work ahead of you."

Ed nodded. "Your woman minding her manners?"

"Mostly," Rod said, nodding in concert with Ed. "I reckon she's worried some about the girl."

"Which one?"

"The older one. To tell you the truth, that's why I come a callin'." Rod drew himself to his full height. "That Tom of yours. Does he have plans?"

☙

Elizabeth Morgan bustled up, followed by her two daughters, Louisa and Melissa. "Just look who is here," Mrs. Morgan crooned. "It is Miss Marie, come for company. Now you get yourself down off that horse, missy, and come along into the house. Is that sunburn I spy? However did you come to be sunburned?"

She looked to Rulon for support, but he raised his eyebrows and shrugged as though to say, "You're on your own with the women folk," and heeled his horse toward the knot of men at the barn.

She slid off Bess, and Mrs. Morgan bundled her along toward the house, despite Marie's intense desire to know what Pa was saying to Mr. Morgan about his errand.

Mrs. Morgan asked, "Whatever are you doin', ridin' astride that horse? Why ever are you here with your papa and the boys?"

"You're all sunburnt," Louisa exclaimed, echoing her mother's tone. "Come out of this heat. You're fixin' to grow freckles on that burnt skin."

"We brought steers down to Mr. Bates," Marie managed to say, removing her sunbonnet in between the fuss Mrs. Morgan and her daughters made over her.

"But your papa didn't need you to shoo them cow critters down the trail, surely?" Mrs. Morgan protested.

"Why were you forkin' a horse'?" Melissa asked. "Don't your pa have a proper saddle for you?"

"I forgot my bonnet," she said. She tried to answer all the questions, first turning to Mrs. Morgan. "It was dark when we left, and I simply forgot to fetch it along." She held up the yellow bonnet. "Mrs. Bates gave me this one." She turned to Melissa. "No, we don't have a sidesaddle. I don't mind. Ridin' astride a horse is simpler than riding sidesaddle. Safer, I reckon." She felt a touch faint. So much attention at one time overwhelmed her, and she wondered if she'd forgotten any important questions. The matter of her being along for the cattle drive remained unaddressed, however, even under further prodding by Mrs. Morgan.

Once inside the house, Mrs. Morgan and her coterie swept her into a small side room that served as a parlor.

"You set down, now," Mrs. Morgan proclaimed. "Tell us all the news. Is it a fact Ellen Bates got herself married to your brother Carl? Ain't he the wrong brother? Weren't she meant to marry James?"

Marie took a seat as Louisa put in her query, "Is it true James took himself off to work in the mines?"

Melissa added, "Did he sock your pa?"

Horrified at the thought, she shook her head repeatedly. "No! He wouldn't. He never. I mean—"

"There now. Drink a cup of tea," Mrs. Morgan said, handing her one. "I made it up this mornin', so now it's cool and refreshin'."

Marie sipped the cold tea, her mouth puckering at the slightly bitter taste while her mind whirled at the notion of her brother doing violence on her father. James couldn't have been that angry! He was prideful, yes, but not violent. Her hand shook and she lowered the cup to its saucer to keep it from spilling. Mrs. Morgan must not have any sweetener. That surely wasn't sweet tea.

When she heard the tread of men's boots in the kitchen, her stomach quaked. The time of reckoning had come.

Even Rulon's recent exhortation couldn't make her raise her head to seek out Tom Morgan's eyes as the men folk trooped into the room.

"Make yourself comfortable, Rod," Mr. Morgan said.

She heard Pa sit down, but Mr. Morgan remained on his feet. "Mrs. Morgan, our neighbor has a proposition," he said.

She wanted to flee. She bent forward to place the rattling cup and saucer on a table that was barely within her reach, as she didn't want to dump the tea onto the floor. Where was Tom? Had he accompanied the two men into the parlor? A hand clasped her shoulder and she jumped.

"Steady," came a whisper.

*Rulon.*

"Chin up."

She tried, but couldn't achieve the task.

"You girls go sweep out the kitchen and wash up the dishes," Mr. Morgan continued.

Marie heard the footfalls as Louisa and Melissa scurried out of the room without saying a word.

"Rod Owen thinks it's time Tom took a wife."

Marie inhaled so violently that she squeaked, but the sound was masked by Mrs. Morgan blurting, "Oh my! That's a bit . . . sudden."

"I understand he's twenty years of age," Pa said. "It's high time he got hitched in double harness."

"He's proposing that Tom ask Miss Marie for her hand," Mr. Morgan said.

When Mrs. Morgan made no response, and no one else ventured to speak, Marie felt as though she could not breathe. The silence continued, except for inhalations. Exhalations. All but hers.

When she could not bear to hear the breathing of the others in the room while she suffocated, she glanced up at last. Tom leaned against the wall, his arms folded, staring at her. His frown was an arrow to her heart.

"He's only a boy," Mrs. Morgan finally said.

"He's old enough," Mr. Morgan answered. "What do you say to that, Thomas?"

"I ain't got a choice?" Tom asked in a clipped tone, glancing at Mr. Morgan.

Marie looked at the man, and seeing his pursed lips, looked back at Tom.

He turned his stony glare in her direction. "It appears to be decided," he said. Ice dripped from his voice. "We're to make a couple, Marie."

Marie's heart sank at the stark statement. Was that how a man asked for a girl's hand? He'd even left off the customary "Miss," as though he spoke to an inferior soul. *He won't love me,* she thought, panic filling her chest. *He'll never love me.* She wanted to melt down into the horsehair seat cover. She wanted to scream, "Rulon, take me home and hide me away." But she didn't. She had no breath for words.

Pa said, "Good. We'll make plans, then. How about . . ."

Marie shut her eyes and finally sucked in a burning lungful of air as others in the room took control of her future.

℘

As soon as she could manage it, Marie got out of the parlor and left the house. She wanted to find Bess, climb on the mare's back, and gallop back home.

Before she could accomplish her desires, Tom came out and joined her in the dooryard. "How about that?" he said. "Me pairing up with you."

His distant tone filled her with rage, and she wanted to lash out at him, but knew it would be futile.

"Yes sir," she muttered instead. "You and me."

Tom narrowed his eyes and put an arm across her shoulders. "They're planning to see us wed this fall, after the harvest."

"That soon?" Marie voice rose in a squeak. Feeling Tom's arm heavy on her, she fidgeted, wondering how best to remove it.

"Don't be nervous, girl. I'm disposed to treat you kindly." He began to walk, and she could do nothing but walk along beside him.

His path took them out behind the barn and into a field of corn. The row was too narrow for them to walk abreast, so Tom dropped his arm from Marie's shoulders and took her hand to draw her along behind him. She followed woodenly, stumbling occasionally on a clod of earth.

"Careful now," he said, turning to her and grabbing her other hand. "Don't be clumsy and knock down the stocks."

*He cares for the corn more than for me.*

56

"You may like it here," he said offhandedly. "That river runs cold. It comes from the high mountains behind the Spanish Peaks over yonder. I reckon the water's snow melt." He let go of her hands and grasped her by the shoulders, rubbing his thumbs along the fabric above her collarbones in a proprietary manner. "It's a hot day. Let's take a wade in the water."

"What are you talkin' about? Right now?" Marie felt her brows drawing together. She wished he'd remove his hands from her.

"You seem a mite warm from your journey. Could be you need a dip in that stream."

"I don't know. I think I hear Pa calling."

He snorted. "No. He'll be busy for quite a spell. We'll go wade in that water." He took her hand again and yanked her into a run down the row. She passed through the stiff stalks, getting silk and pollen all down her sleeves and skirt, and felt her nose twitching. Just as a sneeze gathered, ready to burst out, they broke into the open, on the bank of the river.

Tom didn't stop, but kept pulling Marie behind him down the bank and into the water.

"My shoes," she cried out, stumbling, losing her footing, falling, trying to catch herself against Tom. But he was deep in the stream, too, and there was nothing to keep her from plunging into the chilly water.

Panicked, she flailed against the drag of her clothes pulling her under. Thrashing around, she broke the surface and gasped for air, trying to remember what James had taught her so long ago about moving around in water. *I won't drown*, she thought. *If Tom's trying to drown me out of spite, I won't oblige him.*

Something caught her hand, and suddenly Tom was there, pulling her toward the edge of the river.

"I didn't figure you'd sink like that. Parley and Harry never do."

"Parley likely knows where he's goin'," she shouted, anger finally overcoming her panic as she made it to dry land. "Harry likely doesn't trip on the stones." She fell onto the grass, struggling to arrange her sodden clothing into order, then looked at her soaked shoes. "They likely don't ruin their only shoes."

"You're right. We don't wear shoes in the river. Nor nothin' else," he said, looking her over with bold eyes. "I should have let you shuck your clothes."

"Shuck my—" Marie got to her feet and stormed toward the corn field. "You are a thoroughly crazy man, Thomas Morgan." She stomped away, muttering to herself, "He has his nerve. 'Shuck my clothes!' The idea!"

Tom followed her. "Don't go getting upset. We go dippin' all the time with no clothes on."

"You and your brothers do! I ain't your brother." She wouldn't give him the satisfaction of seeing her red face, so she didn't turn to look at him as she flailed him with her words. "My pa means for me to be your wife." She couldn't bare the shame of his suggestion anymore, so she started to run through the corn stalks.

"What's the harm?" he asked, catching up to her, grabbing her hand and swinging her around to face him. "Once we're married, I reckon we'll see each other with no clothes quite regular."

Rattled by her abrupt spinning halt, but even more by Tom's unseemly words, Marie tried to get the picture of herself lying naked with the young man out of her head. Shame transformed to anger. She breathed hard two times, her breath coming and going with a rasp, then raised her chin and looked him in the eye while she shook her hand out of his grasp with one strong downward swing of her arm. "That time hasn't come. You leave me alone until it does, you hear? My pa won't stand for you foolin' with me, no matter how anxious he is to see us wed."

She stared him down, and he had the good grace to lower his eyes.

"If you reckon he's not man enough to keep you honest, Rulon will back him up."

"Humph," Tom snorted, but didn't object further.

Marie turned and left him, almost frantic to seek shelter until her clothing dried and she could make herself presentable.

&

Pa selected a campsite along the river, in a spot that lay between two fields of Mr. Morgan's corn.

Marie didn't particularly want to speak to anyone while the bitter memory of Tom's behavior sat in the front parlor of her mind. She busied herself with the camp chores, building a fire, cooking a meal, and preparing a pot of beans for their dinner on the journey home.

She thought work was enough of a barrier to keep her family from talking to her, but Pa sat himself beside her while she cleaned the dishes.

"Daughter," he began. "Did you and young Tom get your plans laid out?" He ran his hand through his beard for a moment, then added, "You were gone a long spell, so I went to seek you out. I found only the boy down at the river, chucking stones into the water."

She swiped the tin plate in her hand with her dishrag, watching it go around and around, until she almost felt dizzy. Words had abandoned her. What could she dare tell Pa about Tom's actions and words, his impious suggestions? Although Pa was her father, he was also a man. From the nighttime giggles she'd heard coming from below the loft, she guessed that he and Ma still had carnal relations, even though it was unlikely they wanted more children.

When she realized her father's gaze upon her had lingered long enough to turn into an inspection, she swallowed a couple of times to raise a bit of moisture in her dry throat, but her voice still sounded like a strangled cat when she said, "We had some talk, then I went to tend to Bess."

"Tom was a mite closemouthed. You and he didn't flaunt the conventions, did you?"

"No!" she denied, a bit more sharply than she would have wished. "I'm a proper girl."

Pa looked at her a long time, his gray eyes seeming to read her soul. Then he nodded and got to his feet. "I reckon your ma brought you up right." He reached out and patted her on the shoulder. "Get to sleep. We have a long trip home."

# Chapter 5

The next morning, preparations for the journey home were a misery to Marie. She had no desire to talk to Rulon or anyone else, but went through the motions of making breakfast in the half light before sunrise. After she packed up the remains of the meal, she went to arrange herself for the day. She looked for the hair clasp Mrs. Bates had given her so she could twist up her hair. Failing to locate it in the time she had available, she threw together one long braid to keep her hair in order, and then saddled Bess for the long ride.

For reasons known only to himself, Pa went back to the Bates homestead and stood in the barnyard to chat with Mr. Bates. Realizing that the farmer's kind wife would immediately sense her despair if she came out to talk, Marie forestalled an encounter with Mrs. Bates by fleeing into the wheat field behind the barn. She stood for a long time gazing toward the north. Although she had said her home felt like a prison, she acknowledged that it actually represented her sanctuary after their dreadful trek from Shenandoah County. Melancholy descended upon her like a heavy cloak as she thought of departing that home after the harvest. She scarcely moved until the sun climbed into the sky and Pa called that it was time to leave.

During their brief noon pause for dinner, Marie maintained her silence, spooning out beans and distributing the last of the corn bread, and then packing away the pot and utensils until their arrival home. Even when her younger brothers sought to tease her into joining them in splashing in the creek, she resisted their rambunctious delight.

Without the need to herd cattle, the homeward trek lasted only until sundown. When Rulon peeled her off her horse in the twilight, Marie stubbornly took charge of her horse's care, then hauled the cooking gear into the house. Pleading fatigue, she retired without supper to the loft to be alone. She wrapped her arms around herself as she lay curled on the bed, wishing she could make the nightmare go away.

Her solitude was interrupted a half hour later when Jule climbed partway up the ladder and called out importantly, "Papa wants you. Come down right away." She disappeared before Marie could reply or uncoil herself to throw her pillow at her sister's insolent expression.

Knowing there was no remedy but to go see what was wanted, Marie backed down the ladder and turned to find the entire family still gathered around the supper table.

Pa arose from his chair and said, "Come, come, daughter. Don't keep us waiting longer," and indicated that she was to sit in his seat at the head of the table.

Marie sat, hanging her head.

"There now," her father exclaimed, "what aspect is this?"

She raised her chin and threw back her shoulders. *It's to be an announcement,* she thought. *Pa wants to preen himself.*

"This is a happy occasion," he began. "Tom Morgan has offered for the hand of our Marie, and they will be wed when the harvest has been gathered in." He patted her shoulder. "We'll make the word known at our barn raising."

She turned her head and stared at Pa. *Barn raising? He does like his surprises.*

Throughout the hubbub that ensued, Pa smiled, holding up a hand that called for silence. When the noise had died, he said, "We had a successful journey. I delivered the cattle, and made arrangements with Ed Morgan and his missus for Marie's marriage to Tom. Then I stopped back by and asked Mr. Bates to spread the news down along the Cuchara that I'm planning to build a barn. We'll have a great gathering of neighbors, and construct the barn on Saturday one month hence."

*That's what Pa and he were jawing about. A barn raising.*

Her father addressed himself to the boys. "We have half

enough logs cut for a comfortable building for stock and tack. In the next month we'll finish logging, and then set up the foundation. You won't do it alone. I'll tell Henry to leave off branding, and enlist the hands to cut and haul the timbers."

*I wonder what Bill Henry will think of that?* Marie looked at her hands, gripped together. *Are there trees in Texas? Has he ever cut down a log? Does he even own an axe?* Then she remembered that Bill Henry was not her concern, and Pa was still talking, so she wrenched her mind over to the matter at hand.

"On Sunday, following all the work, we'll hold a Sabbath service. Randolph Hilbrands has come across a preacher in Pueblo Town who is amenable to traveling here from time to time to give us a good sermon. I'll send for him, for I believe we're all in need of a bit of worship."

Ma nodded her head, her hands tightly clasped on the table.

"Our neighbors will bring victuals to feed the workers, but you girls will need to help your ma prepare our share before they come." He looked at the boys. "Let's put in the work, and we'll have a sturdy building before snow flies. Now, prayers and to bed. Tomorrow will be a long day."

Marie went through the motions of participating in the nighttime devotions, but her mind was on the thought of the neighbors who would come to help raise the barn. Within a month, all the world would know she was going to wed Thomas Morgan, farmer. What they wouldn't know was that she would be trapped in an ugly situation for the rest of her life.

❧

Julia drew her shift over her head again, smoothing it down over her body as she glanced sidelong at Rod. He lay beside her, his eyelids only half open as his breathing slowed.

"You're a caution, you know that?" she murmured, wanting to snuggle against his bare chest, but resisting the impulse. The night wasn't as long as it needed to be, and they had best get to sleep.

He took a long lungful of air before replying. "I missed you. I missed my Julie-girl." He slid his arm under her neck and, turning to her, exhaled softly into her ear.

"There now, don't you begin again," she remonstrated, chuckling in a low tone. "We're gettin' too old for that business."

"What do you mean, woman? I can still love you 'til the day breaks."

She wanted to tell him that was nonsense, but knew he would take it as a challenge and that would be that for a good night's sleep. Instead, she gave him his nightshirt and asked, "Did you encounter any difficulties in makin' your arrangements with Ed Morgan?" She waited until he'd put the nightshirt onto his head before she let her fingers explore the red spot at the base of her throat where his enthusiasm had gotten out of hand.

"I did not," he said, his voice muffled by the soft cloth descending over his face. "I believe he took to the notion of joining our families."

She dropped her hand to the bed. "And Lizzie?" She felt a tingle of perversity at calling the woman by the nickname she so detested.

"I've no doubt she'll go along with it. Ed knows how to manage her."

She chuckled. "I daresay she manages him."

He inclined his head. "That may be," he acknowledged. "They're a pair, but good folks deep down."

"Just so she treats my daughter right."

"I reckon she won't hold a grudge against her because of your old quarrel."

"After all these years, you'd think she'd forget an apple pie prize at the county fair."

"You scratched her dignity, winning the ribbon when she'd prepared a place on the mantelpiece for it."

"I couldn't help that my apple crop turned out better that year. You'd think she could be content that she'd won half a dozen ribbons up until then."

"She is a mite prideful, that's true, but I don't see why she would harm Marie. It's not a blood feud between you two."

"I don't count it as such." She yawned. "I can't let that be a-preying on my spirits when it's after dark, husband. We've lost enough sleep as it is." Her words may have been sharp, but she smiled to think that her man still craved her favors after twenty five years.

He rested his hand on her arm, then patted it. "I know you're a-smiling over there, woman. You delight in me. Admit it."

She reached across her body and squeezed his hand. "Good night, husband."

He laughed, and she finally gave in to the desire to nestle against him, just for a moment, but not quite long enough to give his body any ideas.

# Chapter 6

Bill had one leg raised with a foot in the stirrup, about to step into the saddle, when Mr. Owen hailed him.

"Henry!"

Bill had to extract his foot in a hurry. The Old Man's strident tone had upset his mount and it took to bucking, almost getting its chance to drag Bill.

Once he'd got two feet on solid ground, he turned to his employer, hoping the anger he felt wasn't showing on his visage.

"Glad I caught you," the boss said. "I have a new task for you and the hands. I'm building a barn come a month, and we all need to cut timber for the sides. Pine logs. Cut 'em to size, too. Twelve foot, I reckon. Here's the plan." He handed Bill a sheet of paper with figures written on one side and a drawing on the other. "We'll drag the logs out of the woods and stack them there." He gestured toward his chosen spot. "When folks gather to help us with the raising, I want the logs right at hand."

"Lots of folks?"

"I'm spreading the word through the country."

Bill looked at the paper. "Plan for Logging," it said. *Logging? I have no experience of that task.*

His doubts must have shown on his face because the Old Man asked, "You all have cut trees before?"

"In Texas? We was lucky when we had mesquite and cedar. Some live oak. There's nothing like pine in my part of the country."

Rod shrugged. "The same principle applies to cutting one tree as another. Rulon will show you where to begin."

Bill shook his head as the Old Man walked away. The cattle needed tending to, but that didn't seem to matter. Logging seemed to be number one on Rod Owen's chore list.

Bill put on speed to get to where Chico and Sourdough were saddling up. He explained the change in plans, tapping the paper he still held.

"What's that? You want us a-chopping down trees?"

Bill watched as Chico rolled his eyes and groaned at the news. He felt the same, but wasn't going to mention that fact to the cowhand. "It won't last long. We'll be done in a month."

"A month? Thirty days of hard labor on our feet?"

"We'll take Sundays off."

"They won't come near fast enough. I'll get calluses on my feet, never you mind the blisters I'll raise on my pretty hands. Have to soak 'em every night."

"You have a *queja*, take it to the Boss."

"Not me. That's your job. I signed on to work cattle, not make my complaint to the Old Man."

"Shut your mouth and get an axe. Rulon's in charge of the tree felling."

Chico swore mildly. "What's Old Man Owen want with a bunch of logs?"

Bill snorted. "The paper says he's fixin' to build a barn. I reckon he's throwing a regular party to get it done. Inviting the whole countryside to pitch in." He chewed on a loose bit of dry skin hanging from his lip. "You reckon he'll farm us out for laborers come harvest time? He'll need to pay back a lot of favors."

"You're the one with the inside word, Henry. You ask him!"

80

"Daughter, it's time you gave thought to your hope chest."

*Hope chest? Without hope?* Marie thrust aside the bitter qualms and answered, "Pa was too busy going to war to make me one, Ma."

Jule began chanting, "Marie don't have a hope chest. Marie don't have a hope chest."

"Stop up your mouth or I'll put a rag in it," Marie countered, lifting the dripping dish cloth from the tub. "I'll make sure it's slimy with soap."

Jule stuck out her tongue and fled outside, with one last jibing whisper trailing behind her, "Marie don't have a hope chest."

"She's a caution," Ma said, shaking her head. "I don't know what's got into the girl."

"Spite," she answered, biting off the word. "Jealousy. Woman's curse."

"I've never seen it come so early," Ma mused, putting dried plates on the kitchen shelf. "Be that as it may, we've got to find you the necessaries for wedded life." She scratched the base of her neck under her collar. "Linens. Where will we get linens?"

Marie saw the action. "Poison oak, Ma?"

A pink blush rose into her mother's cheeks. "No. An irritation. I'll put a bit of tallow on it."

*Whisker burn, I reckon,* Marie thought. *Pa's been after her again.* Then she felt shame that she was being disrespectful of her mother, and regretted that the notion had passed through her mind. It was no fault of her ma's that Pa had a mysterious, powerful drive to know her. *Know her. Like in the Bible. 'And Adam knew Eve his wife; and she conceived, and bare Cain.' Along with the knowin' comes the begettin'. I don't want to know Tom. I don't want to conceive and bare his sons! I want— I don't know what I want, but he don't have a willing spirit to want me, so I don't want him.* But she was trapped now, bound to marry Tom. Bound to be his wife. *What folly have I done? I should never have cast Pa's failings up to him.*

Ma was watching her, the high color draining out of her face now, watching her like she knew what Marie had been thinking about.

"You've seen the horses breed," Ma said, after she'd stared at Marie long enough to make her squirm. "And the cattle."

Marie's suspicions were confirmed. Ma had read her mind. Hands of guilt clamped around her throat so tightly that she couldn't speak. After a lengthy pause, she nodded, feeling her own blush suffusing her face.

"Human folks do the same to breed children." Ma's voice

scarcely reached above a whisper. "It's needful, so as to keep the race of man alive."

Marie nodded again, mortified that she'd been caught with her mind fixed upon carnal thoughts.

"Time to time they do it for . . . for pleasure, for enjoyment." Her voice was even lower now. "They do it to show they care, one for another. I don't hold that a sin, like some folks do."

Marie's mind took hold of a dreadful notion. "Is Mrs. Morgan of that persuasion?"

Ma nodded. "I reckon she is."

The two of them merely breathed in concert for a while.

"Most men ain't persuaded of that idea," said Ma. "They have a need in them that makes them fairly fools from time to time. It takes hold of them, deep down, and there's no denyin' that . . . desire." She whispered the word as though it burned her lips. She licked them.

Marie felt like she was caught in a whirlpool, listening to her mother give voice to the forbidden subject. Her head swam.

"Some women feel it too. Strong." Ma bit her lip as though she didn't want to let out more of these searing words.

"You?" Marie wasn't sure she had actually asked that, for it felt more like she'd only breathed out.

Ma turned her head away, then after the air in the room felt thick as syrup as it entered her chest, Marie saw her look back.

"Yes," she said. Then she did a surprising thing. She smiled. "Call me a fool. Call me a sinner. Your pa can turn me to liquid butter with a touch. The yearnin' to join with him is." She stopped talking and bent her head to the side. She sighed. "There ain't no words, daughter. There ain't no more words to tell you." She shut her eyes. "I'm hopin' Tom can bring that gift to you."

෨

Several days went by, as the cowhands engaged in their unfamiliar logging task. It wasn't like they were alone doing the chore, Bill reflected. The Owen brothers matched the hands tree for tree. Even the Old Man pitched in, with an air of nervous excitement. The only Owens not turning up for the work were

Carl, who was taking his ease with a new bride while he recovered his health, and James, who had quit the place just in time to avoid this spate of labor.

*Well now, that's not fair of me. Mining's no easy task.* His axe thumped solidly into the pine trunk he was undercutting. As he worked, he likened his own situation with the fairer sex to that of James, whose fiancée had married another man, and worse still, his own brother. Bill had heard tell the Old Man had pressed the betrothal on James against his will in the first place. The whole business had gone bad for James. He wondered if the young man would ever come back and reconcile himself with his father. *I don't reckon he will. Rod Owen can be a hard man.*

It was that hard man's words that haunted him now. *I'm matchin' my girl up with a Virginia boy.* Bill wondered if the match had indeed been made down country, for Miss Marie had come home in a mighty sour mood, and she hadn't yet shook it off. Had the Old Man's matchmaking gone awry? All the family members did seem exercised about something.

He loosed his axe from the tree and stood it upright, leaning on the end of the handle for a brief respite.

"Hey, Henry. Hey! You sleepin'? Shake your tail!"

Bill looked up to see a tree falling toward him, and he turned and ran from death.

The pine hit the earth where he'd been standing—limbs crashing and tearing—and bounced once before it settled amid a cloud of dust and pine needles.

He bent over, hands on his knees, and panted, trying to catch a breath, coughing out the dust he inhaled along with the air, shaken by the close call. With the pounding of his heart filling his ears, he could barely hear Chico razzing him, Rulon's concerned voice, and Albert's cat calls.

Chico sprinted to his side, his pale face belying the curses he let fall upon Bill's head.

"You got a death wish, *hombre*? Git your head outta the clouds and pay heed!"

An exhaled "Yeah," was all Bill could respond as he tried to will his heart to slow to a normal rate. He still felt the evil swish of a branch clipping his rear as he tried to get out of the way.

"Close," came Rulon's voice above him. It had a slight quiver to it.

"Yeah," Bill said again, not able or willing to speak more for fear of hearing his own voice break.

He raised himself up, feeling Rulon's light touch on one shoulder at the same time as Chico belted him on the opposite arm.

"Ow! I got clear of the tree, and you want to make me dead?" Anger firmed up his voice, and as he fended off Chico's next punch, Rulon walked away to continue felling his tree.

"Oh, git over there and pick up your axe," Chico countered.

"You the *segundo* now?"

"If you're dead, I'm the next man for the job."

"That's a likely tale," Bill muttered, but picked up the tool and went back to work.

❧

Late that afternoon, after Bill had stripped his upper body to the skin to remove chips of wood and pine sap with a good scrubbing, he stood beside the door of the bunkhouse, drying his chest with a piece of Turkish towel. He heard the jingle of spurs and the thud of hooves on the path behind him, so he looked around to see the Dominguez brothers ride into the clearing. He found his clothing and covered himself. Waiting until they were within earshot, he stepped forward and greeted the pair with, "*Buenas tardes.*"

Patricio responded in kind, and sat his horse until Enrique drew up beside him.

Bill told them to alight and care for their horses, and the brothers took to that business. When they had finished, they tied their mounts to a tree nearby and walked back to the creek to freshen themselves.

Squinting at the sun sliding behind the mountain, Bill buttoned his shirt and tucked it into his trousers while he tossed the idea of inviting the brothers to stop over for the night from one side of his mind to the other. He concluded that it was the polite thing to do, despite his reservations about the men's moral character, and waited until Patricio returned from filling his skin canteen with fresh water from the creek.

Bill extended the invitation, and the man accepted with a big smile and effusive thanks.

Then Enrique came up, bearing his own water container. Patricio let him in on the plan, and Enrique joined in the "gracias" giving.

"*Que Dios te bendiga.*" Enrique added a wish for heavenly blessings on Bill.

"*Muy amable,*" Bill thanked him, and bid the brothers come inside for supper.

After Sourdough's filling meal of beans and cornbread, Enrique piled his utensils on his plate and looked at his brother, who grinned back at him.

Enrique turned his eyes upon Bill. "You desire to have a leetle game?" He pulled a deck of worn cards from the inner pocket of his vest and wiggled them enticingly in front of the cowhands. "We play for esmall ante, *sí*? A penny only."

"That's about all I have left," said Chico. "Payday don't come around 'til the end of the month."

"I sure you have the luck," Enrique encouraged him. "Eet ees your time, no?"

"*Seguramente,*" added Patricio, nodding and smiling. "*Nosotros,* we have the luck turning, *este,*" he turned to Bill for help. "How you say *'mala suerte'*?"

"Bad luck. Taking a turn for the worse. Turnin' sour." He got up with his utensils and plate and carried them to the washtub, then headed for his bunk, thinking to get a full night's sleep.

"Ah, *gracias señor,*" Patricio said to Bill's back. "We, eh, our luck ees taking a toorn for thee worse. That mean your *suerte* ees turning *buena,* good." Patricio's brows knit as he struggled with the language barrier, but he ended his inducement speech beaming broadly at Chico.

The cowhand pursed his mouth to the side, then arose, picked up his and Sourdough's plates, and nodded. "I ain't got but a little coin, but on the other hand, I ain't got no place to spend it this minute. Go ahead and set up the game while I wash up."

After the supper dishes were washed and put away, Bill

changed his mind, dug into his saddlebag for a couple of dollars in coins, and drew up a chair to the table. The other men pulled out what little money they possessed and put it before them.

"Go easy on me," Sourdough said. "I ain't held pasteboards for longer'n I can remember."

"We play a friendly game," Patricio assured him. "The esmall ante, *sí*?"

The game commenced, and Bill found himself winning a hand, then losing a pot. He was about to quit the game in favor of sleep when a voice spoke from the doorway.

"Kin I play?"

Bill turned, irritated from his recent loss. Bertie Owen stood inside the half opened door.

"Ain't you supposed to be in your cradle by this hour?"

The boy hunched forward at the reply, his face pinking up a bit.

Bill knew he was being unkind, but sometimes the kid rubbed his fur wrong, and this was one of those occasions.

But Bertie wasn't through. He unfolded his shoulders and glared at Bill. "I've got cash and I know how to play."

"This is a man's game," Bill replied. Then he repented of his hard stance and said, "I suppose you can watch, if you don't interfere." He looked to the other players for backup.

They all nodded, and Bertie seemed to accept the decision. He hung an elbow over the spindle back of Chico's chair and settled himself to observe.

Bill played what he thought would be his final hand, but Lady Luck seemed to favor him at last. He won the pot, kept playing, and soon began building up a little pile of coins on the table before him.

When the hour had advanced beyond a time later than he was accustomed to being awake, sleep threatened to overcome him. He yawned as Chico folded, leaving Patricio as the only other player. With two aces and two kings, Bill figured this pot was a sure win, but to his chagrin, he lost it when Patricio displayed three twos that beat his two pair. He shrugged, pushed the money over to the man, and chalked it up to carelessness brought on by exhaustion and '*mala suerte*.' He'd sure enough had plenty of that lately.

❧

Patricio and Enrique had almost reached the bunkhouse with their bedrolls when Albert stepped into their path. He looked back over his shoulder to make sure none of the hands were in sight, and said, "I saw what you did. Teach me that trick."

The brothers looked at each other, shrugged their shoulders, and made as though they would walk around Albert, but he forestalled them by acting out his demand.

"I saw you," he said, pointing to himself and then to his eye. Then he pulled on his shirt sleeve and appeared to be putting something into it. "I saw the trick," he repeated. "I want to know how you done it."

"No, *muchacho*," said Patricio in a patronizing voice. "*No hize nada*." He tried again, in his muddled English this time, but his tone was still superior. "I do nothing."

"Don't you go lyin' to me. I saw that two card drop. You're a card sharp."

"*No soy trampista*," Patricio declared. "I no cheet."

"Yes you did. Teach me, en-sen-yar-meh, or I'll tell Mr. Henry you're a crook."

Patricio looked at his brother and shrugged, then addressed himself to Albert. "Come leetle boy. I teech."

# Chapter 7

When Monday rolled around, Bill had scarcely set foot out of the bunkhouse when Albert Owen approached him.

"Nice day," he said. "You got a hankering for tradin' a chore with me?"

"Depends," said Bill. "What you tryin' to pawn off, Bertie?"

"Just a little light work carrying a bucket or two of water for my Ma. She says it's wash day. I'd druther chop and haul trees than spend my time listening to my sisters jaw at me. How about it?"

Bill's heart rose tight against his throat. He harumphed a time or two to get his voice back, then asked, "A bucket or two of water, you say?"

"Maybe four or five." He looked around, then spoke again. "Ma's not bad. It's Marie bossin' me around that raises my hackles. I reckon she'd speak softer to someone besides me."

Bill tried to keep his face smooth. "I could use a break from stinking up my clothes with sweat." He put out his hand and shook the boy's. "I'll do it. Let Rulon know I switched with you so he doesn't think I'm sick in my bunk, or playing hookey."

*The lad's got a future in wheedling folks to his will,* Bill thought as he walked toward the Owen cabin to present himself for work. *Not that I mind one bit. This is a prime chance to talk to Miss Marie.*

Since the Old Man had rearranged the chore schedule, Bill had not been able to get close to the girl to find out what had her upset. She no longer took her horse out early for exercise, but stuck close to the main house, involved in a multitude of chores he could only guess at. Now, if he could get a minute alone with her, he might be able to discover if she was spoken for, or if he still had a chance to woo and win her.

By the time he'd come upon Mrs. Owen at the back of the cabin, his heart had worked itself up into his mouth. It took a fair bit of swallowing to do more than croak when she smiled briefly at him, raised her eyebrow, and said, "Mornin', Mr. Henry. How can I help you?"

"It's my chore to bring you water, ma'am. I traded the job with Bert—Albert."

"Hmm," she said. "That young'un will do anything rather than carry water. I hope he's in for a good lot of work." She sighed, nodded toward the door, and said, "Yonder's the buckets. First, hang the wash kettle over the fire, then you can fill it 'bout midway. After that, bring up water for the rinse kettle. I haven't built the fire for that yet, but by the time the wash is boiling, I'll have it ready."

"Do you need help with the fire, ma'am?"

"No. Marie can help me with that task."

Bill glanced around, but Marie was nowhere in sight. As he drew near to where the buckets sat alongside the open door, he heard her speaking sharply to her sister.

"Pick that up, Jule. We can't waste it."

Julianna protested, but Marie continued, "Oh, brush it off. No, use this cloth. It's damp."

Bill caught up the buckets and headed for the creek, wondering what fair tidbit of food had fallen on the floor.

On the return trip, he saw Marie come out of the door and speak to her ma. Before he reached the kettles, she had gone back into the house.

That seemed to be the pattern for the day. He would go to the creek to fill another pair of buckets with water, and Marie would come outside. Before he returned, she had retreated.

*A body would think she's avoiding me*, he thought.

When Mrs. Owen bid him rest for a bit, Marie had gone up into the woods on an errand. When he went back to work, she came back to the house, but made no eye contact with him before entering and going about her own tasks.

Mrs. Owen added to his duties by giving him a long stick. "Stir the clothes around a bit, if you would. The water's boiling right nice, but the soap works better if it gets to all parts of the batch."

"Yes, ma'am." Bill stood over the kettle, stirring according to her directions until she put him to work rinsing the soap out of a batch of clothes.

When noon came, Mrs. Owen told him to go into the house and eat. Marie was alone.

Bill doffed his hat and held it in two hands. "Miss Marie," he said, feeling his heart thumping so hard he feared she could hear it. "Your ma sent me to eat."

She looked surprised, but recovered enough to point out the chair he could use. "Take Pa's seat, Mr. Henry. He won't be back for dinner."

He hung his hat on the back of the chair and seated himself. Marie brought him a plate of beans and cornbread, put a tin cup beside it, and indicated the milk jug on the table.

"Thank you kindly," he offered, but she didn't reply.

Before the silence got too awkward, Mrs. Owen and the younger sister joined them, and Marie finally sat opposite him to eat.

As he ate, he glanced at her from time to time, hoping he didn't seem overly-occupied with doing so. Mrs. Owen inquired about the progress of the logging operation, and he took care to answer as much as he knew.

One of her questions caught him off guard.

"Is Mr. Owen treatin' you well?"

"Ma'am?"

"He can seem harsh, time to time, but he knows you're a good worker. He values that in a man."

He swallowed his food before he could answer, "Thank you, ma'am. I appreciate the sentiment."

She laughed, a muffled sound from her throat. "He got bossy during the Hard Time. Some of his men were out 'n' out scallywags, and he was obliged to speak to them rough to get the lines to advance."

Bill made agreeable noises, chewing his beans and musing that having been an officer accounted for Rod Owen's commanding attitude. That kind of experience had to change a man.

After that, the meal limped along to an unsatisfactory end, to Bill's mind, as he found no moment to speak privately with the girl.

Back at work, wringing out clothes for Mrs. Owen, Bill thought a private time had come when he was paired with Marie to twist the water out of a load of sheets. They were never alone, though, and Bill found no opportunity to engage her in conversation. He finished the day's work with a frustrated spirit.

ℰ

Marie climbed off the stool that stood in front of the kitchen shelf and turned to see Ma through the open door, shading her eyes and gazing into the distance.

*What's she lookin' at?* she wondered, and called to her sister in the loft. "Jule, go find out what's got Ma standin' like a tree in the dooryard."

"Go see for yourself," her sister refused. "I'm busy. These towels are all tangled. Mr. Henry didn't fold them right."

"He's a man. A body can't expect him to know how." She abandoned her attempt to cajole her sister into running her own errand, picked up the washtub and stepped to the door.

She flung the water onto the dusty soil, then put down the tub and approached her mother.

"Someone's a-comin'," Ma told Marie, as though she had eyes in the back of her head to see her. "Drivin' a wagon."

"Settlers?" There was still land to be had south of here. Perhaps they would have new neighbors.

"I don't reckon. I only see the one soul on the seat."

"Hmm," Marie replied. "There's something shiny hanging on the side."

"I see it. Copper?"

"Might be."

"Is that a pot?"

Marie shaded her own eyes, then said, "That it would appear."

The person on the wagon seat drew near enough they could make out that it was a man with a dark, swarthy face and felt hat pulled over his brow. As he come closer, he began to sing a song about the goods he had to sell.

"A peddler? We've got a peddler comin'! Girl, we'll get you the necessaries for your marriage after all." Ma's smiled brightened her face.

"That's . . . good," Marie said, and hoped her voice didn't sound as disheartened as she felt.

The man came on, driving his wagon and singing his song, until he halted the horse, and pots and pans covering the outside of the vehicle clattered and clanged as they settled to a stop.

Jule came out of the house and joined them. Ma put her arm around her shoulders and gave her a squeeze. "Welcome," she said to the man, her voice reflecting her good cheer. "Climb down and take a rest."

"I do not mind if I do," the man replied, suiting his actions to his words, and tipping his hat to Marie and Ma once he was on the ground. His lean face cracked a wide smile. "I am Raphael, ladies, and I wish you good morning."

"And a good morning to you, sir," Ma said, her smile rivaling that of the peddler man. "Can I get you breakfast?"

"No, no, I've feasted long since, madam." He looked around. "A tidy homestead you have here."

"This is Rod Owen's land. You'll never see another man work so hard as he."

"Indeed. Indeed," said the peddler with one name. "I have wares to sell today. Pots, both copper and iron. Muslin and linsey-woolsey by the bolt or by the yard. Scissors, needles, and pins. Foodstuffs in tinned vessels. Beans and bacon. Sacks of salt and vials of spices. Knives and flatware and tableware. Sharpening stones, grinding stones, and stones for the chickens' gizzards. Chickens and rabbits, if you have none. Liniment and ointment and salves to soften your skin and draw your splinters. And trinkets. Mirrors and ribbons and lace. Bonnets and feathers and lockets and rings. Cushions for your chairs or for your footstools. What do you need to buy?"

"I'll be trading for a beef cow, butchered or on the hoof."

"I will trade for beef," the man agreed. "Live on the hoof will suffice."

"Good." She turned to Julianna. "Daughter, go up where your pa is workin'. Tell him a trader's come, and I need a cow."

"Yes ma'am," she said, and ran toward the mountain.

"Now then, tell me when I've reached the worth of a good beef cow. I need sharp kitchen knives. Utensils. Tableware for two. A pot and a spider, both iron. Bed linens. Ticking for pillows." Ma continued with a list of necessaries, and the peddler pulled out a note pad and pencil to jot down her wants. Then he began to fill her order, making a pile beside the door. Marie slipped into the house and put the washtub away, her mind unsettled by the tangible evidence of her coming change of circumstances.

∞

When Marie left the cabin again, Ma was still piling up a passel of goods. Marie headed toward the chosen items, thinking if she had to marry Tom, she might as well have a say in the everyday necessities of life. She would be using them for a long time.

The first thing she spotted was the enormous fry pan among the chosen implements.

"Ma, why did you pick such a big spider?"

Her mother looked her way, puzzlement evident on her face. "You'll be needin' one to cook your meals."

Marie lifted it out of the stack. "I don't aim to do for the entire Morgan family. It'll be just me and Tom to make a beginning." *I may as well accept it. Tom and me.* She pushed away the dark reality and let the power of Ma's excitement catch her for the moment.

"Hmm." Ma appeared to contemplate. Then she nodded. "Go ahead and change it," she agreed. "I had my mind fixed on my heap of young'uns." She gestured to the amassed treasures. "You'd best check over what I picked for you."

"I will, Ma."

Marie dug around and found another few items she thought too big. As she was returning them to the peddler's vehicle, she noticed an array of kitchen cutlery. Among them were several

82

knives in leather sheaths. She picked one up and slid it free of the covering. *How odd. Ma has one just like it in the house. With such a protection, I thought it would be a fighting knife.*

"Mr. Raphael," she said to get the man's attention. "Are these ordinary kitchen knives? I've not seen the likes of this sheath on a trimming or cutting blade for kitchen use."

The peddler smiled and nodded. "That is my own improvement, miss. With so many folks traveling about the country these days, they find there's danger to the small ones if a knife is laying loose. The leather also keeps the blades sharp and free of nicks." He chuckled. "I do sharpen knives, so you might think I'm cutting down my own income, but when I came across a poor little child all cut up from an accident, I got the idea for the leather encasement."

"Who would have thought?" Marie mused. "Is the price much higher?"

"I make the covers myself, miss, so the cost is low."

She picked through the knives and chose one of medium size. She showed it to the man. "I would like this one."

"A wise choice," he said, making a notation on the paper.

༄

On Saturday evening, after a hard week of cutting logs, and with another such week in prospect before the day set for the barn raising, Bill felt ready to cut loose or bust. He started off toward the tool shed, carrying his axe in one hand and a two-man saw over his shoulder. Bertie Owen came up alongside him, matching his stride to Bill's.

"Mr. Henry. You goin' to get up a card game after dinner?"

Not having the patience to fend off the boy, Bill sighed and keep walking.

"Will you?"

Bill shook his head. Maybe he needed a good run on a fast horse to relieve his tension.

"Ah, come on. I still have my cash, and if you don't have any, I'll lend you some."

The idea of taking Bertie's money and then winning the rest

83

of it had a fair measure of appeal. Bill nodded.

Bertie grinned. "I'll bring my cards."

"We have a deck."

The boy's face lost the grin, but he recovered quickly and said, "I'll bring the money."

When he showed up at the bunkhouse after dinner, he had indeed brought money, as the sack he tossed onto the table jingled enticingly.

Sourdough had a few coins, and the previous game having whetted his appetite for gambling, he joined in. Chico went to bed, claiming a toothache.

Bill wondered if he'd get in trouble letting the boy participate and gamble away his money. However, it soon became clear that this wasn't Bertie's first time playing poker. The boy knew the rules. Soon Bill was engrossed in planning his strategy and forgot the boy's age.

When ten o'clock came and Bill had five excellent cards in his hand, he felt comfortable that he would cap off the night with a win. But then Bertie let three cards fall out of his sleeve into his lap, palmed them, and exchanged them for three from his hand that he slipped between his legs.

Bill pretended he hadn't seen the exchange, wondering where the boy had picked up the trick. Then young Mr. Owen's trio of fours beat his own double pair of high cards, and he knew. Patricio Dominguez had to have used the same slight of hand on him two weeks ago.

*How'd the young'un convince the man to show him the trick?*

# Chapter 8

Bill watched from his post at the log pile as neighbors gathered late on a Friday afternoon. He and the hands had barely finished their labors at the unfamiliar tasks: felling trees, lopping off branches, dragging the trunks to a spot on the meadow, and stacking them side-by-side and then cross hatched, all in preparation for the barn raising.

During the past month, he had sensed an undercurrent of excitement from family members, and it piqued his curiosity. Overlaying his intellectual interest, a feeling of anxiety accompanied him each day as he reflected that more than a barn raising was in the offing. Had Old Man Owen succeeded in his matchmaking quest? Not knowing the answer played hob with Bill's mind.

He tried sounding out Rulon, but he was always too busy directing the logging operation for small talk. His stint with the water buckets on that wash day hadn't resulted in a talk with Marie. Bill remained in the dark as to the reason for the heightened emotion about the place. Something new, something different was in the wind, and constructing a new barn should not create such a lot of activity and fervor.

And then, that peddler had come.

The boss had been mighty pleased with himself when he'd put a rope on a fat steer and took it off the mountain to the missus. What lot of goods merited giving a steer in trade?

As he worried on the meaning of the enthusiasm he'd seen in the Old Man after that occasion, he saw Marie leading her saddled horse from the stable. She mounted at the block and rode away, up toward the tree line. He ached to join her, but he was obliged to stay where he was, stacking the last of the logs alongside of Chico Henderson.

"Don't you wish you could fork a horse and follow Miss Marie?" Chico asked in an undertone, his grin almost splitting his face.

Bill knocked hard against Chico's shoulder, the one that had been wounded.

"Ow! There's no call for that, Henry."

"Keep your mouth buttoned. I don't want to hear your palaver."

"Where'd you get that burr under your blanket?" Chico taunted. "Ain't she makin eyes at you these days?"

"I told you to shut up."

"Ohhhh." Chico made his voice scary. "Is she in love with someone else?"

"Get back to work. These logs don't get stacked by magic." He gave a heave and settled another log onto the stack as Chico chuckled. The sound rankled. Bill looked hard at his comrade, then walked away, unwilling to let his temper flare out of control with so many folks about.

A wagon came toward him from the south. Bill recognized the man driving as Ed Morgan, whose corn crop had almost been trampled by the Owen cattle a while back.

His prissy-faced wife sat beside him on the seat, and several children crowded in the back along with assorted baskets and crates. Two young men rode horses behind the wagon. One, the elder of the two, had his face turned about, watching something.

Bill looked in the same direction as the young man. Marie was coming out of the stable. The wagon must have caught her eye. She glanced their way and stopped in her tracks.

She wasn't looking at Bill, hope as he would that she'd take notice of him. Her eyes had landed on the young man riding behind the wagon.

Her head went down, and she made for the house with all speed.

*She don't want him to give her a greeting.*

At that moment, he realized the young man was Tom Morgan. Tom, the Virginia boy Old Man Owen had spoken about. The "known blood." Tom Morgan, whose rapt attention announced him as the bridegroom.

*The bridegroom. Miss Marie's intended husband.*

A white flame of jealousy leaped into his chest as he imagined the girl in that man's house, in his arms, in his bed.

He turned away, icy fingers of despair dumping ashes over the flame. The deed was done, the match made. He was out in the cold.

As he paced heedlessly about the meadow, more clumps of people arrived from the north, on horseback or in wagons, some dressed in sturdy clothing, others in more showy garb. Among the latter, he recognized the Dominguez brothers in their best get-up. *They must have been on another of their errands to Pueblo Town,* he thought. *Gambling again.* With them rode a man dressed in a suit, but he didn't look like the preacher Old Man Owen had said was coming. This man sported a silver chain across the front of his vest and tucked into the pocket. No doubt there was a fine silver watch on the end of it. His moustache was finely groomed into points. *Uses wax on it, I'll wager,* Bill scoffed, stroking his own full facial adornment. *He's a town man. Likely not given to honest labor.*

He shrugged off the disdain he felt toward the stranger and turned toward the shed as he remembered where he was supposed to be now. Mrs. Owen wanted plank tables built for the doin's tomorrow, and he'd best get to work.

❧

Marie hurried into the house. Melancholy, almost despair, had taken her in its grip today of all days. She needed to wash her face before anyone noticed that it was streaked with tears. How unseemly it would be if the prospective bride didn't have a cheerful countenance when mention was made of her coming happy day.

*Happy day!* she thought, and shivered. *I'd best have my happy days while I can. I reckon there's few ahead for me.*

Why had she badgered Pa so strenuously about her single state? She might have chanced upon a beau on her own account. Perhaps.

She climbed the ladder to the loft, poured a bit of water onto a rag, and scrubbed her face until it glowed pink. At least the dead skin from her sunburn had stopped peeling off weeks ago. She could be thankful for that. There was nothing so unappealing as peeling skin.

Marie tried to laugh at her silent word play, but nothing came from her throat but a strangled sound. Tom Morgan had made it plain that he would not have chosen her for his bride. Then he had put his hands on her, caused her misadventure at the river, laughed at her, and made uncouth comments. Remembering the occasion disheartened her anew. What new disrespect would she be obliged to endure this weekend?

"Marie?"

*Ma wants me. Have the Morgans come?* Marie hugged herself in dismay, her shoulders hunching nearly to her ears. *Rulon would say to keep my chin up. How can I do that when my heart is so low?* Marie dropped her arms from around herself, lowered her shoulders and descended the ladder.

"We'll need to begin serving supper before long," Ma said. "Folks are comin' in droves."

"I hope they brought plenty of provisions," Marie answered, attempting to put a lighthearted lilt in her voice, and failing miserably. "Has anyone in particular—have the Morgans arrived yet?"

"If they have, they've not come to the house." Ma's voice lacked its usual sparkle.

*Is she still pining for James?* Marie wondered, and gathered herself out of her own misery to try to lift her mother's spirits.

"Ma, James can take care of himself. I reckon he won't be gone long." She wondered if what she said were true. She might never see her brother again.

Ma laid her hand on Marie's arm. "I wish I could be as certain as you, sweet daughter." She looked searchingly at her, then drew her into a tight embrace. "You miss him too, I reckon. You always thought he hung the moon."

Surprised at the action, Marie patted her mother's back a trifle hesitantly. She wished she could share her thoughts, talk with her about all of them, from guilt over not seeing James's pain, to worry about Tom's attitude and his unseemly advances, and concern that marrying him would not bring her the happiness she sought.

But something now constrained her from sharing such secrets with Ma. Ma had the notion she and Tom were a good match. She couldn't blight her confidence. Not after their talk about— Not now. *I want to confide in her, but there's a gulf between us as wide as the prairie.*

෨

When she heard the creak of wagon wheels, Marie disengaged herself from her mother's grasp and straightened her skirt. "Someone's comin', Ma."

"I reckon they'll be needin' my attention," Ma said, nodding, and patting her own self into a presentable state.

Marie hesitated at the door, then drew it open and stepped outside, Ma right behind her.

Mr. Morgan halted his team of horses in the dooryard of the cabin, set the brake, and looped the lines around the handle. Tom and Parley sat their horses behind the wagon, Parley craning his neck looking around the homestead as though searching for someone. Tom looked her way, displaying a stern expression. Marie decided she would ignore him.

"Lizzie, don't fret," Mr. Morgan said in an undertone, but loud enough that Marie heard it.

*Lizzie? I'd not like to be called that,* Marie thought, biting her lip to prevent herself from smiling. *Good thing my name is plain enough that Tom can't shorten it.*

"Elizabeth," Ma said. "Mr. Morgan."

"Julia, you picked a pretty place to settle," Mrs. Morgan said, climbing over her husband's feet as she got down from the wagon. "Look at this meadow, and you have your own creek!"

"We have a river," Ed Morgan muttered, but his wife ignored him. Parley smirked and Tom forgot himself enough to snicker.

Mrs. Morgan turned to give the house a good looking over, shading her eyes from the rays of the lowering sun. "Your cabin is so sweet, just like your house back home."

"This is my home," Ma said, a trifle stiffly.

*Why's Miz Morgan takin' that snippity tone with Ma?* Marie wondered, then turned her attention to her mother. Her voice wasn't exactly cold, Marie judged, but she seemed a mite restrained instead of being her usual affable self.

"Yes, yes, of course. It's so quaintly situated. Did Mr. Owen pick the location?" She went on, seeming to have no expectation of being answered. "Of course he did. Only a man would put such a distance between the house and the water." She turned on a smile.

"I picked the location," Ma said, and this time, frost crept into her response. "I'm puttin' in a garden next spring between the creek and the house. Bein' close there, I won't have to haul the water so far to the plants."

"Well, I never! You're going to have to bring up the water? Your man won't see to it that the boys water the vegetables?" She turned a circle and faced Ma, her smile broadening. "My man is digging me a well, right there in the yard beside the house."

Ma squared her shoulders. "Come in and quench your thirst, Elizabeth. We have water enough here for that."

"Oh, we couldn't wear out our welcome as soon as we've arrived," Mrs. Morgan answered. "Besides, I can't leave my pies in the wagon for the crows to pick over."

Marie heard her mother's quick inward breath.

The woman continued, "Simply tell us where to pitch our camp, and we'll settle in. Mr. Morgan and the boys need a good night's rest so they can do a good day's work on your barn."

"Suit yourself," Ma said, and waved her hand toward the south. "Pick out any spot." Her voice sounded for all the world as though she spoke through clenched teeth.

*Miz Morgan refused our hospitality! No wonder Ma's cross with her. What sort of family am I obliged to join?*

# Chapter 9

Bill kept his face smooth as Chico threw down his playing cards. It would be unseemly to chortle over his good fortune tonight. Admittedly, he had helped Lady Luck along a trifle, but he didn't want to share that fact with Chico or the other players in the bunkhouse.

*Maybe I'm just an ornery cuss,* he thought. He dropped his hand, took the cards out of his lap, and slid them into his boot top. *I only hankered to know if I could pull off that trick.* He'd find a way to return Chico's cash to him later. He never had intended this game to be like the one when that little scoundrel, Bertie Owen, had cleaned him out. *He* hadn't felt any impulse to turn over his ill-gotten gains.

Chico pushed back his chair, the lamplight flickering over his scowl. "Hang it all, Henry! Where'd you get so lucky? Miss Marie ain't here to plant a kiss on your cards."

Bill raised a finger and tilted back his hat so he could see Chico. "Don't go mixing the lady into our game, Chico. She ain't a factor in your bad luck."

Chico took off his own hat and slammed it onto the floor. "Damn you, Bill Henry! That was my last three dollars! Now I can't—"

He cut off the diatribe by saying, "Have it back, friend, with interest. I don't want a fivespot standing between us." He extracted a five-dollar note from the pile of bills before him and slid it across the table toward Chico.

Chico snatched up the bill, his face relaxing just a mite. "Someday you'll go too far, *friend.*"

Allowing a grin, Bill retorted, "You came all the way from Texas with me, Henderson. You know I'm the best *friend* you have."

"Humph," Chico grunted, picked up his hat, and strode toward the bunkhouse door, stuffing the money into his shirt pocket with one hand and his hat onto his head with the other.

"Have you gentlemen had enough?" Bill asked the other players.

A chorus of agreement met his question, and he took a few greenbacks off the pile and pocketed them as he arose. "Split it up, boys," he said, indicated the remainder. "Be fair." Then he made an exit amidst the cacophony he left in his wake.

He walked out into the softness of the night, the stars overhead shining brilliantly before the moon elbowed its way into the sky. He strolled among the campfires, greeting folks he'd met that day and others he already knew. The Mexican brothers and their compañero from Pueblo town played cards on a barrel fitted with a couple of planks on top for a table, swigging from a bottle passed between them. He felt his moustache twitch against his cheeks as he scowled and passed them by without a word, unwilling to meet the dandified man with the thin, pointy moustache.

∞

Shortly after supper, Marie accompanied her mother as she walked from one camp to another to greet her guests and be sure they had all they required for their comfort.

Ma carried a lantern to light their way. Her steps slowed as they approached a bit of brush that marked the Morgan family's camp, and Marie put a hand on her arm.

"I'll see to their needs, Ma. You go have a good visit with Mrs. Bates."

Ma's shoulders relaxed. She gave Marie a wan smile, and as she patted her hand, said, "Thank you, daughter. Lizzie Morgan got my back up this afternoon."

"I could see that."

Ma sighed. "We had a bit of a misunderstanding years ago that she don't want to leave go of. One year I happened to bake a better apple pie than she did, and took home the county prize she'd counted on winnin'. She didn't take kindly to that. She always thought herself a notch above everybody else in the county, especially when it came to baking apple pies." She snorted and wagged her head. "Do you want the lantern?"

"No. You take it. I have young eyes. Don't you worry none, Ma. There's aplenty of campfires to light my way."

"Bless you, daughter."

Marie watched as her mother hurried off. She steeled her courage, then turned and approached the Morgan's fire.

"Marie," said Tom, stepping into her path from behind the brush. "What a pleasure."

Startled at his sudden appearance, Marie laid her hand over her heart. "I didn't see you standing there." With his back to the fire, Tom's figure was outlined with light, and she couldn't see his face clearly. His tone had not been welcoming, despite his words. She almost abandoned her task.

"I saw you a-comin'. Thought as I'd greet you ahead of the folks." He leaned in toward her.

She took a step backwards. "How nice of you. I come to ask after your comfort."

Tom was silent for a moment, then said, "I believe we're set." He moved forward and took her arm, fitting it through the crook of his. "Come to the fire and say hello to the folks."

Unable to think of a polite refusal, Marie let him lead her into the circle of light.

Mrs. Morgan glanced up from her seat on a log. "Well, look who's here. Mr. Morgan. It's Miss Marie, come to call on us."

"Miss Marie," Ed Morgan said, then stepped away from the fire and into the darkness.

Stung at his abrupt departure, Marie blurted out, "Tom says you're set for the night." The look on Mrs. Morgan's face made her regret that she hadn't started out with pleasantries. Then Louisa and Melissa crowded around, asking questions and diverting her attention as she tried to make up for her mistake with Mrs. Morgan.

"It's a nice evening," she began again. "I trust your journey wasn't taxing?"

"Uneventful," Mrs. Morgan murmured, nodding. "Uneventful, but warm."

"It has been a warm day," Marie agreed. "It's fixin' to cool off, I believe."

"I can only hope it don't get too chilly."

"No, ma'am. It should be pleasant tonight."

Mrs. Morgan didn't reply, but instead examined the hand work in her lap.

Louisa and Melissa went back to their chores, and Marie stood awkwardly beside Tom, her hand trapped between his arm and his body. The rhythm of his breathing pressed against the back of her arm, and his warmth seeped into her skin. Her throat constricted.

After several long minutes of silence, it became apparent that Mrs. Morgan had finished with her. Marie cleared her throat and said, "Well, good evening to you. I must be going." She tried to remove her arm from Tom's grasp, but he kept it tightly bound, even placing his other hand over hers to maintain his mastery of it.

"I'll walk Miss Marie home, Ma."

"Don't be gone all night," Mrs. Morgan said, without looking up.

*What does she mean by that remark?* Marie wondered as she walked away from the fire, Tom moving along with her. Trying to quit his company, she said, "I have to see to the other visitors, Tom. I'll be just fine, walking about by myself."

"It's too dark for you to stumble around," Tom answered. "I'll keep you company."

"There's no need." She tried to disentangle her hand again, and Tom let her slip it from his arm, but grasped her hand as it came free.

"That's a piece of my obligation now," he said, his voice a trifle bitter sounding. "I'll see to your safety." He started off, and Marie, unable to shake off his hold on her, followed along.

"We're practically in my own door yard," she protested. "I dare say no harm will come to me between here and my house."

"This appears to be a rough crowd," he answered. "When folks gather, you can't ever tell who they brought with them."

"Don't be a silly." As soon as she finished speaking, she wished she could take back the words, and threw a guilty glance up at Tom.

He glared down at her, pursing his lips. She'd seen that same expression on his father's face. After a few more steps he said, "I saw strangers over yonder."

"I'm sure they're known to my pa."

"I mistrust the look of them, especially those dark folks." Tom motioned to a fire where several men sat around a makeshift table, playing cards.

Marie looked where Tom gestured, and recognized the Dominguez brothers. "I know who they are. They have a place south of here. They stop to water their horses at our creek."

"You can't trust Mexicans. Always taking what's not theirs."

"Do you have experience of that?" Marie asked, looking sideways up at Tom.

"I've heard about them." He turned his head, glanced at her, and laid his finger alongside his nose as if to imply he had vast knowledge of such things.

"That's foolishness. They're like any other folks."

Tom stopped in the dark shelter of the clump of brush and pulled Marie close to him. "You won't talk like that around me. I know better." His voice dropped an octave. "Keep your place."

"Keep my place?" She pulled free of his restraining hand. "Don't dare speak to me like that."

Tom grabbed her arms, though she tried to beat off his hands, and he put his face close to hers. "I'm your man now. You'll do as I say."

"Who commands me so?" She struggled against the hold of his rough hands. "You're not my man until the preacher speaks the words."

"Your pa gave you to me."

"Not yet, he didn't."

"You've nothing to gain being difficult," he grunted, pulling her closer to him. "Heed my words, and I'll treat you well."

"I won't be bullied," she muttered, straining against his grasp, panic squeezing her chest. "Let me go!"

"No. You're not going anywhere." He wrapped his muscular arms around her and lowered his face to hers again. "I didn't choose it, but you're bound to me, and you'll obey." He put his mouth on hers, hot and wet, and kissed her repeatedly, the stiff evening stubble above and below his lips scratching her face.

"No," she cried, although the sound didn't escape her dry throat. She twisted against him, thrashing, her arms thrusting against his chest, until she remembered a bit of advice James had once told her, half jokingly, about how to fight off a Yankee. She bent her knee and brought it up quickly, connecting with Tom's groin, and as he bent double, moaning and covering the stricken area, she fled, straight into the camp of the card players.

&#8450;

She brought her headlong rush to a stop, working to keep upright as she teetered before three men seated around a barrel. Laying on top of it were two planks that formed a rough table, which was littered with cards and poker markers that shook and bounced as the men scrambled to their feet. Marie blinked back her indignant tears. Enrique Dominguez reached forward and snatched a bottle of liquor off the table and hid it behind his back. His brother Patricio removed a cigarillo from his lips and palmed it.

"Señorita Maria, ¿que le pasó? Ah, I say, what ees happen weeth you?" Patricio used a mixture of Spanish and English, his voice raspy with concern.

Marie shook her head, more to clear it than to indicate a negative response. "I— Nothing of— It was a momentary trifle," she ended, flustered more than she would have wished. *That Tom!* She must speak with Pa, as soon as could be done.

"If there's something we can do, miss?" a man asked, his voice low and melodious. He was unknown to her. "We would be happy to assist you in any way." He removed his hat and inclined his head.

She noticed that his hair appeared to be black and wavy in the firelight, not unlike that of her brother James. She put the back of her hand to her nose to mask a snuffle. "Thank you, sir. There's nothing of importance to be done. I thank you all for your concern." She nodded toward the men and turned to go, but the black-haired man grasped her elbow and stopped her.

"Miss. I beg you to sit and compose yourself." He motioned to his recently-abandoned chair as he spoke to Patricio. "Traígame un vaso de agua." He again addressed Marie. "Will you take a glass of water? You seem uncomfortable."

"I— I thank you, sir. And you are?"

"C. G. Thorne, at your service." He bowed as he made his hat cut a figure through the air.

Marie imagined the hat would look quite at home if it had a feather sweeping from the side of the crown. Oddly, the thought did not strike her as ridiculous, but as courtly and comforting. The man seemed genuinely concerned for her welfare. With that, Marie took the chair offered by Mr. Thorne.

Enrique Dominguez brought her a tin cup of water, and Marie accepted it, wondering when Patricio had delegated the task to his brother. She put the cup to her lips, sighed, and took a sip. What did it matter who fetched the water? Her life had shattered into shards around her ears.

"Miss, you truly must allow us to help you if you have trouble to be mended."

It was the same man speaking, Mr. Thorne.

"Sí, señorita," chimed in Enrique. "Queremos— We want to ayud—help you si es posible." He looked at Patricio, as though he were seeking affirmation that his speech was in proper form.

"It was nothing," she repeated. "A slight disagreement."

"Who would offer you such an affront?" Mr. Thorne seemed taken aback at the temerity of anyone to annoy her. "You have but to mention his name." An unspoken threat to the malefactor hung in the air.

"*His* name?" Marie felt a small smile lifting her lips. "You are sure a man wronged me?" Her tears had gone.

Thorne hung his head. "Dear lady, I beg your pardon at making any false assumption." He raised his head again and looked her straight in the eye, one eyebrow raised. "It is the highest dishonor imaginable to distress such a fair creature as yourself. That is my only defense, that I imagined a scoundrel of the male persuasion gave you an insult. Was I not right, dear lady?"

"Sir, you were not wrong, but I doubt the offense will reoccur." Marie heard herself using formal language, and cast her eyes down to mask any delight that might be showing in them at the opportunity. "Once my father takes a hand—" She stopped herself. It was likely that her father would disregard any misgivings she had over marrying Tom at this late date. "That is to say . . ." Again, she felt at a loss for words. What could she say, not knowing where this weekend's events would lead her? Pa was entirely likely to go through with his scheme to announce her engagement to that odious man. Her mouth went dry.

"You are distressed anew," Mr. Thorne stated. "Would a sip of spirits fortify you?" He held up the liquor bottle that had somehow gotten from behind Enrique Dominguez's back into his hand.

Marie first felt shocked by his suggestion, then, as the feeling faded, reconsidered. *Why not? It works for men.* She nodded, not trusting herself to speak.

Somehow, she found herself steadying the bottle that Mr. Thorne had uncorked, wiped on his sleeve and lifted to her mouth. She took a tentative sip. White fire burned down her throat and she almost gagged. Then Mr. Thorne raised the container slightly, and the liquid flowed into her mouth, filling it. Reflexively, Marie swallowed once, then was obliged to do so in vast gulps, twice, three times, before she could thrust the bottle away. She almost choked as she swallowed the liquor remaining in her mouth.

"There." Mr. Thorne said, stopping up the container with a hard thrust of his palm upon the cork. "That should hearten you."

Marie felt herself shudder at the strong taste of the liquor. She licked her lips to cleanse them of a lingering drop. It burned her tongue. She sensed, rather than saw Mr. Thorne tilt his head at the Dominguez brothers, who melted away from the table and left her alone with him.

He placed the bottle on the table and seated himself beside her. He drew the chair close, momentarily bumping his knee against hers. "You must tell me your troubles, my dear," he said.

Marie drew her skirt together at the knees, hands gripping the fabric. "Sir, I don't know what you mean."

Mr. Thorne tilted his head and the corner of his mouth twitched ever so slightly. "Why, Miss Marie, you seem quite vexed with troubles. Won't you allow me to share your burden, even only a tiny bit?" He held his thumb and forefinger together, almost touching.

The fire from the swallows of liquor seemed to be spreading from Marie's stomach to her limbs. She brought a finger to her lips to bite the nail, then thought better of it, and dropped her hand back into her lap. "You are a stranger, sir. How odd, that you wish to be my confidant."

The man drew back a trifle, pressed his lips together, then blurted out, "I beg your pardon for moving beyond my place, Miss Marie. Your beauty overwhelms me." He sucked in a breath through pursed lips, and hung his head. His voice sounded hollow as he said, "I do beg your pardon, very humbly, Miss. Please forgive me."

Marie felt in a forgiving mood. The skin of her hands felt soft enough to run off her fingers like melted butter. *Ma talked . . . 'bout meltin'. Butter, wasn't it?* "I . . ." she began, but her voice faded. "It's not . . . Usually I would not . . ." She shook her head gently, feeling as though her brains would collide with the bones of her skull if she exerted herself overmuch. "You are forgiven, Mr. Thorne," she said in a rush, before her voice failed her again. "Forgiven," she repeated for emphasis. The consonants ran together.

Mr. Thorne raised his head and stared into her eyes. "You are quite magnificent," he said slowly. "Magnificent and magnanimous, together in one generous soul. I feel as though I were in the presence of a royal personage. Such grace. Such charm." He took her hand in both of his, and lifted it toward his lips. He stopped midway and murmured, "I am quite overcome with emotion, Miss Marie. Will you permit . . . ?" and he kissed the inside of her wrist.

Looking at the man's bent head, Marie wondered that his moustache did not tickle her skin. Instead, it felt stiff, yet flexible and yielding at the same time, and his warm lips spread the heat from the alcohol up her arm. She knew she must remove her hand from his grasp, but her strength failed her just as her voice had, and the lethargy caused her head to tilt toward her shoulder.

He made circles on her wrist with the back of one finger, his nail smooth, not catching her skin with jagged edges or nicks, but sliding over her flesh like it rode on a film of sweet oil.

"Sir," she protested, her voice little more than an echo, as he began to place gentle kisses on the heel of her hand. Kisses like the brief touch of a moth's wing. Kisses that progressed slowly onto the sensitive flesh of her palm. Such light kisses, that nonetheless stirred her blood and drove her inhibitions far away, far up the mountain, diving into the depths of a dark pool of water where she had sat once in time, a man bending over her, offering her a cup to dip into the black water. Who had that been? Her head swam as memory eluded her, and she swallowed, no longer fighting the wild pulse of blood that throbbed in her temples.

She raised her head with an effort. The camp fire had gone to embers, no longer lighting the table before her. The man beside her murmured, "So lovely," and placed his hand on her knee.

An internal alarm roused her senses. *This is wrong. I did not tolerate Tom's hands on me. This man is a stranger. He has less right.* She shifted her body so that her limbs slid out from under the man's hand. "I . . . must go," she said, grateful that her voice seemed steady. She pushed herself to her feet against the man's protests. "You must forebear, sir," she added, tugging her hand free. "Goodnight."

Steering herself toward the light of the distant lantern hanging from the door post of her father's house, Marie splashed through the creek and felt the shock of the cold water bring her wits into sharper focus. She grimaced against the headache starting behind her eyes, but made it through the front door and into the loft before anyone greeted her or made note of her wet shoes and hem.

*I'm shameless,* she told herself. *A shameless spinster, acting like a brazen hussy.* And yet, part of the warmth from the man's moth-like kisses had not faded from her body, and she wrapped herself in that warmth as she fell asleep.

# Chapter 10

Marie awoke, her head pounding and her eyes sensitive to light. *What happened to me?* she wondered, trying to think back to last night as she dashed cold water onto her face. *Ma and I. We visited . . . Tom! Blast him! Where's Pa?* She hastily dried her face, dressed, bundled up her hair in the leather clasp Mrs. Bates had given her, and dropped down into the cabin. No Pa in sight.

"Mighty late comin' in last night," Julianna jeered at her. "Made you a slug-a-bed." She raised her chin and sniffed, then swiped at the tin plate in her hands with an old flour sacking towel.

"Leave her be, Jule," Ma said sharply from where she knelt at the fireplace, pouring batter into a heavy iron oven.

"I may, or I may not."

"Don't sass Ma," Marie said. Her voice hardly made it past her lips, and horrors! It sounded like a frog's croak! She cleared her throat and tried again. "You're impertinent, Jule."

"Better'n being a slug-a-bed!" She stuck out her tongue.

Marie reciprocated, feeling foolish but justified.

Ma turned her head away from the fire. "I saved your breakfast, daughter." She gestured with a spoon toward the table. "Under the cloth."

Marie lifted the dish towel, drew up a chair, and sat before a plate of one fried egg, a slice of beef, and a slice of corn bread. The honey pot also sat on the table beside a cup of milk, and she spilled a bit of sweetener onto the bread. "Thank you, Ma," she said after she'd swallowed a mouthful. "I'm sorry to be a slug-a-bed."

"See?" Jule dried another plate and smirked.

"I heard you come in late. Is all well with you and Tom Morgan?"

Marie hastily filled her mouth so she would have an excuse for a delayed answer. She didn't want to talk about the revulsion Tom had raised in her. She chewed. Good thing she'd gotten away . . . from . . . him. . . . "Oh!" She drew in a breath, then choked and coughed out the piece of corn bread that had gone down the wrong pipe.

Jule came and pounded on her back, much harder than was necessary.

When she'd regained her breath, Marie turned around and slapped at her sister's hand, then huddled over her plate, remembering the soft kisses on her wrist and palm that had sent her senses shivering into oblivion. That man, Mr. Thorne, had been making love to her. Had he meant what he'd said about being overcome by her charms? Warmth spread through her body. The man certainly had seemed sincere.

"Marie?" Ma's voice came from close behind Marie.

She looked up, hoping she wasn't blushing.

"Hmm." Ma nodded. "I can see you have pleasant thoughts about your evening."

Marie said nothing, grateful for once that she *was* blushing. Since the coloring spoke for her, she would have no need to comment or to speak a lie.

Ma laid a hand on Marie's shoulder. "Go slow, daughter. Harvest time will come soon enough."

A lump rose in Marie's throat, choking her just as effectively as had the bit of corn cake before. She couldn't make a sound, but reached up and patted her mother's hand as she swallowed hard. She couldn't speak of Tom to Ma. She seemed so sure that Marie was pleased with the recent turn of events. But with Pa it was a different matter. Pa would get an earful . . . just as soon as she could catch up to him!

☙

Bill hadn't seen Marie all morning. The fact that he'd been busy lifting logs and pegging them into place hadn't kept his eyes from scanning the female figures that brought water to the crew. Not one had the dark, waving hair, the winsome smile, the light step of Marie. Not one made his heart swell in his chest. Not one made him ache to converse with her, to touch her arm. Where was she keeping herself?

"Henry!" Mr. Owen bellowed.

Bill looked down at the boss standing at the foot of the ladder and waving for him to descend.

"Yes, sir?"

"Come down."

He went down. Once on the ground, he took off his hat and wiped the sweat out of his eyes with his sleeve. "Yes, sir?"

"Where's that bale of leather thongs you had Carl cut?"

"I wrapped them strings in a piece of holey hide and put 'em on a shelf in the stable. Want me to fetch 'em?"

"No, I'll send Albert. Return to your work up there."

Bill swept his hair back with his fingers and put his hat on his head. He nodded, climbed to his previous position, and grasped the log that was being levered atop the last. He got it on his shoulder and heaved. He still hadn't seen Marie.

The man next to him grunted and swore as he dropped his end of the log onto his own fingers.

"Careful," Bill said automatically.

The man swore again, berating Bill for not catching the log when he had dropped it.

"Beg pardon, friend. I'll do better next time." He gritted his teeth. How was he supposed to know when a man was going to fumble his load?

Although his neighbor groused for quite a spell, Bill tried to ignore the man and deal with the unfamiliar work. Give him adobe blocks for a building material any day. This business of constructing with logs was out of his experience.

&

*The girl. Where is the girl?*

C. G. Thorne sipped from the dipper, wiped a drop of water from the corner of his mouth with his handkerchief, and looked around the meadow again. It was becoming quite a chore, moving from spot to spot to avoid being assigned to a work crew. He continued to walk about as though he had a purpose, and came upon Enrique Dominguez, who was engaged in trimming the end of a log with an adz.

"Oye, hombre," Thorne said as he drew near. "¿Dónde está la chica de anoche?"

Enrique looked up and surveyed the crowd. "No sé, señor. No la he visto. She no work here."

"¿Sabes quién es?"

"Sí, señor. Ella es la hija del patrón Owen, el gran dueño en estos lugares." Enrique raised his eyebrows and waggled them.

Thorne swore. *Old Man Owen's daughter.* "¡No me digas!" He preened his moustache. "¿El Viejo tiene dinero?" He rubbed his fingers together in the age-old sign for money.

"No sé. El patrón vino aquí el año pasado. Pero yo sé que él compró mucho ganado en Tejas." Enrique shrugged. "Tal vez todavía tiene dinero. Es seguro que él tiene que pagar a los vaqueros."

*So the old man has money.* Thorne rubbed his chin. *Enough to get himself a herd in Texas and pay the help. Those cowhands wouldn't stick if he didn't pay them.* "Gracias, amigo," he said, clapped Enrique on the shoulder, and moved off.

೫

Engaged as she was in helping Ma cook for the noon meal, Marie didn't get out to locate her father until it was nearly time for dinner. However, a need to visit the outhouse finally took her outside, and she ran up the trail into the woods.

As she did her business, she heard voices, low-pitched voices, accompanied by long pauses and suspicious noises. Fearing what she would find, she carefully closed the door, rounded the wooden structure, and followed the sounds.

Her ears led her toward a nearby copse of oak trees. When she got closer, she identified one male and one female voice, and inwardly groaned as she hurried toward the source.

Parley Morgan! He was crooning to her sister, "Come on, girl. No one's going to know. I can't stand bein' so far away when I love you so much."

Kissing noises. Rustling of fabric. Halfhearted protests.

Marie burst into the clearing, yelling, "Oh, no, you don't!" She skidded to a halt beside Jule. Her sister's bodice was open, and Parley had one hand where it had no right to be.

Jule looked up, saw Marie, and her face went pale. She began to scream and Parley swore and jumped away from her. Then he high-tailed it down the trail.

Before Marie could grab Jule's arm, the girl fled in another direction, sobbing and clutching her bodice together. Marie stood in the clearing, panting, wishing she were a man so she could swear as Parley had done. What was her sister thinking? Had she no shame, no pride, no sense of decorum?

Feeling her strength leave her, she sank down on the dense carpet of decaying leaves and fallen pine needles, holding herself and weeping.

She didn't know if she wept because Jule was shaming the family, or for her own pain in knowing Tom wanted to do those same things to her, as soon as he could, and without benefit of marriage words and vows. *What makes men such beasts?* she wondered, and cried harder, rocking, barely feeling the beetles that crawled up her limbs and into her stockings.

When she had cried out her anger and sorrow and her focus widened to include the world around her, she finally felt the scurrying on her flesh. Shuddering as she leapt to her feet, she yanked down her stockings and swept the insects into the leaves.

Marie straightened, breathing heavily, and looked around. Jule was long gone and she couldn't berate her, so the next order of business was to find Pa and tell him what his younger daughter was up to. Pa would put a stop to that!

# Chapter 11

Time and again, Marie missed finding Pa. *Where is he?* she asked herself as she looked into the stable. Then she ran to the house and put her head inside the door, but Ma was the only one in the room. She had expected to see Jule clinging to Ma, making her complaints, but evidently the girl had felt some shame and hadn't come here.

"Have you seen Pa?" she barked more than asked, but Ma only shook her head as she lifted a kettle off the andiron at the fire. Fearing she would ask her to stay and help, Marie shut the door and ran toward the crowd raising the barn.

The first person she encountered was Patricio Dominguez, who swept off his hat and nodded to her. "Señorita. Cómo le va? How you do this fine day?"

"Hello," she said, looking about. "Have you seen my father?"

"El patrón?" The man also looked around. "No sé dónde— I don know where he be, Mees Maria. Perhaps . . . at . . . thee . . ." Struggling with his English, he described the log pile with his hands.

"Thank you, sir. You are most kind." She dashed in the direction of the logs, but Mr. Thorne, the man she had met the night before, stepped into her path and she had to stop short to keep herself from ramming into him.

"My dear Miss Marie," he exclaimed. "Where can you be off to in such a hurry? May I assist?"

His eyes were so expressive, so keenly trained on her, that she almost squirmed with unease at the attention, but she kept herself from being impolite, and nodded her head at him in greeting. "Mr. Thorne. I seek my father. I can't seem to find him anywhere."

"There, there," he said, taking her hand and fitting it into the crook of his arm. "He must be somewhere about. We'll find him in short order."

Hesitating to be burdened by a companion when she was in such a hurry and on such a delicate errand, Marie tried to pull her hand free, but Mr. Thorne's grip was firm, and she finally ceased resisting. "Thank you, sir," she forced herself to say. "I have urgent business with him. The sooner we can find him, the sooner my errand will be accomplished."

"Well then," he said, looking around again. "Perhaps he's off under the trees seeking shade. It's been a hot morning." He started to walk toward the edge of the forest.

Not able to feature her father taking his ease when everyone else was engaged in a task, Marie started to shake her head, but Thorne's grip on her hand persuaded her to accompany him, and they soon gained the shadows under a stand of pines.

"Hmm," Mr. Thorne grunted. "He doesn't seem to be here. I was sure I had seen him walking in this direction." He stroked his moustache. "I must have been mistaken, or he returned to the building enterprise while I was otherwise engaged."

Marie tugged Thorne in the direction of the meadow. "I must find him, sir," she said, but the man touched her hand briefly, as though he meant to further restrain her. He ending up pausing, then patting the back of her hand.

"Wait a bit, Miss Marie. The sun is hot. You will burn your lovely face." He left off patting, and reached up to touch her cheek with the backs of his fingers. "You must not ruin such beauty."

Thinking of the dreadful molting process she's undergone after the journey to the Cuchara, Marie felt herself blushing.

"Ah, there. Have I said something rash? My dear, you are such a marvel. Stay and cool yourself." He let go of her hand and drew a flask from his pocket. "Would you care for a bit of lemonade? I only just filled up my flask." He handed the container to her, and she took it automatically.

"I don't know—" she began, but he cut her off.

"You are flushed, dear Miss Marie. The drink will cool you."

"Perhaps a little taste," she conceded, and unscrewed the lid. She took a hesitant sip, but the fluid was clearly lemonade, and would not compromise her thinking as the liquor had done. She took a large swallow, then another, then removed the flask from her lips, secured the lid upon it, and returned it to its owner.

"That is good," he said, then reached out and removed a lingering drop of lemonade from her lip with a light touch. He put his finger into his mouth and drew it out in a long motion. "Sweet," he said, drawling the word into several syllables.

Marie watched him, fascinated by his action. Again, his touch had been light as the wing of a fluttering moth. Certainly a too-familiar gesture, much more familiar than the length of their acquaintance warranted, but certainly it reflected care of her feelings, and tenderness.

"You quite take my breath away," he murmured, closing his eyes, and sighing heavily.

Not sure how to react, Marie stood frozen, awaiting she knew not what.

He opened his eyes and looked at her, longingly, it seemed. "I think I've fallen in love with you," he whispered. "Is it possible?"

Marie looked down, a bit frightened to have glimpsed naked yearning in his eyes, and fearing what might be showing in her own. Had she imagined he said that, that he loved her? The growing warmth in her body belied the thought that she had dreamed up his words. He *had* professed his love. Her mind churned. How did she feel about Mr. Thorne? Was it within the realm of reason to suppose that she was falling in love with him, as well?

"Would you permit—" He stopped, hung his head. "I feel it is a great liberty I'm asking. Oh, dear Miss Marie. May I call you 'Marie'?" He looked up again, a smitten expression on his face. "I feel I have known you forever. May I, would you permit me to kiss you, dear Marie?"

She took in a sharp breath of air, but before she could say yea or nay, Mr. Thorne's lips were on hers, soft and gentle, and pressed hers briefly, then released.

Marie breathed out. That hadn't been distressing. Indeed, she felt a longing to repeat the experience, and when he gently cupped her face between his hands, she permitted a second kiss.

This one was a trifle longer, more heartfelt, and caused her knees to quake. She put her hands on his shoulders to steady herself, and he wrapped his arms around her, pulled her against him, and kissed her again, with mounting fervor.

She halfheartedly pushed against him, at the same time as she reveled in the heady sensation of being wrapped in the comforting circle of his arms. Yet, at the same time, she struggled against the enchantment, a part of her not wanting to escape so quickly into the bubble of unrestrained joy.

When she at last broke away from the embrace, Thorne seemed repentant, a little shamefaced. "I— I beg your pardon, my dearest Marie. I became carried away. Your loveliness is as attractive as nectar to the honeybee. I could not resist your charms."

Marie tried to moderate her heavy breathing as she realize that he had dropped the construction of "Miss Marie" and was using her Christian name alone. She hadn't given him leave, but she didn't mind, not a whit. She felt ready to float away from beneath the trees. It appeared that they both were carried away on the wings of emotion.

He sighed and shook his head. "We must return to the building enterprise at once. I believe you were seeking out your father?"

"Ah, yes," she replied, remembering that she *had* indeed been looking for him, but searched her mind unsuccessfully for the reason why. The spread of the warmth that rose into her bosom almost persuaded her that her errand no longer was of any significance. What mattered most to her at that moment was that this man cared for her. She was sure of that. Didn't his manner, his actions speak of it?

Thorne shifted from foot to foot for a spell, then said, "My darling Marie, it would be best if you preceded me alone. If your father—" He left the thought unsaid.

"But—" she began to protest, but he shushed her with a quick kiss.

"It will appear better, my dear. Our acquaintance is a bit tenuous, as yet. I will follow you in a moment." He looked quite crestfallen at the notion that they should not be seen together.

She gave him a questioning glance, but his forlorn expression convinced her that he meant to compose himself before again being seen among the people working on the barn, so she left without him, looking back once at his dear face before she walked out into the sunshine.

☙

Bill looked up from the log he was trimming square and almost cut off his foot with the adz. Marie came toward him, out of the shadows of the trees on the hill above him. She had a faraway look in her eyes, then she glanced over her shoulder toward the forest, and he caught a glimpse of a man standing next to a pine. His stomach clenched. It was the town man he'd seen riding in with the Dominguez brothers. What had she been doing in *his* company? Alone?

He put down the implement and wiped the sweat from his face, lifted his hat, and raked his hair back with his fingers. *Marie Owen, off in the trees with that man?* He swore softly as he jammed his hat on his head. *He's up to no good.*

Marie walked right by him as though he weren't standing there, prepared to speak to her. He pivoted to follow her with his gaze. She seemed almost to walk in a dream state, and he determined to catch up to her to find out why.

Leaving his work, he angled to where their paths would meet, and put on a bit of speed to encounter her.

"Miss Owen," he said when he was near enough for her to hear him. Not knowing what next to say, he ventured, "Have you any water?" Then he felt a fool, for she clearly wasn't carrying anything with her.

She seemed startled at his voice, stopping and looking around as though coming out of a daze. Then she smiled and said, "Oh, hello, Mr. Henry. Water? No. I don't have any with me. I can fetch you a bucket, though."

"Don't go to any trouble," he said. "I reckon I wanted mostly to say 'hello'."

"Hello, then," she said, and walked away.

"You're a fool, Bill Henry," he berated himself in a low tone. "She wants nothing to do with you." He glanced back at the trees.

111

The man who he'd seen a few moments ago was now halfway to the barn site, preening his moustache as he walked.

"Dandy!" Bill muttered, and got his feet moving toward the log he'd abandoned. He would dearly love to put his fist into the man's face, but what would be the point? The dandy had been the one consorting with Miss Marie under the shade of the trees, not him. What would a fight gain him? Exile, most likely. He picked up the adz and began chopping it into the log, thinking dire thoughts about the town man who passed by with clean hands and not a speck of dust on him. Had the man done a lick of work today? It seemed unlikely.

≈

"Pa. I need to speak to Pa," Marie reminded herself as she left Bill Henry. "I need to tell him—" Why couldn't she remember what had been so important this morning? Something had occurred. It upset her, she remembered, but what had it been?

She decided to think back through her day. *I was late rising,* she remembered. *Jule called me a slug-a-bed. Then Ma had me help her all morning. Then I had to use—*

She stopped so abruptly that she almost toppled over. Her memory had returned, with a picture clear as if it were reflected in a good looking glass. *Jule's scandalous behavior with Tom's brother! And Tom!* She recalled the struggle with him from the night before. She couldn't marry Tom. "Where's Pa?" she said aloud, now frantic to speak to him.

People moved by her, jostling her one way, then the other. "Let me through," she pleaded, pushing, shoving, trying to get to the front of the crowd before Pa ruined her life. Then she wriggled herself free of those who had bumped into her, preventing her passage, and she stood on her toes in a vain attempt to gain a better view. She resorted to jumping, but still couldn't see him.

Then she heard her father's voice, and her heart seemed to stop.

"Gather 'round here. I have a grand announcement to make. Attention, folks. Come along over here. I have a few words to speak to all," he was saying, in a voice so loud it broke her heart free from its temporary failure.

Pa had already launched into his speech, and now the crowd shifted, so she saw him, talking from where he stood in the bed of a wagon, one foot perched on the seat.

"When I arrived in this place, I brought with me a host of fine folks. Among them was my good neighbor, Ed Morgan, who settled down the country to grow crops along the river. Now Ed has a strapping son, Tom. He's a fine lad, sturdy and a hard worker, good as the day is long."

*No!* Marie thought, her chest thudding with the renewed pounding of her heart. She threw herself into the press of the crowd. She struggled to get to Pa's side, to gain his attention, to forestall the rest of his words, but folks had again jammed themselves so tightly together that her progress was slow and uneven.

Pa's voice continued to ring out over the heads of the people gathered in his meadow. "I have a comely daughter," he said. "In normal times, she would've been the first of her age to marry. But times were hard in our neighborhood a few years ago, and that chance didn't come her way. It's high time she became a bride."

*What is he saying? Why is he pouring shame over my head?* Marie's soul cringed.

". . . so it is my great pleasure to make known my daughter Marie's upcoming nuptials to the son of—"

*No!* She was too late. And Pa had caught sight of her, was beckoning her up to his side.

All at once, she found herself staring up at her father, and didn't know how she had arrived there, standing below his high perch. Perhaps the hands she had sensed on her arms and body had something to do with her rapid forward movement. Then she was standing beside him in the wagon, stunned as she heard him conclude his announcement, and again, knew not how she came to be there. She felt as though she'd been drenched in icy water. The people below her, clapping and making joyful gestures, had no distinguishable faces, only blurs of pink or brown. A buzzing filled her head from ear to ear, sounding like a giant swarm of bees intent on traveling through her brain. She pulled on Pa's arm, struggled to get out a few words, important words about

Tom, as he leaned over to receive them. Then she was falling, and the last thing she knew was a sharp pain when her cheek met the boards of the wagon bed with a thunk.

# Chapter 12

Bill watched as Marie toppled to the bed of the wagon and heard the sickening thud when she landed. Then he began to push through the crowd, trying to get to her, shoving the milling, gawking onlookers, who shoved back with many a curt comment.

"Watch it, buddy. Don't be pushing on me."

"Hey! Keep your hands to yourself!"

A blow landed on the side of his neck, but he pressed on, frantic to see if Marie was all right. He reached the wagon just as Tom Morgan vaulted into it ahead of him. Then he could do nothing as the young man gathered up the girl and began to pat her cheeks, a bit too roughly for his liking.

An awful truth engulfed Bill, and he shrank into himself, feeling bereft, empty. Tom Morgan had the right to be up there in the wagon, holding Marie Owen in his arms, and he didn't. Hadn't her father just announced the couple's betrothal?

The Morgan youth was shaking Marie now, and Bill couldn't help himself. He leaped onto the wagon tongue, over the seat, and into the wagon, then began to pry the boy's fingers off Marie's shoulders.

Mr. Owen said, "Here now!" and grabbed Bill's arm. He shook off the man's grasp, and kept trying to get Marie out of Morgan's hands.

"Leave her be!" he cried out. "You'll hurt her."

Tom blustered, "She's mine," and struggled against Bill's intrusion.

Old Man Owen leaned in and tried to intervene, but Tom's elbow found his stomach, and he backed away, clutching his middle.

Then Mrs. Owen fired a shotgun into the ground, which got

everyone's attention. She stood enveloped in a cloud of dust while silence fell over the crowd. Finally, she broke the stillness, speaking in a quiet but intense voice that throbbed with anger.

"You men unhand my daughter," she said. She lifted the firearm, put it in the wagon box, and climbed up.

Bill backed away and over the wagon side, giving her room as he recognized that his dog was no longer in the fight. At least Marie was in good hands, with her mother taking over the situation.

Tom attempted a protest, but the missus turned on him.

"You was shakin' her," she said, glaring at Tom, her eyes fierce as fire. "Do you have a brain in that head of yours, boy? She's passed out cold, and you was likely doin' more damage than good. Get out of here." She waved her hand, and Tom got.

&#8413;

Julia glared up at her husband, who looked down at her and Marie, furrowed eyebrows topping his puzzled countenance.

"You and me are goin' to have a conversation," she said in an undertone, mindful of the crowd surrounding the wagon. Her face felt as though it were setting into stone as she continued her baleful glare. She watched his reactions flickering in his eyes: first shock, then dawning comprehension, and finally, defensiveness and bluster. She held up a hand in a shushing motion before he could propel himself into speech and murmured, "Later. We'll talk on this later, you may be sure."

&#8413;

Bill watched Tom descend from the wagon. The farmer glanced around the crowd, and when he had found Bill, he locked eyes with him. He stalked closer, and as soon as he had his face up next to Bill's, he growled, "You keep away from my woman. You ain't got any claim on her, filthy cowhand."

He wanted to deck the man, but balled his fists tightly at his sides instead, to keep from flinging himself into a fight. Brawling wouldn't help Miss Marie, and it might upset her if she came to herself to hear a ruckus going on. He compressed his lips over clenched teeth.

116

Tom, evidently thinking him a coward, made a derisive noise, roughly barged into Bill's shoulder as he passed him, and started off through the crowd.

He let him go on his way without a word, but moved up toward the wagon again, kneading his arm to release the pain. It was much less than the pain in his heart, knowing Marie was lost to him, but neither one could match the anxiety he felt for her welfare now. He reached the wagon and saw that Marie lay—still and pale—on the floor of the wagon box. A wash of nausea attacked his stomach. Then he saw that her chest moved slightly, and he let out the breath he didn't know he was holding. She lived!

Mrs. Owen sat herself beside Marie and gently lifted the girl's head into her lap, talking softly to her all the while. She pulled a small vial from her apron pocket, unstoppered it, and held it in front of Marie's nose.

After a short pause, the girl reacted, pulling away from the strong odor of ammonia that he could smell from where he was standing. Marie's hand came up, futilely batting at the vial.

"There now, easy, girl. Come back to us," Mrs. Owen crooned.

Marie opened her eyes and said, "Ma?"

Bill's heart stopped beating for a moment, then lurched back into rhythm. She knew her mother. Mayhap she would recover.

℘

Marie's throbbing cheek brought her to awareness, but the pain was second on her list of importance once she gained consciousness. The first item was the awful stink filling her nose, and she turned her head aside to avoid it, batting at the source to get it away from her. The odor faded, and Marie opened her eyes to see Ma removing a vial from underneath her nose and corking it.

"Ma?" she asked, and touched her cheek, but it was too tender to permit exploration, and she couldn't restrain a small moan.

"Daughter."

Marie began to shake her head to drive away the pain, but

117

stopped after one movement when it felt like her brains might spill out onto the wagon bed. Her cheek hurt, but so did her head. She wondered if she were concussed. That was the least of her worries, she decided, trying to pull her random thoughts into order. Why was she lying here in a wagon? The sun was high overhead in the bright bowl of heaven, so it was time for dinner, and Ma should have been presiding over the victuals, with Marie at her side with a utensil in hand, ready to threaten her younger brothers into going to the back of the line. *Like I did when Carl wed Ellen.*

Then her father asked, "Is she waking?"

Marie went still as memory sharpened.

Pa had only just made his horrible announcement, binding her to that loutish Tom Morgan. She remembered coming out of the crowd and climbing into the box of the wagon, intent upon lighting into her father, then she had collapsed. Why? She didn't have a tendency toward fainting. However, she had felt strange, a bit lightheaded. Was that due to her distaste toward Tom? It didn't seem logical.

Ma and Pa were discussing her in low voices. Marie sat up. Her cheek still throbbed, but her senses were clearing, probably because the headache pain had lessened a bit. Now annoyance at the hubbub and the attention on her took its place alongside of the pain.

"Are all these folks to be kept waiting for their meal?" she asked, gesturing to the people beyond the sides of the wagon, and made a move to get to her feet. Pa took her hand and helped her up, his face a study in confusion.

"Daughter?" he said, his voice raising a question, but since she didn't know what it was, she didn't answer him.

Before she could scramble down the spokes of the wagon wheel, Pa found his question.

"What of the celebration I planned?" he asked. "We owe these folks that."

Marie looked over at her father. "Celebration?" she asked in her turn. *More like a wake*, she told herself, but then spoke in a soft but firm voice, "Pa, I'll not be marrying Tom Morgan." Before he could respond with the full force of blustering fury, she was off the wagon wheel and hurrying away toward the food tables.

❧

C. G. Thorne pretended to examine his fingernails. The action kept his head down so the satisfaction he felt would not be plainly visible for all to see. He had gotten as close to the wagon as he could to find out what was important to the old man to make such a fuss. This engagement uproar would play nicely into his hands. He must get the girl alone again to talk. Ten minutes should do the job. He'd have to keep a sharp eye out for an opportunity. He didn't want the farmer to interrupt his plans, but the mother had helped by sending *him* scurrying away. *While the boy licks his wounds, a man will step in and gather up the prize.*

C. G. felt like laughing, but resisted the urge. Instead, he surreptitiously scrubbed his lips with his handkerchief. It was good to know the drug worked as well as he'd been told. It appeared there were plenty of rich pickings to be had here, if the Mexican was right about the money. The girl was nice enough looking. Pleasing figure. Clear skin. Seemed to be clean. He lifted his head and surveyed the meadow until he caught sight of her. *Nice walk*, he thought, and let himself go into imaginings that would have horrified her and sent her mother into a fit of vapors. After a few moments of musing on the possibilities, he thought, *I'll spend a few dollars of her old man's money on making her fancy. Time I got back in the game.*

# Chapter 13

At the beginning of the dinner break, Bill looked for Marie to find out how she fared. When he located her, he was surprised that she stood alongside her mother at the plank table under the oaks, serving up the victuals. He had thought she'd be resting in a chair under the oaks.

Her cheek hadn't turned black from the fall yet, but the bruise was a deep red color, and must be giving her a deal of pain. His stomach lurched in sympathy and began to ache.

He got into the line and moved forward toward the table. He wondered if he would even be able to eat with his gut acting up in such a treacherous way. Then Miss Marie asked, "What's your pleasure?" and gestured toward the array of dishes on the table. He stopped looking at her and took a look at the food. It didn't much matter what he picked, as anything he put in his mouth would surely taste like ashes.

He frowned, studying the choices, then pointed toward a hot dish the likes of which he'd never seen before. Through the sinkhole of previously-removed food, he could see it was brown in the interior, with layers of something that was not quite white, covered with what appeared to be white cheese. Miss Marie dug into the cheese with her spoon and plopped a hearty portion on his plate. Mrs. Owen added one or two other bits of food, then he was through the line, his heart aching as much as his stomach.

Marie Owen was pledged to another man. Her pa had made the public announcement, speaking words that scourged Bill's soul. "What was his pleasure?" she had asked. He gritted his teeth. His pleasure would be to scoop up the girl and take her home with him to Texas. They could find that priest who did the marrying for Carl and Miss Ellen and get the holy words said over them.

He mumbled an unholy word. That option was as far distant as the moon. Miss Marie would marry the farmer when the upcoming harvest was done.

ဢ

Despite the throbbing ache in her cheek, Marie stood beside her mother and handed out chicken, spooned up hot dishes made of the most amazing ingredients, and felt her nose twitch as she served highly spiced dishes brought by the Mexican families who had come to help. As the parade of strangers from around about passed before her, her stomach began to greet them, and she bit her lip for the shame of it.

Then the line dwindled to nothing. Ma wiped her hands on her apron, smiled at Marie, and said, "I appreciate your help. You're a good worker." She looked Marie over, then continued. "You don't appear to suffer lasting damage from your fall. God is gracious."

"Yes, Ma. You need to eat now."

"We both do."

"Oh drat," Marie said.

Ma laughed. "Nothing can control those noises but a bite to eat, girl." Her face went sober. "How's that cheek farin'? Can you chew?"

"It hurts some, but I can talk fine, so I don't reckon any bones are broke." She touched the area carefully, then grimaced. "I will have a nasty bruise."

"It's formin' up now. Put a cold cloth on it when you can."

Marie dished up a plate of food for her mother and then one for herself, and found a seat against a tree. She was just biting into a chicken leg when Mr. Thorne spread a handkerchief on the ground and sat beside her, his face crestfallen. Her brow furrowed. He'd caught her with her mouth full.

"My darling," he whispered, looking around furtively. "My sweet Marie. I am gratified that you are well. However, I cannot believe what your father said. You are marrying that farm boy?" He gulped convulsively. "I had such hopes of a future with you."

Marie choked. Thorne gently patted her on the back until she

122

recovered. She drew a deep breath, and finding her voice unimpaired by the passage of the chicken, said, "I won't marry him. Pa has put me in an impossible situation." She lowered her voice and hung her head. "I own a mite of fault in the matter. I pressed Pa to think about my need for prospects."

Thorne screwed up his face in obvious agony. "What will you do, my darling? The wedding has been announced. The farmer's parents will expect—"

"I don't know, but I can't marry him. He's vile."

Thorne sat back.

Marie stole a look in his direction. He seemed to be gathering his thoughts. She waited.

"It was he you were fleeing. It was he who caused you grief." He paused again, then said with some heat, "That simply will not do, my darling. It will not do!"

Marie shivered. No light dawned to brighten her path. Without a doubt Pa would bring pressure on her to fulfill his commitment to the Morgans. Her head began to ache again.

"Oh," said Mr. Thorne, a long sighing vowel. "I have it, my dear. A plan."

Marie hardly dared breathe, waiting for him to enlighten her.

"We will go away. We will ride to Denver and be married there. I have a lovely home in the foothills." He spoke rapidly, breathing hard. "My dear aunt died recently and left me the house. There will be quite a bit of money, by and by. We will be well situated, my love." He took her hand. "Say you will do it. Say you will come away with me!"

Marie's breath was shaky as she inhaled. She hardly knew this man, but he seemed to be over the moon in love with her. Surely this was her salvation. She would not need to marry Tom if she went away with Mr. Thorne.

She looked at him closely. He was well groomed. There were no bits of food in his moustache. His clothing was clean and well kept. His fingernails were trimmed and clean. His breath was sweet. His hands were soft and gentle, and not at all sweaty. She remembered that merely being in his presence often caused her bones to melt. Surely that was a sign she loved him.

She let out the breath. "Yes," she said. "When can we leave?"

Thorne looked around again. Then his gaze returned and he lowered his voice, almost to a whisper. "Tonight. We will make our escape when everyone is asleep." His face looked pained for an instant, then it cleared as he obviously made an effort to shake off a doubt.

"What's amiss, dear Mr. Thorne?" Her voice shook as she tried out the endearment.

"I am ashamed to say that I have no money for our expenses. I was foolish and played poker with the Dominguez boys. They are sharper players than I." He looked down.

"Pa has a bit of money." She clapped her hand over her mouth, horrified that those words had escaped her lips.

Mr. Thorne gently removed her hand and patted it between his. "That is a fortunate happenstance. You can bring it along tonight."

"I cannot simply take it." Marie's head swam at the thought of stealing the remaining gold dust in Uncle Jonathan's box.

Mr. Thorne's chin came up. His eyes narrowed. "Does not your father owe you a dower price?"

The words hung in the air between them for a long moment.

Marie thought of all the grief she'd had to bear in the last year. She thought of her father's lack of concern for her needs. She thought of the pain of becoming a woman without a future. She thought of Jule's taunting words and scandalous behavior.

"Yes," she said in a burst of emotion. "He does, and much more. He owes me respect, and he doesn't give me any."

Thorne shook his head. "A dowry doesn't make up for a father's lack of affection, but it goes a long way in soothing hurt feelings."

Marie began to protest, but Thorne shushed her with a lingering kiss, hidden behind his hat.

"We haven't more time to plan. Put a bundle together, bring food and cooking tools, and get the money. Meet me at that lightning-struck oak on the north side of the clearing at ten o'clock. Bring a good horse." He finished his instructions and rose easily to his feet, bending down to retrieve his handkerchief. "Until then, my sweet Marie." He gave her a wistful look, gently squeezed her hand, and left.

When Mr. Thorne had gone, Marie's head swirled with details, the warmth of his kiss spreading through her body. *This is right*, she thought. *He loves me. He will treat me gently. Yes, this is the right thing to do.*

ॐ

This time when Thorne had slipped deep into the forest, he gave himself up to great peals of mirth. *That was easy as eating pie,* he thought, wiping his eyes when he had recovered his equanimity. *The girl is sitting in the palm of my hand.*

He composed his face, straightened his waistcoat, and strode off in search of the Dominguez brothers.

# Chapter 14

With dinner out of the way, Marie was gratified that Ma sent her back to the cabin with a load of dishes to wash.

"If you don't mind, daughter, start the fire under the wash water. I'll be along by and by, after I visit with Mrs. Bates. I won't tarry long."

*Here's a blessing,* Marie thought. *I'll put together the things I want to take. Just a change of clothes. A pot and the spider, will do, I reckon. Food will have to wait until Ma brings back the leftovers.*

She hesitated, not wanting to think yet on the other item she must put in her bundle of necessities. Mr. Thorne had the right of it. Pa owed her a dowry. Even though he had put the gold aside to pay the cowhands and purchase supplies, she surely wasn't stealing if she took the portion that he would have used to marry her to a proper suitor back in the county.

And yet, the thought of carrying a sack of gold dust away with her, even a part of a sack, squeezed her chest, leaving her without breath.

How would Pa react? Would he be sorrowful? Angry? Bluster about for days, castigating her name and memory? Disown her?

Ma would bite her lip, then mourn silently for weeks. At least four. Maybe five. How many weeks had it been since James had left?

The thought of causing her mother to mourn threw Marie into a frenzy of activity to fend off dwelling on it. She found a gunnysack and put her new fry pan and stew pot into the bottom. Then she put half a sack of cornmeal into the pot, and a sack of beef jerky beside it. She moved about the kitchen corner mechanically, gathering a few of the cooking implements that Ma had gotten for her from the peddler. She smiled as she included the sharp new knife in the leather sheath. That covering was going to be handy. Into the sack the knife went, along with a spoon and fork from her new flatware set. She assumed Mr. Thorne had his own utensils, so she limited herself to one set. When he and she were established in their new home, she would send for the other items that made up her hope chest.

Marie steeled herself and went to the mantel. Uncle Jonathan's small, but heavy leather-bound box had sat for years on the mantelpiece of their home in the Shenandoah Valley of Virginia. Marie had dusted it a thousand, thousand times. Only after his death had Ma opened it to find a cache of gold nuggets and dust. Now the box occupied the same place of honor upon their Colorado mantel, although it was somewhat lighter in weight.

For several moments, she stared at the box. Pa had shot off the lock, since Ma accidentally left the key to it behind. It had taken a few bullets to sever the steel, so chips and slivers of wood were missing from the front. She finally lifted the box down and put it on the floor before the fireplace. She opened it and looked for the smallest poke. She didn't want to leave her family destitute and unable to pay its obligations. At the same time, resentment surged through her chest.

"Pa owes me something," she said hotly. "There must be a price for having Tom Morgan's hands wandering over my body." She paused a moment, cringing at the thought of taking Pa's money in exchange for serving as the young man's plaything. She wondered if that made her a wanton woman.

"No," she decided aloud, "not now, nor ever!"

࿏

Once she'd sent Marie on her way, Julia didn't seek out Muriel Bates, but instead went hunting her husband. She found him walking around the far side of the halfbuilt barn, inspecting the sheathing timbers. Chester Bates strode beside him, looking skyward while engaging him in talk.

Julia approached the men at a fast walk to catch up to them.

"Mr. Bates, Mrs. Bates needs you over to the horses," she lied.

The men halted in their tracks.

"Well, that's a caution—" Chester began.

"Now!" Julia barked.

Chester looked at her in surprise, but after nodding a goodbye to Rod, he hurried off.

When they were alone, Julia turned on her husband.

"What were you thinkin', makin' a grand public announcement thataway? Did you see the look on my daughter's face?"

She paused to draw a breath, and Rod found his voice.

"Wife, I did what seemed the right thing at the time. There's no harm in spreading the news so folks can give thought to coming for the wedding." He pulled at his collar and cleared his throat.

"I reckon she don't want a big gatherin'." She set her hands on her hips and glared at him. "I reckon she's simply pleased to make a match and get on with livin'."

He squirmed. "She said something different before she tumbled over."

"What did she say? She does seek a crowd?"

He shook his head, pursing his lips before he spoke. "She said she won't marry Tom Morgan."

She felt her face slacken as her jaw dropped, her mouth falling open. For a moment, she couldn't even move, let alone respond to her husband's astounding news. She finally got her mouth closed and swallowed, cleared her throat and asked, "You heard her right?"

"There's no question, Julie. She said it to me again after she come to herself. Something's gone awry."

"Land a mercy! She won't have Tom? What is in that girl's mind?"

"I reckon it's your job to find out, woman. I've got fences to mend."

She turned her back and stared toward the mountain. "I fear I told her why Lizzie and me don't see eye to eye." She bit her lip. "Is she scared that woman will mistreat her?"

He put his hand on her shoulder, hesitantly, she thought, and she covered it with her own.

"I don't reckon the fault lies with you," he said quietly, his voice a bit rough around the edges, as though he had forgotten how to use it to express tenderness. "The girl's been acting a tad off ever since we come back from down south. It would appear something went amiss there. I should have asked her straight out what was plaguing her mind."

She turned, still holding his hand under hers as she pivoted to face him. His countenance twisted.

"She bears an air of," he paused, considering. "Dread," he said at a low volume. "She's a strong girl, but something has her spooked." He paused, but then merely exhaled and pressed his lips together, his jaw thrust forward.

She patted his hand, squeezed it once, then released it. "I noticed she and Jule have been squabblin' more than usual. The girl's in a dither." She turned and took three steps away from him, then retraced her path. "She don't confide in me, Rod. Not for quite a spell now." She left him again to pace. When she drew near again, she wiped an eye. "I miss talkin' secrets with my girl."

"She and I had quite a lengthy talk back when she dressed me down for not fixing her up with a husband." He shook his head. "How'd she get to be woman-grown?"

"That war took the years," she said, and heard her voice break. "It stole a piece of our lives and our young'uns lost their childhood." By the time she finished speaking, it was all she could do to hold the tears in check.

He put his arms around her. "Woman, don't you cry." He nuzzled the top of her head. "You'll unman me, here in front of the folks."

"I don't care," she snuffled. "I'm worried about my girl."

৪৩

Rod held Julia close as long as he dared, knowing that at any time, Chester would be back to help him inspect the construction work accomplished during the morning hours. Just as he was fixin' to go about the process of getting his wife back on track with the chores of the day, he noticed a movement at the barn's corner. A head popped around it, then disappeared again. When this had happened for the third time, he patted Julia on the back and, sidestepping around her, strode to the corner, reached around it, and seized the collar of his youngest son, Albert.

"Confound it, what's the problem?" he asked, dragging the youth around the corner.

"I gotta talk to you." Albert shuffled his feet as Rod pulled on him, finally digging in his heels against any further movement.

Rod tugged again on the back of Albert's shirt. "Come along here and talk."

"Not to Ma. To you."

"Humph," he grunted, and stopped trying to haul the boy toward Julia. "Speak up."

"She'll hear me."

Rod pivoted. "Julie, are we talked out?"

She looked steadily at him for a moment, nodded once, then turned and left.

He watched until she turned the far corner of the barn, then gave his attention back to Albert. "She's gone. Speak your piece."

Albert looked at his toes, breathing noisily for a few moments as he fidgeted, then looked up and sighed.

"Sister's been foolin' around with Parley Morgan."

"What?" His hand tightened on Albert's shoulder. "Why would Marie—"

"Nooo," Albert said, drawing out the word as he shook his head with vigor. "Not Marie." He clasped his hands together, moving one within the other. "It's Jule. I caught her half dressed, kissin' Par—"

"Where is she?" Rod started to shake Albert by the shoulders.

"Pa! Leave off! Let me go!" Albert's voice rose until it cracked.

"Where's your sister?"

"She's hidin' in the stable."

Rod let the boy go and stalked away, feeling cold rage swelling up through his chest and into his throat. What was the girl thinking? She was just a baby. *I won't stand for outrageous fiddling of that sort. Parley Morgan is going to pay the piper.*

Marie cut a length of string from the ball Ma kept, threaded one end through the two drawstrings holding the small, but heavy leather bag closed, and tied it to the other end. She slipped the string over her head, lifted her hair to hide it, opened the top button of her bodice, and guided the poke underneath her camisole so that it lay between her breasts. She had just replaced the strong box on the mantelpiece and turned away, when Jule threw open the door and stomped into the room.

She looked a sight, her eyes red and puffy as she screamed, "You told Papa! You told him about Parley." She rushed at Marie, and began to pummel her on the shoulders.

Startled, Marie grabbed at her sister's fists and held them fast. "I didn't," she grunted, struggling with the girl. "I would have, but didn't get a chance."

"You're lying!"

"No." Marie lost one of Julianna's hands, and took a fist on her sore cheek. "Ow! Stop it, Jule!"

"Papa's angry at me 'n' Parley, so you must have told him." The girl flailed about, hitting Marie wherever she could.

Marie caught the errant hand again, and held it away from her face. She said, "Hear me. I didn't have a chance to tell tales. Ma's had me workin' the skin off my bones. Besides, I don't want to talk to Pa just now. I'm plenty annoyed with him."

Jule stopped carrying on, seeming to realize at last that Marie was speaking the truth. "Humph," she snorted. "What do you have to be annoyed about? Papa made known your betrothal and I reckon you should be dancing a jig. You won't be an old maid after all."

Marie realized that the gunnysack lay on the floor next to the table. She had to keep Jule from seeing it. She racked her brain to find an answer that would turn away her question, and an errand to send her on.

She finally arrived on a plausible answer and said, "He cast a heap of shame on my head the way he did it, before all and sundry, makin' it sound like I was already ripe for the shelf. He could have been more closemouthed about my affairs."

Jule's eye grew huge. "Do you reckon he'll stand up tomorrow and make me a laughingstock with another announcement?"

Then she mumbled, "He says if I'm going to pretend at being a wife, I ought to get married when you do. He's awful mad. He says he's going to cut Parley." She furrowed her brow, scowling. "I don't know what he means, but I reckon I shouldn't marry Parley after all. He did disgusting things to me." She stopped and hung her head. "I thought getting married meant going on picnics and kissing and holding hands."

Marie almost let pity curb her indignation. "When did you ever see Ma and Pa going on a picnic? I swear I don't know where you acquire such notions." She let loose of Jule's hands and continued in a softer tone. "I reckon there's a long sight more involved, like the disgusting things Parley wants to do to you. Tom has those same notions in his head." She gave a shudder.

"Sister." Julianna's voice took on a whining characteristic. "Please talk to Papa. Tell him I'm too young to make a marriage. Tell him I don't hanker to carry on with Parley anymore. He'll listen to you."

Marie wondered why Jule had that idea. To her great chagrin, Pa had never much listened to her until just lately. It was a fine thing that she was getting out from under his thumb tonight. Before she could build a head of steam at the thought of his overbearing nature, the remembrance of Mr. Thorne's kiss warmed her, steadied her.

"Please talk to him for me," her sister begged.

She blinked, remembering that she was conversing with Jule and needed to get her out of the cabin.

"I got chores to do and don't have time to find Pa this minute. I got a blinding headache, besides." She touched her cheek. "I'll try to get Pa to see things your way later on, but I swear I didn't tell him about your little escapade."

Jule's face wore a scowl once more. "Wait a minute. If you didn't tell Papa about Parley 'n' me, who did?"

Marie let loose her own "humph," then added, "I reckon you can lay that to Albert's door. He's always sneaking around, gettin' secrets, and workin' blackmail on folks. Why don't you go pull his nose for being a pest?"

Jule appeared to be letting her anger come back in full measure, for her face grew red and blotchy. "I will do that," she said, and stormed out of the door as upset as when she'd come into it.

Marie grabbed the gunnysack and hid it behind the wood box. Only then did she begin the task of getting a kettle of water hot for cleaning up.

ॐ

Marie finished washing the dishes, curious and a bit concerned that Ma still had not returned. After she had worked herself into a fret, she set off to find her.

That task wasn't hard. Suddenly hearing a wail that could only have come from her mother's throat, Marie broke into a run. The continuing anguished sound came from the meadow, and as soon as she could, Marie arrived and found the source.

Ma would have crumpled in a heap, save that Pa was holding her up, his arms wrapped around her in a tight embrace. Mr. and Mrs. Hilbrands from Pueblo Town were standing nearby, Mrs. Hilbrands wringing her hands, and Mr. Hilbrands stroking his chin and muttering, "I didn't think she'd take it so hard," over and over.

Another man stood behind Mrs. Hilbrands, patting her shoulder and crinkling his eyebrows.

Pa caught sight of Marie and motioned her over with his head.

*Does he think I won't come near because she's crying?* Marie thought, still regarding her father in a poor light. She looked a question at Mr. Hilbrands, and stroked her mother's cheeks, saying, "There now, Ma. It can't be that bad."

Ma answered in a high, thin voice, "He's been shot, daughter."

"Who, Ma?" she asked. A chill passed through her body, and she knew full well the commotion must have something to do with her missing brother.

"It's James."

The chill settled in her stomach. "What about him, Ma?"

"He's been boarding with the Hilbrands, but he's shot to pieces."

Marie looked at the Hilbrands, and then at the stranger, gauging which of them would tell the clearer story, and decided to query the missus.

"Ma'am, is it all that bad?" She looked toward the Hilbrands's wagon. "Did you bring him with you?"

Mrs. Hilbrands quit the hand-wringing and seemed to pull herself together. "He was hurt some bad, with two wounds that I stitched up, but he is not in danger of death. Mr. Hilbrands wanted to inform your folks, but James refused to let him write a note. He left a few days ago, and I do not know for sure where he went."

"He was much improved when he left after a few weeks with us," Mr. Hilbrands chimed in. "He sat the saddle fine."

"Julie," Pa murmured. "You hear that? He could ride when he left Pueblo Town."

Mr. Hilbrands continued. "A week ago he decided he'd had enough of bed rest. Mandy said the daughter told her he was fit enough to stretch and turn without showing any pain. He seemed fine when he drove a mule team for me before he took out. Well, maybe not in the best of spirits, but not favoring any of his parts. I reckon he's on the mend, Miz Owen."

Ma wiped her eyes and straightened in Pa's arms. Marie stepped back, glancing at the stranger again and wondering who he could be.

"I regret fussing so much," Ma said, her voice still thin and whispery. "It came as a great shock to learn he had been doin' so poorly and I didn't know of it." She took a gulp of air and continued. "I should have felt his wounds in my body."

"Julie, you can't sense everything," Pa protested.

"I should have known," she insisted. "I've felt your pains."

"Ma, Mr. Hilbrands says he's on the mend now," Marie said. "Take comfort in that."

Ma stood still, breathing deeply. "It appears he's not going to come home soon as I'd hoped."

"No, Mrs. Owen," the stranger said, speaking for the first time. "He seemed intent upon a journey, perhaps a spiritual progress of sorts."

*This is Pa's preacher man. I wonder what sermon he'll*

*preach tomorrow when they know I'm gone?*

"He did ask about a job with Angus Campbell," Mr. Hilbrands said. "I figured he came south. He didn't stop in to give you greetings on his way?"

Ma shook her head. "He did not," she said, with a return to a moaning sound.

"There now, Ma," Marie said, stepping up to touch her cheek. "He'll come back when he's calmed down some. A body must be a tad bit angry when he's been shot up."

"It was a drunk Irish did it, I was told," the preacher put forth.

No one had anything to say in reply to that, but Mr. Hilbrands spoke up after a pause. "I think the worst of it was over when young James left town."

"The worst of what?" asked Marie.

Mr. Hilbrands shook his head. "There's still sentiment against those of us who, ahem, who took sides against the Union," he said with a shake of his head. "There are saloons in the town that cater to Unionists, and others who serve Southerners. The folks don't mix freely."

"Oh dear," Marie said, mostly to herself. She'd have to pass through the town on the way to Denver City. Then she spoke up in a firm voice. "Ma, he's out of the town, and it's good and proper that he left. We will hear from him by and by, I know it."

Ma gave a moaning sigh, then drew herself up and shook off Pa's arms. "We will pray fervently for that," she said. "The Reverend will surely help us in that respect." She turned to Mrs. Hilbrands. "Amanda, despite the news you bring, you're welcome to our homestead. Rod, help Mr. Hilbrands unload his wagon."

# Chapter 15

Marie's stomach roiled with nerves as she backed down the loft ladder. Clay's canteen hung by its strap from the shoulder of her coat, and she carried her shoes in her hand, hoping her stocking feet would make less noise on the floor. There was one plank to be avoided at all costs. It would simply shriek if she stepped on it. Although she could hear Pa's regular snores now, if he heard that plank! Well, she'd be discovered, and all her plans would be for naught.

She had traversed halfway to the door in safety when she remembered she needed her sunbonnet. Without it, her face would surely suffer a recurrence of the burn it received on her trip to the Cuchara land. Even though Mrs. Bates's strong leather clasp would keep her hair in order, it would not help with the sun.

Restraining a sigh, Marie finished her trek to the door and placed her shoes beside the wall. She unlimbered the canteen and put it atop her shoes, taking care that it did not bang the wall. Then she retraced her steps across the room and up the ladder. Feeling her way in the darkness blacker than stove soot, she found the article and put it on her head, tying the strings under her chin. This severely restricted her sight to the sides, but at least she would have the bonnet when she needed it tomorrow.

In her haste to get back to the door, she almost stepped on the squeaking floorboard, but stopped herself in time, rocking in her abrupt halt, and holding her breath as Pa snorted in his sleep.

Would he wake? Was her escape to be thwarted? She didn't dare breathe until the sonorous exhalations became regular again. Then she let out her breath slowly, sidestepped to avoid the villainous board, and resumed her trip across the room.

Now she had to get out the door. The hinges sometimes made

noise, but Marie hoped the oil she had put on the leather that afternoon would keep that from happening. She picked up her shoes and canteen, took a shuddering breath, and pulled the latch.

The wooden stop lifted, the door opened soundlessly at her touch, and then she was free.

Pausing only long enough to sit on the bench beside the door to put on her shoes and fasten them, Marie hurried across the yard toward the creek. She tiptoed across the plank bridge toward the stable, her mind whirling with a mixture of relief and concern. She still hadn't decided whether to take her black riding horse or Bess, the gentle mare she'd ridden on the Cuchara expedition. Both were good mounts, but the remembrance of Bess's easy gait and comfortable ride weighed heavily in her favor. Besides, the black could be uppity of a morning, and Bess never had been.

In the end, Marie woke the more comfortable horse, took the tack she needed, then put it all on Bess, arranging her bundle and supplies on the mare.

*Do I have all I'll need?* she questioned herself before she mounted. She'd brought no trinkets or baubles, but only a change of clothes, the cooking utensils, the poke of gold dust around her neck, a bit of grain for the mare, and food and water for the first few days of the journey. She left behind a letter she'd written on the sly upon the last piece of the pink stationery she'd hoarded since the war. She simply said she was heading north with her own true love, and that the next time anyone from the homestead saw her, she would "be a married woman."

Once in the saddle atop Bess's broad back, she surveyed the meadow with the embers of all the campfires scattered across it, looking for the surest route through them. If she bent her way south around the Bates's camp, then between the Campbells and the Hilbrands, she should soon be out of harm's way.

Gently putting her heels to the horse's sides, she sat forward, and Bess moved out into the vastness of the night at a walk, nickering softly.

"Oh hush, Bess," Marie whispered. Perhaps she should have blindfolded the mare and led her? *It's too late for that,* she acknowledged, and resorted to patting the mare's neck and whispering soft encouragement instead.

Once she heard voices and froze, reining Bess to a halt. She listened, and located the sounds as coming from the far side of the meadow. *A couple up late, romancing?* She couldn't tell, as no clear words came to her ears. Finally judging the late-night chatterers to be no threat to her, she clicked her tongue at Bess and got the animal moving again. In only a few moments more, she would be through the visitors' camps, and well away.

Although she didn't actually hold her breath as she guided the mare between the intervening campsites, when she reached the appointed spot beside the lightning-blasted oak near the road to Pueblo Town, Marie felt as though she'd gone far too long without air. She slid from the saddle into Mr. Thorne's arms, stumbling a bit, but with his aid, she recovered herself.

Mr. Thorne then clasped her tightly, pressing kisses on her brow, her cheeks, then finally, on her lips. Marie responded, relief at getting away clean feeding her fervor. At last, they broke apart and looked at each other.

"I am so gratified that you came," Mr. Thorne murmured, holding her face between his palms. "Yes. Most gratified." He dropped his hands and looked her up and down. Drawing a deep breath, he said, "We really should be on our way." He hugged Marie again, then whispered, "My companions may miss me. I'm not sure they were asleep when I left the camp."

A tingle of fear swept down Marie's spine. "Let us leave now," she agreed, shivering.

She remounted with a boost from her swain, then Mr. Thorne got up on his horse, signaled with his head the direction they would take, and they left the meadow for a path through the trees and out of the Owen claims. Soon they arrived at the well-traveled road, and started their journey north.

෨

Within an hour, Marie was thirsty, and leaned over the pommel to retrieve her canteen. Not knowing how long Mr. Thorne had it in mind to travel that night, she took only a shallow sip of water. That served to refresh her though, and she continued to follow the man ahead of her on the moonlit road.

Finding herself yawning, Marie closed her eyes for a moment and let Bess follow the other horse. The gentle gait of her mount soon had her fighting to stay awake.

She must have slept, because the next time she opened her eyes, the moon had risen higher in the sky than it had been before. The flat landscape, broken by the occasional stream bed and butte, glistened here and there where minerals lay exposed on the earth. Marie gave herself a little shake as she endeavored to awaken, but soon, she was nodding in concert with the horse's easy movement.

Bill Henry soon joined her, in a dream so vivid that she might have said his name in her surprise. He talked of her Pa's heavy-handed ways, and Marie could only nod vigorously, given the recent events that had caused her such grief. He lifted his hat and raked back his hair, and then reseated the head gear. Suddenly, she was rebuking him for calling her foolish. The light in his eyes faded and his expression grew guarded. His grave voice echoed in her mind, "I didn't mean you, I didn't mean you, I didn't mean you."

The next thing she knew, Marie opened her eyes to find Mr. Thorne standing beside her stirrup, shaking her shoulder and muttering her name.

"Come on, wake up. I don't have all night to stand here."

Marie pulled away at the frank irritation in her lover's voice, straightening her torso from her sleepy crouch. Guilt at dreaming of another man at the very onset of her elopement made her cautious, and she replied tersely, "I'm awake. Are we camping here?" *Did I speak his name aloud? Did Mr. Thorne hear? Did I upset him?*

"No. We'll rest the horses for a spell, then travel along for a while longer." The irritation had left his voice, and he smiled at Marie. "I apologize for being short with you. I fear I'm not at my best tonight. It must be nerves from the anticipation of having trouble getting away." He helped her dismount, then continued. "I must say, I'm vastly relieved that no one was about to stop us from leaving."

Marie nodded, feeling a release of her anxiety, and smiled back. "I reckon I'm a bit unsettled myself. It was quite unnerving riding between the camps. I feared a dog would bark and set up an alarm."

"We've had luck on our side tonight. That is sure." He kissed her on the brow, gently, tenderly, briefly.

Marie yearned for a further expression of affection from the man, but Mr. Thorne took himself away to tend to the horses. She found a suitable place on the ground to sit and rest, a hummock of earth crowned by a sparse grassy growth, and lowered herself onto it. She reminded herself that she must bridle her passions, as the Bible counseled, until she was a married woman. When that moment came, she could enjoy all the expressions of affection with which Mr. Thorne chose to favor her.

Marie sipped from her canteen, trying to cool the rising warmth of her body. This ardor would never do. It was unseemly. Even though she had run off with a man she barely knew, she must uphold the standards Ma had drummed into her from childhood. *I can wait a bit longer for married life*, she told herself, reluctance tingeing her thought. *We'll be in Denver inside of a week.*

Once the horses were sufficiently rested, Mr. Thorne prepared them to get on the move again. He first saddled Bess and brought the mare to Marie's side. Then, as he tacked up his own horse, Marie noticed for the first time a coil of rope that he tied onto the right side in front of the stirrup, and she idly wondered if he had worked cattle sometime in his past. She mounted, clucked Bess into movement, and followed behind the man into whose hands she was entrusting her future. She had left her past behind. She had all the time in the world ahead of her to study Mr. Thorne's many sterling qualities and savor stories from his youth. A fascinating new life opened before her.

She'd never seen much of how others lived, spending all her formative years on a farm and interacting with the small community in Shenandoah County. Her journey across the Great Plains had been cautious, as her pa hadn't wanted to draw attention to their party. Not much had happened to her personally in Colorado, beyond that horrid outlaw encounter and Tom's outrageous behavior. One thing she did know. She looked forward to the adventures ahead.

For the moment, however, nothing much was occurring, beyond sitting her horse and fighting off her tendency to yawn and close her eyes. From time to time, Mr. Thorne glanced at her over his shoulder, and she endeavored to smile reassuringly at him. Her fatigue was stronger than her resolve, however, and again, she slept.

Bill slipped back into her dreams, and for a spell she enjoyed watching the way his moustache turned up on the left side of his mouth when he smiled. Then her inner self realized she should be leaving Mr. Henry behind to do his chores with her father's cattle, and not tug him along on what would soon become her honeymoon. She struggled to cast him out of her mind, and finally slept deeply and alone.

When she next awoke, Marie noticed that the moon was in the wrong section of the sky. The trail beneath them had disappeared, and it looked as though they were traveling overland.

Marie urged Bess to greater speed to overtake Mr. Thorne. When she had come alongside him, she said, "We're off the road, and we're not goin' north."

Thorne drew up his horse and smiled at her. "No, my love. I've been pondering. I heard talk of a priest living in a town south of here. It occurred to me that you might prefer being a married lady for the rest of our journey."

Marie drew in a sharp breath. She hadn't given the timing or location of her marriage much thought, beyond having a lovely wedding somewhere in Denver City once they had arrived and made arrangements. "We won't wait until Denver?"

Mr. Thorne seemed unsettled. "My love, I can scarcely hold my ardor in check. It would be much better to marry soon. A day or two more, and we'll be man and wife."

"We're not going back through the homestead, are we?" she asked. The thought of encountering Pa dried her throat. The thought of encountering Bill Henry raised gooseflesh on her skin.

"No. We'll swing wide to avoid it. Showing ourselves there at this time would perhaps be unpleasant."

And yet, there was a preacher already at hand, if Mr. Thorne was in such a hurry to wed. After only a second of reflection, she knew she'd make no mention of the reverend. There was little chance he would be willing to fly in the face of her father's agreement with the Morgans and marry her to someone else. Besides, she was not ready to face her father's wrath, even with her beloved Mr. Thorne at her side to bolster her courage. *And Bill Henry's eyes would go dark as midnight.*

Marie swallowed hard and nodded her agreement with the plan, so they resumed their journey.

℘

It seemed to Marie to be a shameful thing that she kept nodding off, especially when she began to dream again, but she couldn't help it. Bess's gait was most easy, and she was so tired. The strain of the day's events, not to mention the aftereffect of the blow to her face when she fell, had built up a great lethargy, and she kept giving in to the need to sleep.

She awoke with a jolt when a chill wind hit her cheek. She shivered. The moon's light had diminished due to an obscuring bank of clouds. With the wind blowing stronger each moment, she feared it would soon rain, so she urged Bess to overtake Mr. Thorne once more.

"Will we camp before the storm comes?" she asked him, a note of anxiety making her voice sound high and thin to her ears.

Mr. Thorne looked up and tilted his head. "I imagine we do need to seek shelter. Look for any trees, or a butte we can camp beside." He patted her hand. "We'll be safe. Don't worry."

"I can't help a bit of nerves."

"So you cannot. Let me relieve your mind. I'll do the worrying from now on." He smiled in the dim light and gave her hand a final pat before turning away.

Marie heaved a sigh and let Mr. Thorne take the lead again. It made good sense that all would be well with Mr. Thorne doing the thinking. She had cast her lot with him, and looked forward to their future together, did she not? She felt a bit of her burden lifting from her shoulders. *Yes, all will be well.*

After a while, she heard Mr. Thorne laugh from ahead.

"See there? I believe we've come upon a stream. We will have good shelter there."

Soon they were dismounting near the bank, and discovered that the stand of oak trees lining the creek served somewhat to cut the wind.

"I'll water the horses. You find wood and build a fire," Mr. Thorne said.

Marie nodded, grateful that the rain hadn't yet started. She'd still be able to find dry kindling and branches for her fire. She hurried to her task, and within ten minutes had gathered enough fuel to start a small fire. Mr. Thorne could search out more wood later, if they needed to keep the fire going for long. She hoped he had a hand ax in one of his saddlebags, in case he needed to cut a large branch. Then she thought that if the trees were dry enough, he could pull off a branch with his rope.

She scraped a patch of earth until it lay bare, and arranged the tinder and kindling to her satisfaction. She put a piece of cotton wool underneath, and struck flint and steel together until the resultant sparks set the tinder to smoldering in a couple of places. She carefully blew on the best spots, then pulled back when they burst into flame. She pushed the tinder together so the flames would intensify, and soon the kindling was ablaze. It didn't take long until the sticks she had found were also afire, and she rocked back on her heels to admire her work.

Mr. Thorne came up and laid his hands on her shoulders. "That's a fine fire," he said, his fingers squeezing.

"We'll need more wood if we're to stay here for a while," Marie answered. "Would you fetch a few larger branches?"

"Isn't that your task?"

"Not if we need a quantity of logs."

Mr. Thorne made a sound that Marie thought expressed dissatisfaction, and she frowned. She didn't want him to think ill of her. She moderated her voice to be soothing as she said, "I can gather a few more fallen limbs, but if wood must be cut, it's a task I can't accomplish."

"I'll do it if I must," he said in a surly tone, his fingers digging into Marie's shoulders. "Put food together. I'm hungry." Then he released her and stalked off.

Marie hunched her shoulders, rubbing the abused muscles alternately to ease the pain he had left behind. *What have I done* to make him angry? she wondered. *I hope he doesn't know I've been having scandalous dreams. Aside from that, in my family it's a man's job to cut wood.* She got to her feet and moved toward the bundles she'd brought. *Perhaps his mother and sisters did that chore? I will have to be more careful from now on not to cause him grief.*

# Chapter 16

Bill awoke before dawn with an uneasy feeling. As he sat on the edge of his bunk, he paused before pulling on his second boot. What was bothering him? It didn't take much pondering to know that the path he had planned for his life had gone terribly wrong. Marie Owen was promised to that wretched farmer, Tom Morgan. That was enough to bother anyone.

"Tom," he growled, yanking on his boot. "What a puny excuse for a man!"

He rose and slammed his hat onto his head. *Why did she choose Tom Morgan? Doesn't she know how I feel about her?* Anger battled grief in his body, his heart pounding like galloping hooves on a hardpan road. He took several deep breaths, trying to get the emotions under control so he could get about his day, but the sense of wrong, the sense of foreboding wouldn't leave him. Maybe something else was gnawing at him.

Try as he would to shake off the feeling of disaster that lingered like a bitter aftertaste in the mouth, Bill went to breakfast without any relief from the sensation. Even three spoonfuls of sugar mixed into his coffee didn't take away the dread.

A heavy hand came down on his shoulder from behind, startling him. Immediately the hoarse sound of Chico Henderson's morning voice cut through what remained of his reflective fog.

"Sorry I was a porcupine the other evenin'," Chico said. "You don't usually take my money so handily."

Bill attempted to add a light tone to his reply. "You're a sore loser, Henderson." He failed. His voice grated in his ears as though he were drawing a rasp over a tin washboard. He clamped his jaw shut.

"I ain't so much, old son. You were on a winning streak the likes of which I ain't seen before." Chico sat in the chair next to Bill's and lifted his mug toward his mouth. "It took me by surprise, I got to say." After a slurp or two, he cut his eyes toward Bill. "What's tuggin' on your brainpan?"

Bill shrugged.

"Somethin' has you befogged. Out with it."

"I can't say." He shrugged again. "I don't know." He chewed on his lip for a moment, then blurted out, "How could she up and get herself promised to that lump?"

Chico wiped the last sip of coffee from his moustache. "Was you makin' plans with her?"

Bill hesitated. Then, remembering that Chico Henderson had saved his life on several occasions, he acknowledged that the man was indeed the closest thing to a good friend that he had. He spoke in the direction of his coffee cup, "It didn't get that far along. I was hoping, but—" He stopped short when the cook, Sourdough Smith, slapped a plate of eggs and beans onto the table before him.

Chico waited until Sourdough stepped back to the stove before he spoke again. "Uh-huh?"

"I had no chance to speak to the girl."

"Why's that?"

"She went on that little expedition with her pa and the boys."

"She come back."

"Maybe so, but she's mighty changed. She's put up a wall betwixt us the size of the Guadalupes."

"You sayin' you ain't much of a mountain climber?"

Bill snorted derisively. "Chico, you trying to make me smile? I'm not in a cheerful mood."

"I'll say you ain't!" Chico took a plate from Sourdough's hand and shoveled a mouthful of eggs beneath his moustache. Then he mumbled through the food, "You oughta talk to her. Speak your mind."

"You think Rod Owen would stand for that?"

"The ol' man don't got to know."

"Humph."

"You got to gather the reins and use the spurs to make the

horse run, Henry. I know you ain't afeared of a little slip of a gal, nor her pappy, neither. Speak at her."

Bill chewed a mouthful of beans. "I ain't usually a coward, Chico," he said once he'd swallowed it.

"No, you ain't. Not in my experience of you."

"I'm unmanned by the cold she breathes out."

Chico stared at Bill for a while, then swallowed his own mouthful. "It happens. A girl has the power. Howsomever, you know you're a better man for her then any mule-eared farmer boy, and mayhap she knows it, as well. Tell her you got feelings. Show her you got the grit to be tender."

Bill exhaled a long breath. "It's got to be done. Today's as good as tomorrow." He arose and gripped Chico's shoulder, then left the bunkhouse with long strides.

℀

Marie rose shortly after dawn to build a fire. Thank the Lord she hadn't had any more of those disturbing dreams! She hauled half a potful of water from the creek, which she set beside the fire to boil. After that, she dug into the gunnysack for the cornmeal, and salt to add to the water to make it boil sooner and season the mush so the taste would be appealing to Mr. Thorne.

She readily found the cornmeal and set the sack to the side, but couldn't locate the packet of salt.

*Drat*, she thought, feeling around in every corner of the sack. *Why can't I find it? I surely remem—* That thought dried up as she froze. Slowly, she withdrew her hand from the depths of the sack. *I forgot to bring salt. I'm a silly goose. How can I make a decent pot of breakfast without salt?* Anxiety crowded through her breast and tightened her throat. *Mr. Thorne will think I don't take care for his comfort.*

She went back to her exploration of the sack. Had she brought an onion? That would add savor. But after checking every possible cranny of the provision sack, she discovered she had not put an onion into it. Just as exasperation threatened to overtake her, she had a welcome thought. *I did bring jerky. I'll cut it into pieces and mix it into the mush.*

Feeling among the utensils in the gunnysack, Marie located the knife and slipped it into her pocket. As she searched for the bag of jerky, she heard a rustle from behind her, then a loud voice startled her.

"Marie!"

After her initial jolt from hearing Mr. Thorne call her when she thought she was the only one awake, Marie answered, "Yes?" thinking his voice sounded unusually stern this morning. Perhaps he hadn't slept well on the stony ground.

"What's the delay in getting food together? We have to be off soon."

Marie looked over her shoulder. Mr. Thorne was still abed. Irritation at his brusque manner warred with the anxiety she already had to deal with. *Goodness sakes! He should be up and feeding the livestock.* "I'll have breakfast very soon," she told him. "It will be ready after you tend to the animals."

"You will do that," he replied, lying down again.

"I have this chore to do," she said, not very loudly.

"What's that? Speak up when you address me. I can't come over there merely to listen to you prattle on."

Marie felt her eyebrows draw together. She turned her face away so he wouldn't see her expression of dismay. Mr. Thorne really must have slept ill to be so out of sorts with her today. Their elopement wasn't starting off very smoothly. Her shoulders tightened and drew forward, but she stopped herself from crossing her arms in front of herself with a conscious thought. *I must make a better effort to be pleasant to him when he's tired. He had such a long night, guiding us overland, and he wasn't able to sleep in the saddle like I did. No wonder he's a grump today.*

"Marie!"

She jumped at the urgency in his tone, then calmed herself and spoke up in a more or less steady voice. "What is it, my darling?" At least her voice was audible this time; she felt sure of that.

"Roll up your bed!"

"What? You see I'm busy with the meal."

"That doesn't concern me. This mess offends me. Take it out of my sight."

The unreasonableness of his request puzzled her. "Ain't you hungry? You spoke up for a meal."

"Leave it! I can see you are not competent to boil up a simple pot of mush in time to eat and be gone."

"I'm sorry," she said with a conciliatory tone, feeling her shoulders hunching. "It won't take much longer. See? The water is boiling now."

"Pour it on the fire," he demanded. "Get up and do as I told you."

She did so, racking her brain to determine what she had done so poorly as to make him unhappy and so stern with her. Steam enveloped her as the water doused the flames she had so carefully coaxed to life just minutes before.

"I don't understand," she ventured, but regretted it a moment afterward when Mr. Thorne jumped to his feet, shedding bedclothes in his wake as he ran upon her and gave her a sharp slap across the cheek.

"Don't answer back," he thundered. "My wife must be meek and compliant."

"Yes sir," she whispered, trying to swallow a sob.

"Stop your sniveling. I can't abide sniveling."

"Yes sir. I won't snivel, sir." She held herself very still, not daring to cross him again.

"Put those things away, then tend to your bed. You have the horses to saddle, and it's almost daylight."

She hastened to restore the cooking utensils and meal to the gunnysack, tie the neck, and hoist it toward the animals, then ran to scoop up her bedding before he had time to think of another chore.

As she rolled up her blanket, she craned her neck to see what was occupying the man in silence. He sat astride his saddle on the ground, smoking a cigar.

&

Bill's long strides took him within earshot of the Owen's cabin before he paused and took off his hat. In the half light, he noticed that his hand was shaking, making his hat shiver like a giant aspen leaf. He ran his other hand through his hair, re-seated the hat, and took several deep breaths to steady himself.

As he was about to move toward the cabin to have conversation with Marie, he heard a cry that reminded him of those of the panthers he hunted in Texas as a boy. Even as he squinted towards the woods behind him, he realized the sound hadn't come from that location. It had come from the cabin, and it continued as he gathered his wits and sprinted across the meadow, leaping the creek to arrive in the yard.

Bill barely knocked before he threw caution to the wind and hauled on the latchstring to open the door. He put his shoulder against the wood and, as it swung open, abruptly stopped himself from falling into the room.

Mrs. Owen stood nearly in the fireplace, her head bowed over a piece of rosy-colored paper. All her energy seemed absorbed in making a keening wail. The younger Owen girl knelt beside her, face in her hands, sobbing. Mr. Owen bent over his wife, his brows drawn together, strong emotions chasing themselves across his face. The two younger sons, Clay and Albert, stood frozen at their places at the table, breakfast abandoned. Then Clay broke the tableau when he bent to right the chair he must have overturned just moments before.

The Old Man looked up at Bill's intrusion, blinked, then barked an order at him. "Take Clay. See if that blasted Tom Morgan has lit out with my daughter!"

He felt the blood drain from his face and arms, chilling his skin. "What?" The strangled word sounded like a groan.

The man snatched the paper from Mrs. Owen's grasp, crossed the room, and thrust it into Bill's hand. "Read it. She's run off. If that young pup took her for his pleasure, I'll hound him to Hell and back."

Bill almost dropped the sheet, but got his fingers pressed onto it in time to keep it in his grasp. He brought it up where he could scan it.

*Dear Ma and Pa,*

*I cain't bear the thought you would stop me, so I have stealed away with my own true love. We aire going North to Denver, where we will be wed. The next time you see me, I will be a married woman.*

*Always your loving dauter,*
*Marie*

He stared at the paper until the lines of script began to wiggle before his eyes, pain surging throughout his body, from the part of his hair to his toenails. He knew he looked a fool with his mouth open, but if he was going to breathe again, the happenstance of his jaw having gone slack might help him drag in a little air, if only he could remember how that was done.

Bill shook his head and read the note again. Then he crumpled the paper and shoved it into his pocket. He turned and left the house, his heart pounding as though it would escape his chest.

&

Bill could hear footsteps behind him, and supposed they were Clay's, but he couldn't stop to talk to the boy with the wind knocked out of his body by the grim news. He struggled to inhale, then to get that lungful of air back out and suck another one in. Did it matter to keep breathing? Marie was gone. Life didn't seem worth the struggle. Then he thought if Tom Morgan was to blame, yes, he'd need all his faculties to find the kid and beat him into the ground before Rod Owen did.

Now Bill's breath came easier as deadly resolve took hold. He'd catch the scoundrel and bring Marie back home. He had to get her back. The phrase repeated in his brain, pushing against his skull, crying from every corner of his soul to be screamed aloud: *got to get her back, got to get her back, got to get her back.*

Clay shouted, "Hold up."

Bill slowed his pace a fraction to allow the youth to join him. Without a word, he began to run in the direction of the Morgan family's camp, Clay beside him.

When they skidded to a stop beside the Morgan's wagon, the family seemed barely to have risen. Bill looked at the figures in front of him: Mr. Morgan yawning and stretching his arms above his head, Mrs. Morgan bent over the fire, the two girls looking at him with wide eyes, the boys . . . he counted. The youngest one with the limp, Parley . . . and Tom.

"Where is she?" Bill shouted at Tom, drawing near enough to yell the question again into his face.

"Who the hell you talkin' about?" Tom blustered.

"The Owen girl. Marie. What've you done with her?"

Tom gave no quarter. His body arranged itself into a crouch and he spit his words back at Bill. "I ain't done nothin' with her."

Tom's fists were coming up quickly, guarding his face, poised to strike, and Bill backed off a pace, puzzled at this outcome. "You ain't seen her today?"

"It's none of your affair had I done so, but no. I ain't seen her."

An odd wash of disappointment enveloped him, primed as he was for battle, hating Tom for being Marie's betrothed, hating him in this moment because he was here instead of being the proper object of Bill's wrath, that man who was absent with Marie.

Voices surrounded him then, buzzing in his head: angry, concerned, shushing, petulant.

"My boy was here all night," Mr. Morgan said, a brittle edge to his speech. "When I arose to . . ." His words drifted into an uncomfortable silence. Then he spoke again. "He was here."

Bill flung himself in a circle, taking in all the eyes staring at him. "Well, Miss Marie ain't. She's . . . gone." His voice sounded tinny in the silence of dawn.

Then the uproar began again, but sounded different this time, more muted, cautious.

"What you mean, gone? Not dead?" Mrs. Morgan's voice quavered through an ascending octave.

"If it's not Tom—" Clay began in a strident tone, then looked at Bill and shut up.

"Here now," Tom started, then his face went dead white. He gasped out, "Check the Mexican's camp." He took a harsh breath.

"She was havin' some truck with them."

"Mexicans?" Bill could scarcely get the word out.

"Them Dominguez dandies. I don't trust 'em."

Bill remembered the brothers and the town man who had ridden in with them, the man he'd seen lurking in the forest on the occasion when he'd made a fool of himself asking Marie for water when she'd not been carrying any. The idler. The smooth, soft-handed man who'd been consorting with Marie in the shade. Was he a seducer as well as a lay-about? Had he convinced her to leave with him on such a vile pretext as being her "true love?" Bill's stomach clenched over his breakfast, and he had to take a moment to will it into submission.

Conviction growing that he was on the right scent, Bill lowered his chin and spoke softly. "It's not the brothers. I reckon it's their *compadre*, that man playing cards with them the first night. He must of took her."

"Thorne. His name is Thorne," Clay murmured. "Pa asked."

Bill swore softly. The name fit. He was surely the wily beast who had stolen the girl away. He looked around at the Morgans again, then asked, his voice barely above a whisper, "Who'll join a search party?"

Mr. Morgan tilted his head. "Tom and me will come."

Parley tried to speak up to go along with his pa and brother, but was shushed by Mrs. Morgan with a single "No!"

Mr. Morgan added, "We ought to check if Thorne is here. Mayhap he's not the one."

Bill said, "I'll go find out." A curious calm settled over him now that he had a clear task. "You and the older son gather your gear and go down to the main house." Even nestled within the calm, he couldn't bear to speak the young man's name just now. "I reckon Mr. Owen will want to set off as soon as may be." He focused on Clay and motioned with his chin. "You go report to your pa."

Clay absorbed Bill's look and hunched into himself. Then he turned and ran toward the Owen's cabin.

80

Bill set off for the last place he'd seen the town dandy, the camp where the man had been playing cards with the Domiguez brothers. The fire lay dormant, ashes and half-burned sticks in a circle. Beside it, two bedrolls manifested by their lumpy appearance that the brothers favored sleeping late. He nudged one of them with his toe, just forcefully enough to show that he meant business.

"¡Maldito seas, hombre!" came from the folds of the quilt. "¡Déjame dormir en paz!"

Bill ran off a string of border Spanish, and the bedroll creased into an "L" shape as the occupant sat up, flinging out new curses.

"Where is the man?" Bill asked again, his foot in action once more, a bit more urgency in the nudge this time.

"¿Quien?"

"El hombre feo que no está aquí," Bill replied. "Where is he?"

"No sé. ¡Déjame solo!" A face appeared, and Patricio Dominguez didn't carry a smile.

Continuing his conversation as he rousted the other man from his bedroll, Bill discovered that neither the elder nor the younger brother could remember a thing about the previous night's events.

"Tomé mucho anoche," Enrique complained, holding his head and almost whimpering. "¡Ay, que dolor de cabeza!"

"Your hangover is your concern. How do you know the man Thorne?" Bill demanded. "Where is he heading?"

This time, Enrique screwed up his face and appeared to be attempting thought. After carefully managing a headshake, he replied, "Thees man Thorne, Geraldo Thorne, I theenk he say, he come to town a while ago."

"¡Basta ya!" cautioned his brother. "Say no more."

Bill hauled Patricio out of his bed and held him by the front of his shirt. "Where is he heading?"

"Cálmate, hombre. No sé. He ees an estranger to we . . . us."

"Not last night, he wasn't. You know him well. I saw you ride in together."

"We solamente ride in at thee same time," Patricio insisted. "He no ees un amigo."

Bill dropped his grip on the man's shirt, but gave him a little shove to distance him. He didn't want to breath the same air as a liar.

"Get your gear and clear out," he growled. "We don't want you around here."

The two men cast dark glances at him, but began to gather their belongings. He watched for a moment to be sure they had a good start on packing up, then turned and hustled toward the bunkhouse.

# Chapter 17

Although he spent several minutes comforting Julia and their daughter, as soon as Clay brought the news that Tom Morgan was not involved in Marie's disappearance, Rod became the commander.

"It was Thorne, you say?"

"Mr. Henry's making sure of that. He headed for the Dominguez brothers' camp."

Rod scowled and took a few paces toward the fireplace, then returned to where his sons stood. "The man don't have that much of a head start, maybe six or seven hours. We need to raise a party to get Marie away from him. Are any of the Morgans with us?" He massaged his chin.

Clay nodded. "The mister and Tom will join us. Miz Morgan wouldn't let Parley come along."

Rod's mouth tightened, and he grunted, "Not surprisin', but I won't allow him to hang around here to—" He broke his sentence off sharply, and narrowing his eyes, nodded toward Clay. "Go inform Mr. Bates of the situation. Ask him if he'll accompany us. If he will, he'll know what to bring along. I'll deal with Parley Morgan."

Clay nodded and then bolted out the door. Rod turned to his youngest son. "Albert."

"Yes sir?"

"Tell Mr. Hilbrands he's wanted. Tell him to bring a pistol and provisions. Tell him it's a manhunt. That should excite his blood."

"Yes, Pa."

"Tell him Mrs. Hilbrands can stay with your ma until we get back. Tell him to invite the preacher along." He rubbed his whiskers again, then continued, "I wager Muriel Bates will stay over to help out. She'll be a comfort, and she can visit with the daughter a mite longer." He nodded once, dismissing the boy.

"Yes, Pa." Albert scurried off on his errand. Rod looked over at Julia. She huddled into herself, one arm around Jule and the other raised, with the back of her hand covering her mouth. Her face looked as gray as though she had scooped up a handful of ashes from the hearth and rubbed them into her skin. If only he had time to enfold her in an embrace and give her a mite of comfort.

"Woman," he said in his gruff voice, rubbing his finger against his thumb, "we'll find her. By all that's holy, I vow he won't have her long."

෨

When Bill arrived at the Owen cabin with his horse, his gear, and the cowhands in tow, it appeared that Old Man Owen had affairs well in hand. The Morgans had shown up, including a surly-looking Parley; Mr. Bates stood in the yard tightening his cinch; Mr. Hilbrands stroked his chin and decided to mimic Mr. Bates' actions; and two other men who had volunteered for the search party sat their horses nearby.

Bertie Owen led up three horses from the stable and threw himself aboard a buckskin. Mr. Owen came out of the house, followed by his son Clay, Mrs. Owen, and the little girl. Carl hobbled after them with the aid by a handfashioned crutch and stood in the doorway, grasping hold of the frame. He had gumption to come down from his cabin to see them off. His red-headed wife appeared to have a firm grip under his elbow as she shielded her eyes from the rising sun with her other hand.

One of the Morgan's horses raised its tail and did its business, forcing Mr. Morgan to dance out of the way. Chico's rude comment resulted in a retort from Tom.

*We're off to a good start*, Bill thought, his mood as dark as the droppings.

Old Man Owen held up his hands to quiet the hubbub. "Hilbrands, is the reverend accompanying us?"

Mr. Hilbrands looked startled at the notion. "No. He said he'd stay behind to lend comfort to the women."

The boss made a face, then continued talking. "We'll head north along the road. The man strikes me as a townie. I don't reckon he'd head off across the country, so it's most likely they took the road." He looked up as Rulon rode into the yard. "Good. Rulon is our best tracker. Son, you take the lead."

Rulon nodded. "Ready to go?"

"Soon as we're all in the saddle."

As the remainder of the men got on their horses, Mr. Owen gave his wife a quick embrace, rested his hand briefly on the young girl's head, and strode to his horse. Once mounted, he looked around at the searchers, his mouth a grim slash across the bottom of his face.

Rulon led off, his father right behind him. The rest of the searchers followed.

Bill clucked to the horse he'd chosen, and it responded smoothly without the use of spurs on its flanks. *At least one thing is going well*, he thought, trying not to gnash his teeth at the delay occasioned by rounding up the men. *I should have taken out after that gambling lay-about an hour ago.*

Before too long, the horses and riders began to string out along the road according to the swiftness of each mount. Bill soon surged to the front, just behind Rulon, his gut seething with anger as well as the dread he'd felt upon awakening. Maybe his place in Marie's future wasn't as secure as Tom Morgan's, but if he could bring the girl back home, that surely should count for something.

He shook his head, despairing of his chances. On the other hand, the girl hadn't liked the arrangement enough to stick with Tom. She'd lit out with Thorne, even though she'd only known him for a day. He sighed, sucking part of a bean from where it had stuck to his back tooth.

His see-sawing emotions caused an about-face. Evil intent wasn't in her. He was sure of it. More likely, Thorne had seduced her into fleeing with him, probably telling her a pack of lies to achieve his ends.

His ends. What ever were the man's ends? What advantage had Thorne gained from stealing off with Marie Owen? He had no feelings for her. Of that, he was sure.

*The man is a bloodsucking leech.*

Bill looked back at Tom, riding at the rear of the pack, a scowl firmly in place on his visage. Without a doubt, the farmer was not happy with the situation. *I reckon he's irked that Miss Marie spurned him in so public a fashion.* Out of the blue he chuckled, relishing the man's discomfort. The humor didn't last. His mind turned again to puzzling out what end Thorne had sought.

After a few miles, Rulon called a halt, and everyone dismounted to rest their animals. Rulon knelt on the ground, touched a hoof print, and contemplated it for a time. Then he raised his head to scan the area.

Tom led his horse around the outside of the group, cooling it down.

"Stop!" Rulon thundered, getting to his feet, and Tom jumped backwards, scuffing the earth as he landed on his backside underneath his mount.

Bill watched Rulon bow his head and gnaw his lip, seemingly trying to keep his temper. But then the man's teeth released his lips and they moved silently. Not in prayer.

Tom frantically tried to get out from under his horse before it panicked and trampled him. When a hind hoof clipped his shoulder, he swore and batted at the animal's legs.

Rulon ran over, bent down, and hauled Tom to his feet. He spoke to him quietly, but anger was clearly upon Rulon, even when he kept the rest of the men out of his quarrel with Tom.

The farmer raised his shoulders in denial of his wrongdoing, whatever it was, but Bill was able to approach the two before Rulon had made an end to it, and overheard his forceful complaint.

Bill let out a slow breath. The farmer had wiped out the tracks Rulon had found, tracks he evidently thought were vital in discovering the route the couple had taken.

Rulon left Tom and stalked over to Mr. Owen. Bill was too far away to hear their talk, but after a heated discussion, Rulon stamped over to his horse, got aboard, and led off, following the road as before.

ℰᴐ

Hours later, Marie sighed with relief when Mr. Thorne called a halt. She had followed his horse across a very broken land with her saddle slipping back and forth because she had not had the time to cinch it securely before Mr. Thorne had thrown her on top of it and started off at a trot, holding onto a lead rope attached to Bess's bridle.

Now he approached her horse, and she shrank away from him as he put up his hands and smiled.

"There now, my love. Why the curdled expression? Let me help you alight. You need to rest yourself." He wiggled his hands in a fashion designed to draw her near so he could get her off the horse. "Look around. There's a brook just over there, and a lovely stand of shade trees beside it. You must come off the horse and take rest."

Not knowing what to expect from the man at this moment, Marie slid from Bess's back, feeling as though spiders crawled on her flesh as he solicitously took her elbow to guide her.

"There now. Sit yourself down and take delight in the shade. I'll draw you a cup of cool water." He took a collapsible silver cup from an inside pocket, pushed it into shape, and smiled over his shoulder at Marie as he approached the bank of the stream.

She sat.

He sloshed the cup around in the water for a few seconds, then pointed off to the side, where the horses had gathered in the water, muzzles down, attempting to drink. "The gait of your mare is quite comfortable?"

Marie looked at Bess, the gentle Bess her father had picked for her to ride on the journey to the Cuchara. "Yes, she is a good horse with a good gait." She glanced back at Thorne, who finally seemed satisfied with the cupful of water he had acquired.

He lifted the cup, got to his feet, shook out the handkerchief he pulled from a pocket, and laid it over the cup. "That is good. Yes, that is very good," he crooned, coming toward her with careful steps, as though the water he bore were precious mead instead of the most common of liquids. "Now you must slake your thirst, my dearest heart. See, I have kept any insects or leaves from falling into the cup." He knelt beside Marie and proffered the drink, bringing it close to her mouth before he whisked the fabric off.

Marie closed her eyes and sipped. The water was cool. That was a help. It tasted slightly alkali, and she hoped it didn't contain an overabundance of the stuff. She surely did not need any stomach aches or worse maladies on this journey.

∾

Julia stopped stirring the pot hanging over the fire and returned to her seat. Gripping one hand with the other, she set her mouth and waited, her head inclined so she could see an area on the floor about fifteen inches in front of her shoes.

"It won't do to fret, Julia," Elizabeth said. "If Mr. Morgan catches up to them today, we'll know by nightfall."

"Leave her be, Lizzie." Muriel Bates stood from her chair and went to Julia's side, gave her a pat on the shoulder, then turned to remonstrate with Elizabeth, whose face had turned ashen. "Yes, you know I call you 'Lizzie' whenever I've a mind to. This is one of those times when a body ought to be allowed to fret all she wants, and I'll stand here and tell you so to your face."

"Well! I never heard the like in all my days! I've a mind to get in my wagon and go home, if this is the treatment I can expect hereabouts."

"You know you're blowing hot air, dearie. You've never hitched up a team in your life. Mind your manners and leave Julia to have as many dark thoughts as she's willing to bear."

"You really are being dreadful to her, Muriel," Julia said, not moving a muscle beyond those necessary to talk. "I grieve in the open. Elizabeth hides her feelings behind charitable acts."

"Charitable acts? Pshaw!" Muriel strode to the fireplace and stirred the pot. Then she rounded on Elizabeth again. "I don't blame the girl for running off when her expectations were wrapped up in living her life under your thumb."

"Stop it, Muriel!" Julia arose and felt her cheeks burning. "I don't reckon quarreling will help me or you or Elizabeth abide the waitin' with any hope of decorum or calm. It's not your dog in this

164

fight, much as I value your friendship and good sense." Seeing Muriel's crestfallen countenance, she took two steps and folded her in a tight embrace. "Oh, you know I mean you no ill will. I do need all the peace I can muster." As the gravity of the night's events overcame her again, she dropped her arms from around her friend and moaned, her voice breaking, "My girl. My girl! Will I ever see you again?" Her shoulders slumped and her head hung forward. "Please, pray with me."

A voice came from the doorway. "I will join you. It is but the least thing I can do for you, Julia."

Julia turned and saw Amanda Hilbrands coming toward her, and she swiped at her eyes. "Yes. Thank you. Ladies, please pray for my girl, and for my wounded boy, for that matter. And for Lizzie's boy. His feelin's must be mighty raw, Marie treatin' him thataway."

&#8473;

After an extended time spent beside the creek drinking several cups of water borne to her by an exceedingly attentive Mr. Thorne, Marie wondered if he expected her to make a meal for them, since it was drawing close to noon. It only made sense. There was good grass for the animals and a water source. *But please,* she thought, *no more water to drink!* She had but to get the necessaries sack off the back of her horse to begin. But before she could even think about approaching Mr. Thorne with the idea, he lifted her bodily from the ground and threw her into Bess's saddle. While she was getting back her breath, he tied a length of rope around one of her ankles, then ran it under the horse's belly to wrap around her other leg, and knotted the end of it to the stirrup. Then he mounted his own horse.

Without a word, he set off at a rapid pace, whipping the free ends of his reins against the neck of his horse.

*I must have said something wrong,* Marie thought, alarmed by his odd actions. *I didn't mean to. Did I complain to him that I was getting over full of water? What did I say?*

When Mr. Thorne suddenly slowed to a trot, Marie found herself leaning forward so she could grasp Bess's neck in order to stay on the horse. With the cinch still loose, the saddle had canted precariously to the off side. Although her left leg was encircled with a rope loop, her right leg was tied in place, and it was all she could do to keep her body weight from dragging her to the side and underneath the horse.

Her arms soon ached from encircling the thick neck of the old mare. Her right leg felt like it was tearing from her hip socket. The rope chafed the skin of her ankles. She also had an urgent need to dismount and seek the shelter of a large bush to perform personal business.

*Dear God, tell me how to make amends! I'm so sorry! I didn't mean to offend him.*

Resorting to prayer gave her comfort, but no immediate physical relief. Her position caught the saddle horn between herself and safety. She dared not release her hold around Bess's neck. The horn pressed upon her intimate reservoir, which seemed to continue filling with fluid as each minute passed. "I'm sorry," she sobbed, and knew she had said that aloud. Ashamed, she gritted her teeth to keep from crying out again, but pain welled up with another bounce, and she could no longer maintain control of all her muscles.

Warm liquid flooded from her body. *He will beat me for ruining the saddle*, she mourned, and almost let go so she would be trampled, rather than endure Mr. Thorne's wrath. But just as she was willing her arms to loose themselves from their frozen encirclement, he pulled his horse to a halt.

# Chapter 18

After the search party had ridden for several hours under an increasingly somber sky, Rulon called a halt to rest and eat. The horses badly needed the break.

Bill led his animal to water, but glanced around as his ears picked up the mutter of one man speaking to another in an undertone, complaining about the possibility of being caught out in a storm.

"More fool you if you didn't bring your oilskin," his companion replied. "I knew this hunt might take a day, or two at the most, but I taken a look at the sky and brung my rain gear."

*We might lose several days' time if we're on the wrong trail,* Bill fretted, remembering Rulon's thunderous voice and stormy aspect, and not at all sharing the speaker's confident assessment. When his horse had begun drinking, he pulled the pink paper out of his pocket and read it over for at least the tenth time. *Miss Marie thought she was headed to Denver. Who knows what that louse planned instead?*

Rulon must have seen the note before Bill jammed it into his pocket again. He came loping over to the stream bank to stand beside Bill, and put out his hand. "Can I take a look?"

"It's spare on clues." Bill retrieved the letter and gave it over, albeit with reluctance.

Rulon studied it out for a time, nodded, and looked up at Bill. "You have that right. She says 'Denver,' but I was almost convinced the tracks turned off the road onto rock before the Morgan kid spoiled 'em."

"Could you be wrong?"

Rulon tipped his head to the side and cocked his brow. "I could be. They might only have rested off the trail for a spell." He lowered his eyes to the note again. "Pa said Marie was clear, so here we are, headed north." He shrugged.

"You think he took her south?"

Rulon shook his head. "The tracks were ruined, so I can't say for sure. There's plenty of traffic on this road, heading both ways, so I can't trail them with any certainty." He spread his hands. "I just don't know. There was nothin' left to see."

Bill felt his heart sink into his nether regions. *If Rulon doesn't know* . . . "So we'll go to Denver?"

"All the way. Pa won't quit the hunt until the scent dries up. Even then . . . he can't go home to my ma without something to show for his efforts." Rulon's shoulders slumped and he looked at the stream.

Bill directed his gaze in the same direction for a long moment. The cloudy water burbled over a pebbled bottom for a stretch, then fell, splashing, about a foot into a pool that took shade from a large cottonwood tree. Although he recognized the beauty in the spot, the sight and sound had no power to raise his spirits. Marie was gone, and these men could be on one of the wildest of misdirected chases known to man.

After a time, Bill turned back to Rulon and asked in so low a voice he hardly could hear himself, "Do you mind if I keep the letter?"

Rulon held it out, catching Bill's eye. "You're fond of my sister." He had no hint of a question in his words.

"I am," Bill said, almost whispering the acknowledgment.

"When we retrieve her, make your play, and I'll back you."

Bill took the paper, feeling a flood of emotion coloring his face. "I'm a hired hand. You'd favor me over your pa's chosen 'known blood'?"

"I favor Marie's welfare above all else. I reckon you feel the same."

Bill kept Rulon's eye as he carefully folded the note. Then he nodded in thanks, replaced the paper in his pocket, and walked into the water to get the horse.

∞

Thorne wheeled his horse back toward Marie, gathering the slack in his lead rope as he came. She began to shudder from anxiety. With his hat shielding his face, she had no idea of his mood.

Then he lifted his head and drew his horse alongside Bess.

"What's the meaning of this? Your clothing is totally sodden!"

"I'm sorry, I'm sorry." She couldn't keep tears from dripping down her cheeks from her overflowing eyes.

"You're quite askew as well. Straighten up!" He moved his hand as though he would strike her.

"I cannot reach," she whimpered.

He hit her then, once, the back of his hand across her cheek. Thorne spoke in a soft, caressing voice. "You look frightful. Pull yourself together."

The tender voice made Thorne's words doubly frightening, and Marie struggled to haul her torso up onto the horse's neck so her legs would drag the saddle into place. With rubbery arms, she could not achieve her goal, and sank back to her original position, sobbing, and growing chilled as her saturated skirt and petticoat cooled.

Thorne clucked to his horse, and letting the lead rope droop, moved around to Marie's other side, pulling the slack out of the rope so as to catch her around the waist. Then he heaved her back into place. Bess whinnied in protest.

Marie cried out as the rope dug into her flesh. But the movement brought her atop the horse again, and she could finally unclasp her arms from about its neck.

She lay against the mare's warm hide, sobbing from pain and embarrassment. Never had she wet herself with an audience, certainly never in the presence of a member of the male sex. She couldn't fathom any such occasion in her life since childhood, and no one but her mother would have seen her in a similar condition.

"Get off the horse," Thorne directed.

Marie, disbelieving her ears, raised her head and looked at him.

"Don't play dumb. Dismount."

"But the rope . . ."

He bent and fiddled with the knot, then yanked the rope from around her ankle, scraping it through her stocking in the process. "Get off that horse," he shouted.

Marie cowered toward the off side, dragging her free leg over the back of the saddle. She still couldn't dismount with her left foot tied to the stirrup, so she curled her body and clung to the horn, getting as far from Thorne as she could without actually falling to the ground.

"Do you think I'm a fool?" he yelled.

Marie dropped her body lower, her arms aching anew and her legs in pain from the unaccustomed crouch in the air.

He clucked to his horse again, and Bess took a step forward.

"No!" Marie batted at the mare's neck. "Stop!"

Thorne had circled to a spot behind her, and was breathing on her neck, pressing his lips against her ear. "What is this contretemps?" he crooned, leaning over and reaching beneath her.

Marie wondered what he'd done, but then figured he had to have untied the rope, because she felt her foot slip in the stirrup, and knew she was falling.

Thorne's hands remained below Marie's body, as though he was preparing to catch her. "You must trust me, my darling," he whispered. Again his mouth was at her ear, his hands now upraised and supporting her body weight in a fashion that would not bear her mother's scrutiny.

She tried to keep her hold on the horn, but the sweat of her hands had made the leather surface slick. She fell against his chest, onto the neck of his horse, and one of his arms snaked around her, holding her fast.

"There now," he said, his breath like a feather tickling her neck. "You are where you ought to be, my sweet. Safe in my arms." He clasped his other arm around her and rocked her a bit, planting light kisses on her ear lobes, on her jaw, on her neck. "Safe in my arms," he repeated, and then let her slide a bit. "Oh, that won't do." He tightened his embrace around her and drew her up against his chest again.

She stiffened as his fingers brushed against her breast, but then he readjusted his hold, and his hand ceased the brief exploratory movement. Perhaps she had imagined the touch. *Yes.*

*Probably so*, she thought. *Mr. Thorne was merely keeping me from slipping.*

Bess sidestepped away, the saddle again leaning off center, the lead rope dragging the ground. Marie watched the mare move off, and experienced an odd sense of abandonment. She was beginning to feel awkward locked in Thorne's encircling arms, and wished she were safe on her gentle horse's back once more. But of course that would not be possible unless she were given a moment to tighten the cinch. Otherwise, she knew she could not chance mounting Bess.

Thorne moved his head to the other side of her neck and began to nuzzle her again.

Marie closed her eyes and slipped into a sort of trance. *He does love me, but I have been a great trial. I must try harder to please him.*

Her stomach rumbled.

"Thunder!" he cried, and dumped Marie onto the ground.

∞

"Is that man joining us for dinner?" Julia asked Muriel as they put plates on the tables set up within the shelter of the new barn. She'd commandeered Parley and his younger brother to construct the tables despite Lizzie Morgan's strenuous objections against working on the Sabbath, and they'd done a credible job of the chore.

"What man?"

"The reverend Amanda brought from town. I'm sure he was hoping to send around a collection plate during a sermon Mr. Hilbrands enticed him to prepare. I've half a mind to send him on home."

"Why would you be inhospitable, Julia?"

Julia stopped her task and gazed at her friend. "He makes me nervous, prattling on about James's spiritual progress and Marie's misdeed, and always patting and touching a body. Gives me the shivers."

Muriel laughed briefly, then her mouth fell into a slight frown. "I reckon he's either freshly embarked upon a new career of ministerin', or he hasn't suffered any pain in his life. How do folks go through life skipping along the top of troubles?"

Julia snorted. "I haven't. You haven't. Who do you know who hasn't suffered loss and grief and the like?" Then her voice broke on her next words. "I'm full up, I tell you. Marie going off is such a blow to me, comin' on top of James leavin' us." She sat down in a heap, as though she had no more strength in her body.

Muriel hastened to her side. "Julie, don't you give up hope. Your man is as good as any hound dog in keeping to the chase. He'll bring her home in good order."

"He'll bring her home, but he'll be shamed. When a child takes a notion to disobey him, he does not take kindly to the slight. No, not at all." She pinched the bridge of her nose between two fingers, eyes closed tightly. "He'll drown the girl in cascades of silent reproach."

Muriel kept quiet.

"On the occasion that Carl enlisted, I thought Rod would never get over it. 'Course he was off fightin' most of the time, but he wrote home, and I could hear his voice as I read each letter. Bitter. Yes, downright impolite, he was." She shook her head and dabbed at her eyes with her apron. "Then we thought we had lost the boy. That cured Rod of his pique mighty quick."

"I remember Carl's homecoming. All the excitement, then getting fixed up to come west in such a hurry."

"I hope to goodness Rod's learned a lesson from that time. We'll see, we'll see." Julia got up and resumed setting the places, then stopped again, holding a plate in the air. "Lawsy me, I hope he's learned something," she said, shaking her head and swiping her eyes again with her other hand.

∞

Marie landed hard on her side, and the pain radiating to every part of her being seared away any action but to curl into as near to a ball as was possible and lie still. Her head swam. Her breath had escaped her. She felt as though she would surely suffocate before she could draw another one into her lungs.

Thorne kicked his horse into moving over to where Bess was

standing, shaking herself to get rid of the unbalanced load. He leaned down and caught the dragging rope, then led the mare back to where Marie lay. Bess quit trying to shake off the saddle and stood still, but seemed to quiver.

"My darling, your wicked horse threw you. That cinch is a menace. Get up and tighten it so you can ride in security."

Marie remained where she was, struggling to get air, trying to block the pain.

"Did not you hear me? Arise and commence the task. We must be on our way."

She didn't move, although the thought that she should make haste to do so niggled at the margins of her battered mind.

Thorne started to dismount, throwing his right leg over the back of his saddle. Before he could finish the action, Marie whimpered and rolled onto her knees. She heard him settle back into the seat as she reached upward to get her hand through the stirrup that dangled nearby.

"That's my good love," she heard him croon, and she hauled herself to her feet with all speed.

Clinging to the horse, trying to will her hands to tug the saddle into position and find the buckle on the cinch, she wondered why Thorne had blamed Bess for throwing her. Hadn't the man been clutching her? Hadn't she been sitting atop his own horse? Marie's head refused to offer up the correct answer.

"We're late," Thorne barked. "Hurry it up."

She gained a purchase on the saddle and yanked on it, again and again, her arms burning and her ribs hurting her so badly that she wanted to scream. Her legs felt like rolls of muslin, and she struggled to stay upright on them. Finally, the leather sat upon Bess's back in the correct position. She slumped against the mare, catching her breath, but a movement she sensed behind her drove her to reach for the buckle.

"Bess," she whispered as she loosened the strap, "Let me draw this tight. Don't, no don't fill your belly."

The horse rolled her eye to look back at Marie, who patted her and encouraged her to stand still and exhale. Her own stomach cramped, adding to her anxiety.

"This must be tight. I can't slip again." Marie's crumpled

voice sounded to her ears as though it came from someone else, some cowed, whimpering soul in dire straits. She pulled the cinch strap as far as her straining muscles would allow, then fought the tongue into the buckle and secured the end.

The second she had done so, arms snatched her up and flung her toward the saddle. Terrified at the consequences if she landed in it on her side, she managed to kick her legs apart against the mass of her skirt. The arms released her above the horse, and she fell, hitting the seat awkwardly, but at least she was astride. Before she had gained a good seat, they were moving again, Thorne dragging Bess forward by the lead rope.

Marie hung on to the mare's mane with a frantic grip as they picked up speed. She gasped at the jolting ride, racked with pain from her head to her toe. But before they had gone too much farther, she finally got herself properly adjusted in the saddle, with her feet shoved firmly into the stirrups.

Rain began to hit her back with soft drops, then hard pebbles, then stinging nettles.

80

Nigh onto dusk, the search party reached Pueblo Town with not a moment to spare. As soon as the men had crowded their way into the livery barn, the skies opened and let fall a torrent of rain.

Bill dismounted and strode to the open door. Rulon and Chico joined him, and Bill looked over to see a forlorn countenance steal upon the former man's face.

"Still been tryin' to track?"

"Some. All sign is gone now."

Bill looked at the sky. He sighed. "I reckon it's fixin' to snow at the homestead."

"Maybe here, in an hour or so," Chico said. He turned up his collar and moved away from the incoming wind.

Bill gripped the door jamb. "Think we're bunking here overnight?"

"Likely," said Rulon. "I don't reckon Pa's going to stand us to hotel rooms."

"Ain't Hilbrands your father-in-law?"

Rulon put a shushing finger to his lips, looked around, and craned his neck until he located Randolph Hilbrands. He turned back and lowered his voice. "Yes, and tighter'n a Yankee drumhead. You won't catch me asking him for a favor."

Bill chuckled. "I knew a man like that once. He'd squeeze a penny 'til it barked, then save the sound to chase away thieves."

Rulon cracked a smile. "Good story, Henry." He cuffed Bill on the upper arm.

"I keep it in my vest pocket for use. Sometimes it's worth a drink in the right saloon."

Once the conversation with Rulon had run its course, Bill turned to the interior of the barn to care for his mount. The Old Man and Mr. Hilbrands moved toward the door, speaking with a tad bit of agitation. Bill got out of their way.

"They should know of the man." Mr. Owen turned up his collar.

"But they don't like to meet unless it's town business," Mr. Hilbrands protested. "I doubt the mayor will summon them."

"Time is running on. What's the quickest way to get answers?"

Mr. Hilbrands wiped under his nose with the back of his hand. "The saloons. If he's a gambler, he'll be known there."

# Chapter 19

When Old Man Owen and Mr. Hilbrands returned from their foray into the rain, Bill couldn't help noticing the sour expression shared by both men. Mr. Hilbrands carried a pot smelling of beans and pork, which he apportioned out to the men.

Bill sat crosslegged on the floor beside Rulon, Chico, and Sourdough. They ate plates of beans and hunks of bread from a loaf Mr. Hilbrands had taken from inside his coat. He'd said the food came from his hotel restaurant.

Chico looked up, his mouth full of half-chewed beans. "You reckon Hilbrands will pass a cup for us to pay for this here grub?" he mumbled over the food.

"Humph," Sourdough grunted, sopping bean juice with a crust of the bread. "The bread's stale. I wouldn't pay a penny for it."

"It's wheat bread," Bill observed.

"It ain't decent wheat bread," Sourdough claimed.

Bill managed half a smile at the outrage in the cook's voice.

After the meal, he stood beside the open door, watching the clouds to the west brightening a bit just before the sun went down. He turned away. Mr. Bates and the stable hand were lighting lanterns.

Rulon, who was sitting against a wooden upright in the open alleyway between the two rows of stalls, beckoned to him, and he walked over to join him.

"Thorne ain't anywhere in the town," Rulon said as Bill took his seat on the floor. "Nobody has seen him since he left here in the company of the Dominguez boys a couple of days ago." Rulon rubbed his thigh. "Pa says there's some talk he was forced out of town."

"Any idea why?" Fear clutched at Bill's throat, and he swallowed a couple of times, trying to clear it off as he waited for the answer.

Rulon's face had darkened in the lamplight. "Something about mistreating a girl."

A thick chill swept over Bill. "We should leave tonight," he muttered.

He started to get to his feet, but Rulon put a hand on his arm and pulled him back down.

"There's no sense freezing yourself in that rain. You'll be cold enough tomorrow when we head out for Denver City."

"Early?" Bill heard in the pitch of his voice the fear, the anger he was trying to hold back.

"I reckon. Pa will leave plenty early. Bunk down and sleep."

Bill shook his head, meaning to reject the advice after all, but Rulon persisted, and he finally agreed.

As Bill wrapped his blanket around himself and began to wiggle a space for himself between Chico and Sourdough on the floor of a stall, raised voices attracted his attention.

Old Man Owen and Mr. Hilbrands sat in a stall across the alleyway, consulting with their Virginia comrade, Mr. Bates. They spent the next half hour in a discussion that frequently escalated toward an argument.

Bill tried to block out their voices by tying his neck scarf around his ears and pulling his hat further down onto his head. Then he attempted to find a bit of sleep atop the dusty hay, jammed in among other men trying to achieve the same goal.

When the search party mounted up early the next morning, it was evident that Mr. Hilbrands had no plans to continue onward. He and Mr. Owen exchanged a few heated words, then they parted ways as the mounted men rode into the teeth of the wind-swept rain.

The initial rainfall let up toward midday, but began to came down again in fits and starts during the afternoon. Riding in the wet was pure misery to Bill. The only things keeping him going despite his sodden exhaustion were recovering the girl and taking vengeance on the man.

He found himself riding alongside the boss a few minutes

later, and was surprised to recognize the same ends reflected in his haggard, tightly set expression.

*He is her pa. If Marie was my daughter, I reckon I'd take it mighty hard to have her stolen away.*

The possibility that the vile scoundrel had taken the girl's virtue crossed his mind. Anger flashed with the power of lightning through his veins at the repugnant thought of another man, especially *that* man, possessing Marie against her will. He knew he'd been avoiding letting the idea out into the open, realizing that rage would paralyze him. As he struggled to concentrate on the obscure trail ahead, he thrust the fury down into his gut where he could bring it out later for examination.

The rain ceased again late in the day, about the time they found a wide spot in the road that consisted of a pair of saloons, a couple of bathhouses, and a few outbuildings. The Old Man called a halt.

As Bill climbed off his horse, he noticed a peculiar rumbling sound. It was not loud, but continuous, like a chorus of men humming at a low pitch.

Rulon and Mr. Bates accompanied the boss into one of the establishments while he and the other men looked around for accommodations for the night. Quiet, persuasive Clay got them the use of a stable behind a bathhouse, and found Bill and Chico together near one of the saloons.

Clay imparted the news, then added over the low rumble behind him, "They call this Boiling Springs, on account of the noise the gas makes rising up through the water. Folks come here to sooth themselves and drink the water. It is plenty tasty." His morose expression didn't harmonize with the good cheer in his words. He showed them the way to their lodgings.

Rulon came later, and drew Bill out of the stable where they could talk in private. He bore a visage carved from equal parts of anger and despair.

Bill's limbs began to quiver as he eyed Rulon. "What did you learn?"

Rulon's voice came slow and steady, but with an edge of steel. "He called himself Thornecroft hereabouts. Set up a poker table in one of the saloons for a spell."

Bill sensed there was more, and waited for it with a feeling of dread.

"They say he's cold, not right in the head." He paused, gazed at his toes, then raised his chin and looked Bill in the eye. "He abused a girl so bad it killed her."

Bill reached behind him, feeling for the stable timbers to hold him up as his legs threatened to fold.

"They was fixin' to string him up, but he got away clean and headed south. I don't reckon he'd come back this way, nor head to Denver."

"You argued that to your pa?"

"I did. He's seen the error of his ways."

Bill sucked in air through clenched teeth.

Rulon gestured toward a stall. "Rest up. We're turnin' south at first light."

&#8449;

Marie awoke to half light with hunger clawing at her innards. She clutched her abdomen, her head feeling as though her thoughts were wrapped in cotton wool, and her body shouting against any movement that would stir up more pain.

Where was she? Why did she have a rank barnyard odor clinging to her clothing? She looked around at the gray surroundings, hesitant, frightened, but not even sure why she was fearful. Why was she lying in the open, the ashes of a campfire beside her? Who was that wrapped in a blanket, snoring softly?

*Why can't I think?*

She strained to bring back any memory, and grabbed at a passing notion that she was camped with her father and brothers. Something about cattle brushed against her mind.

She lay still and listened for a moment. No. There was no sound of cattle bedded down nearby. She could see only two horses standing hobbled, each one nose to tail with the other. As she continued to listen to the noise coming from the blanket, she became convinced that the sound was unlike that which her father made at night.

Who kept her company? Why were they alone?

She lay still, letting her mind do its best to clear through the pain and the fog and the fear.

Slowly, slowly she walled the pain into a tidy compartment of her brain, straining to keep it intact with mental arms encircling it. Then she felt a light memory touch, very like a feather, stroking the back of her hand: a man with a waxed moustache bending over her hand, kissing it. The dream image faded as stark terror chased it away. She was bouncing crazily on a horse's overset saddle, and she couldn't draw rein to make the animal halt.

A tiny moan escaped her throat. Her stomach burned with acid. Her arms flailed as she fell from the horse, trapped in soaked skirts. A man reviled her for wetting herself.

She no longer wanted any part of memory, and retreated inside the pain, letting it flood over her until she had no more thoughts.

She didn't know how long she lay encased in pulsing agony, welcoming it to overwhelm her. But when she could no longer bear it, at the point where she knew she must die, her mind cleared and she could think again.

She had chosen to run away with a man who said he loved her. She swallowed down the mouthful of gall that rose to choke her. Doubt grated her thoughts as surely as though a rasp had been applied to her brain. The man who called himself C. G. Thorne lay just beyond her, snoring. She didn't even know what those initials signified, yet she had entrusted her life to him.

She turned on her side and threw up bitter acid.

When she had passed through the vomiting to dry heaves, she lay back on her bedding, taking in rapid, shallow breaths. Last night was very clear to her now. Last night, after riding for hours without a break, Mr. Thorne had finally stopped to make camp. When he insisted that she put together a meal, she had felt heartened. But when she had finished preparing the food, Thorne took it away and consumed the whole of it. He had only allowed her a sip of water that he tipped from his flask into a cup. She had grasped it tightly, shaking in her eagerness to ease the dryness of her mouth.

*Drugged!* She was sure he had drugged her. What poison was in that flask of water? She realized the man never drank from it now. On one occasion, it had contained lemonade. She wondered if that had been drugged, as well. Had she taken that unexplained fall in the wagon because Thorne had poisoned her?

*What a fool I am!* she thought. *He has no plan to marry me.* A chill swept through her. If not that, what base scheme had he devised? *A man this foul will sink to any depths. He wants to sell my body.*

The blinding conviction that her thought was the true case made her want to vomit again. But when she tried, she had nothing to expel. Nothing but foolishness. Nothing but folly. She berated herself for trusting a man with such vile intentions.

When she sank again onto the bedding, her hand flopped against her skirt and it struck a hard object. Puzzled, she untangled the fabric until she could put her fingers into her pocket to investigate.

Leather. Wood. She froze. She had the sheathed knife in her pocket.

&#8494;

Old Man Owen was as good as Rulon's word, Bill reflected as he saddled up by lantern light. He had no pocket watch, and could only guess at the hour, but from the aching in his limbs, he figured he hadn't slept very long. *Midnight, maybe?* It could be later, but he was sure it wasn't nigh on to dawn.

His horse was just about played out, as were the other mounts. The thought that they couldn't go at the speed he would have liked galled him. There was nothing he could do about the situation. Thorne was getting away from them.

"Steady there," Sourdough spoke from behind him.

Bill thought he was talking to his horse, but when the man's hand settled on his shoulder, he knew the advice was for him.

He glanced around, and yes, the old-timer was looking at him.

"I know you're in a rough spot, Henry. Keep in mind, the girl has spunk."

"Thorne's pulled the wool over her eyes."

"It won't take long for her to see through it. Them swindlers can only run a confidence game on a body for so long before their victim's good sense kicks in."

"What day is it now?" Bill tried hard to keep desperation out of his voice, and nearly succeeded.

"What does that matter? I didn't know what day it was yesterday. If this ain't still yesterday," he muttered.

Bill doffed his hat and had a try at hand-combing his hair. "My brain's a muddle. How many days since he took her?"

"Well now," Sourdough ticked them off on his fingers. "This is the third day." He pursed his lips. "Don't give in to despair, boy."

Tom Morgan let go of his mount's bridle and pushed his way between Bill's and Sourdough's horses, glaring at Bill. "I told you. Marie is my woman. You ain't got any claim to plow that field." He shoved Bill on one shoulder for emphasis.

"Keep a civil tongue," Bill growled, and shoved back. "She surely don't want you. She left with Thorne."

Tom went after him, fists flying, howling curses.

"Boys, boys!" Sourdough shouted, but stepped back out of the way, pushing on his animal's rump to clear more room.

Before the Old Man and Mr. Morgan could stop the scuffle, Bill landed a few good blows, but received five or six himself. He backed up, one ear ringing from Tom's strike as the farmer's father pulled him off and muttered warnings at his offspring.

"We have business!" Mr. Owen barked, his furious face not two inches from Bill's. "Get mounted!" He spun about and stomped away to take his own advice.

Bill swiped at his trickling nose, then yanked at an edge of his neckerchief to sop up the blood. "Damned corn farmer!"

The ride back to Pueblo Town commenced without further incident, but Bill avoided the spurned farmer as they traveled, hunching himself against the wind and rain that persisted to torment them.

Chico approached him as he leaned against his horse when the party rested at noon.

"Why you want to tussle with the farm boy?"

"He threw the first punch. I had to defend against it."

"Keep your head clear, Henry. He's a thin reed, easy to break.

The big stick is the con man."

Bill heaved a sigh. "I reckon you have the right of it."

"We'll catch up and break him over our knees."

Bill nodded. Then as he caught sight of Old Man Owen's example, he swung into his saddle. "He's got a long lead on us. We've wasted good horseflesh on a false trail." His belly ached at the misuse of their resources.

"Yep," Chico agreed, his mouth twisting down as he got his own foot in the stirrup.

They entered Pueblo Town after dark, to discover that Mr. Hilbrands had gone south to retrieve his wife.

"No fine food tonight, boys," Rulon announced in a rueful tone. He handed around two loaves of brown bread.

Sourdough yelped, "Weevils," in high indignation when he tore himself a chunk.

"Hand it here," Chico said, chuckling. "Extra meat."

"I fancy my meat on the hoof," the old cook replied, digging into the bread with the tip of his knife and flicking out the insects. "Catch 'em, if you want 'em so bad."

∞

At noon the next day, Marie huddled beside a fire sheltered under an overhanging rock, stirring gruel. The never-ending rain dripped off her sunbonnet onto her shoulders. Thorne sat wrapped in his blanket, watching her, the once-elegant hat atop his head now drooping and sodden. Yesterday, he had allowed her to saddle Bess properly, but once again tied her ankles to her stirrups for the cold, wet ride. He'd also persisted in denying her nourishment, and her stomach felt as though it must be grinding against itself. Other than that, the journey had been unremarkable.

Except for the daydreams. She couldn't get Bill Henry's harrowed countenance to leave her alone.

Then, at day's end, she had discovered large holes in her stockings from binding against the rope, and despairing of any chance to repair them, removed them and tossed them behind a bush.

Today her muscles trembled from fatigue and weakness, and her legs felt the cold more intensely due to her hasty action. She wasn't used to so much horseback travel, and she certainly wasn't used to starving.

Thinking she must do something to preserve her strength, she plunged her hand into the sack lying beside her leg and took a bit of cornmeal between her fingers. She crammed it into her mouth on the sly, holding the lump in her cheek, hoping it would soften enough to chew, terrified that Thorne would discover what she had done.

The gruel had thickened, so Marie removed the pot from the fire and glanced at the man. He got to his feet, came to the fire, grabbed the pot, and carried it away.

She remained beside the fire, trying to raise saliva in her dry mouth so the cornmeal could soften. She had drained her canteen long since, but didn't trust the contents of Thorne's flask. Perhaps she should spend the afternoon's ride holding the canteen to collect rainwater.

Idleness brought back her daydream, strong and almost tangible. Bill Henry sat beside her at Ellen's wedding dinner, smiling and chatting at her, pausing from time to time to take a bite of chicken or cornbread.

Marie fought the temptation to put out her hand, to see if she could touch the image of Bill's face. *He's just a fancy, my tired mind playin' tricks.*

She'd had plenty of the dreams, waking or sleeping. They must have a meaning. Surely she wasn't conjuring them herself.

When Thorne had eaten, with much slurping and lip-smacking, he grunted at Marie and made a gesture toward her horse. She got up to make ready for the journey, chagrined that she had been caught idle. It was a wonder that the man hadn't got up and backhanded her.

Carefully, whenever her back was turned to Thorne, she ventured to chew the corn, one motion at a time, as she packed away the implements and sack of cornmeal. Then she saddled Bess, taking care to tighten the cinch.

She held her breath when he wrapped her bare ankles with the prickly rope and secured her on the horse, fearful of what new indignity he might visit upon her. His imagination seemed to have failed him, however, and he did nothing more to add to her present uncomfortable state.

As they rode, Marie stared at the deep hoof prints made by Thorne's horse in the mud through which they rode. How much longer would it rain? She swallowed the corn meal. It seemed to form a lump in her stomach, but at least it was there to give her the power to sit the saddle.

After several hours of travel, Marie wondered if they were going in circles. With no sight of the sun behind the constantly weeping clouds and no road to follow, it was highly likely that they were lost. One scrawny creosote bush passing beside her foot looked like another. Even the tracks looked the same, chewed up by the horse ahead of her.

She asked herself why she stayed with Thorne. Couldn't she escape? Couldn't she whip Bess into a run and outdistance the other horse?

Her spirits sank as she looked at her horse's lowered neck. Bess had no more reserve than she. The mare's strength was near to failing.

As the miles piled up through the day, miles that she was almost certain they were traversing over and over, Marie began to lose any hope that her world would ever consist of anything but riding in circles in the rain, soaked to the skin, with a madman holding the upper hand. The thought wore on her soul, chafing her spirit as much as the rope running beneath the horse's belly chafed her skin.

Late in the afternoon, she could bear no more of the endless plodding, and she kicked her heels against Bess's flanks, yelling to the horse to "Giddyup."

The startled mare leaped a foot forward, and Marie rejoiced in finally getting away from the man.

She made no great progress in her attempt to escape. Thorne still had control of the lead rope, and he'd dallied it around his saddle horn. Although Bess's yank caused him to lean precariously to one side and cry out, he regained his balance, hauled on the rope, and pulled Marie to his side.

"You can't get away from me," he yelled, slapping her until

she covered her face with her arms. He flung himself off his horse, dug in a saddle bag, and pulled out another length of rope. Then he snatched one of Marie's wrists. She struggled with him, shrieking with rage and fear, but he soon overpowered her and immobilized her arms, tying them to her own saddle horn.

೪

Marie lay on her side in the brightening morning light. She could see well enough to realize that the clouds had moved off during the night. Sunshine at last! Perhaps she would be able to gain her bearings and make another attempt to escape from Thorne. This time, she would take care to slash the lead rope just before kicking Bess into flight.

Thorne had tied her wrists and her ankles last night. He'd told her she had been a naughty maiden to try to get away, and then roughly shoved her onto her blankets.

If it hadn't been for yesterday's rain that left the ground a quagmire, Marie would have cut her bindings and left under cover of the night's darkness. She had only resisted the notion because she knew he would have no problem finding her tracks in the mud when he awoke and found her gone. A sense of despair chilled her heart. Until she could find a way to make good her flight, the constant belittling mixed with the sudden bursts of strange behavior that so frightened her would continue.

Her heart sank at the predicament in which she had put herself. Why had she listened to the man's silver words, trusted that he cared for her? The immensity of her folly loomed over her, further diminishing any sense of her own worth. What a fool she was!

Thorne moved in his sleep, and Marie froze. The man finally lay still again, and Marie relaxed her tightened muscles. There was little point in trying to cut her way out of the knotted rope restraints with escape so fruitless.

She realized what little esteem she retained, and the thought rankled her. That lack of gumption had enabled Thorne to keep her captive. His prisoner! And yet . . . She felt the return of her resolve like little iron bars slipping into place within her spine.

The time would come. She would get free of him and his despicable plans.

This time when Thorne stirred, his eyes opened, and he raised his head and looked at her.

"Don't think it, little Miss Owen." His voice was rough with sleep, but well conveyed his power over her. He closed his eyes, and seemed to sink into slumber once more.

She quaked at the chilly threat in his voice. Would she never get free of the man?

She started to imagine ways to disable his horse so he couldn't follow her. It pained her to think about hurting an animal, but if it were necessary—

He was on her in an instant, his knees astride her body. She began to scream as he tore at the neck of her dress. She struggled with the man, frantic that she hadn't wiggled the knife out of her pocket and cut her bonds. Her screams diminished to sobs. She would lose her virtue today. She renewed her fight against him. Better she should lose her life.

When Thorne had gotten her bodice open, he reached down between her breasts and grasped the sack containing the gold dust. "I thought so," he growled, and yanked the string until it broke, leaving a welt on the back of her neck.

He got off her, thrust the poke into his pocket, and went off beyond the boundaries of the camp to perform his morning business.

Marie lay as he left her, sobbing into her bound hands, relieved that after so long a forbearance, he hadn't attacked her virtue, but distraught that he had robbed her of Pa's gold.

8

Rod arrived home Wednesday night in the forefront of a footsore party of complaining men leading played-out horses. The situation he found was no less grim.

Rand Hilbrands, having deserted him in his hour of need, had fetched Amanda and the preacher back to town, upsetting the remaining women.

Julia, who he'd always counted on to be levelheaded when he

flew into pieces, clung to him, weeping.

Lizzie Morgan jumped up and demanded of her husband to be taken home as soon as horses could be hitched to the wagon. Ed refused her, showing either exhaustion or a surprising rise of gumption. Their quarrel could be heard across the meadow for what seemed to Rod to be hours.

Chester Bates got pulled off to one side by his wife, and they conversed for quite a time until Chester returned and made the excuse that Muriel was worried for the wheat crop. He said he was heartsick about the whole affair, but he owed harvested wheat to quite a number of folks, Rod included, and had best get home tomorrow.

And Mary was sick. Rod had no more than put Julia to bed after dosing her with laudanum when Rulon, looking more peaked than he had since healing from his war wounds, came to the big cabin. He paced back and forth outside until he poked his head in the door and blurted out that he couldn't ride on the morrow.

"We need to fetch your sister back." Rod slammed his hand into his fist, catching himself before he let a curse escape his lips.

Rulon stood in the doorway and appeared about to collapse. "I'm feeling mighty low about turnin' you down." His voice was so cowed Rod could barely hear it. "I'm obliged to choose my wife and young'uns."

"What ails her? It can't be more than your ma can deal with." Then he realized that his own wife was unlikely to be of any assistance, given her present state of emotional disarray.

Rulon crossed his arms, pressed his lips together and lowered his head. He gazed at his toes for quite a spell, then shrugged his shoulders and let them fall.

From his discomfiture, Rod guessed the problem. "She's increasing?" He turned and paced across the room to the fireplace, and then turned back to stand in front of Rulon. Then, before he spoke in haste and blundered into the middle of his son's private affair, he took another circuit.

Rulon was ready for him now, and said merely, "Yes, Pa."

"She's not feeding the babe? Preventing another?"

"She is." Rulon shook his head ruefully.

"Well, I'm gratified the mumps didn't steal your vigor." He took another walk across the room, an undercurrent of pride in his son swelling from his toes, but uppermost in his feelings was slashing anguish that his daughter was still in the clutches of a dangerous man.

Rulon left to return to Mary's side, and Rod was halfway across the room when he heard him speak out in the yard. "Henry." And a second later, surprise in his voice, "Morgan?"

Rod steeled himself to break up another row. One of the men knocked on the door, and at his invitation, Henry opened it and stood on the doorstep. He removed his hat.

Rod beckoned him in, and the man looked over his shoulder, then took a step inside the door, holding his hat at his side by the brim. "There's one horse fit to travel tomorrow," he reported.

Rod inhaled sharply. *As bad as that?*

Tom Morgan pushed his way into the house, knocking sideways into Henry.

The cowman straightened his shoulders and stepped back out of the way, but his dislike for Morgan showed plainly in his glower.

The boy had wrath written up one side of his face and down the other. "I've come to call off the wedding," he said in a voice louder than the location warranted.

Rod looked over his shoulder to see if his strident voice had awakened Julia. Not seeing her face peering from behind the curtains that enclosed their bed, he turned back to Tom, an angry retort on his lips.

Cutting him off, Tom declared, "Thorne's had her too long. She's damaged goods, not fit to be my wife."

Henry stirred behind him, and Rod barked at him, "No!" Then he directed his anger and frustration toward spoiled Lizzie Morgan's spoiled son. "You pompous, craven, doghearted lout! If General Lee himself sent orders my daughter was to marry you, I'd tell him no to his face." He took a raspy breath. "My daughter is worth any ten Morgans, and you can tell your mama I said so. Get out of my house! Be off my land by sunup!"

Tom's face blanched, and he balled his fists, but he took his leave in haste, slamming the door behind him.

Rod felt the anger draining from him, leaving him feeling slightly lightheaded.

Henry cleared his throat. "Sir?"

He looked at the man and nodded for him to speak.

"I'm asking to draw my pay. I beg leave to take that sound horse at first light and track down Miss Marie. If I can't..." He paused for a moment to clear his throat again. "If I can't recover her, I'll light out for Texas. I reckon I..." He couldn't finish his thought.

Rod's own throat tightened. He'd judged the man a poor match for his daughter, dazzled by pride in his own connections, yet as narrow-sighted as though he'd donned horse blinders. If he'd only seen the man's affection for Marie before now— Rod abandoned that train of thought. Fact was, he had seen it, and discarded it as a matter of little weight.

He drew himself up, filling his lungs with air. *I can't dwell on my past sins*, he thought. *I'll send Henry after my girl. If he can't bring her back, nobody can.*

# Chapter 20

The last thing Bill packed into a saddlebag the next morning was the deed to the Texas ranch that he'd hidden away under the mattress of his bunk. The action brought a wave of melancholy flooding over his churning thoughts. That paper represented failure, his failure in the past to get enough work to keep the place going, and a pending failure if he did not succeed in his quest to find the girl, wrench her out of Thorne's hands, and bring her home. Not for a second did he contemplate leaving the deed behind. He couldn't be sure he would return to this place. If he didn't, he'd battle all the carpetbaggers in Texas to get the ranch back. Henry blood had been shed to gain it. His folks now lay beneath its earth. It belonged to him.

After eating a hurried meal, he embraced Chico silently. Choked up as he was, he dared not risk saying a word. Then he departed from the bunkhouse and mounted, feeling the weight of his revolver in one coat pocket, and the heft of his wages in the other.

Rod Owen had paid him off with a mixture of bills, coins, and gold dust. When the man had opened the box in which he kept the gold, he'd turned back from it with a grim set to his mouth. "It appears the scoundrel talked my girl into helping herself to a small poke I had in here. As you ask after them, it might aid you to know that. He'll leave a trail if he's spending my dust."

The wages had to last him for a good length of time, either on his desperate manhunt, or on a long journey home to Texas.

&

Marie had not yet seen a chance to get away from Thorne, but he had finally led them back to the road that ran south. During the early afternoon, he stopped at a farm to buy food. That night, Marie devised a soup by boiling a handful of the beef he had bought, along with a turnip and a potato, which she cut into the broth. Afterward, she took care to sheath the knife and furtively place it back in her pocket.

The man surprised her greatly when he left soup in the pot and bid her eat it.

"You're losing flesh," he said. "That won't do. You're of no use to me if you're skin and bones."

She took the pot and spoon, wiped the utensil on her skirt, and ate the soup, trying not to gulp it down. As she savored the hot liquid, she pondered on his choice of words. She had escaped what she had thought were his advances earlier in the week. However, his comment supported her fear. It appeared he intended to make his livelihood by offering her to be used for men's carnal pleasures. She shuddered. It was entirely likely he would yet take it into his head to use her himself as a prelude to the degrading life he had chosen for her.

When he tied her wrists that night, Marie followed the pattern she'd set at their previous night's encampment of making sure there was slack in the bindings so she could free her hands during the hours of darkness. This time, she distracted him from the task by asking him annoying questions about the people at the farm, and managed to keep her wrists slightly apart as he secured them. She didn't fancy being helpless if this was the night he tried to assault her. She had to have her hands free to wield her only weapon.

She had almost dozed off when a slight noise alerted her that Thorne was awake. She strained to see into the darkness as she slipped the blade free of the leather. He would not catch her vulnerable.

He tried, clasping his hand over her mouth to silence her. But she didn't want to scream. She wanted to cut him, hurt him, cause him great discomfort.

And she did. The faint contrast of his grotesque white appendage against the dark fabric of his trousers was a good target, and she poked and slashed at it, sending him howling away. She hurriedly got up from the bed, trying to locate Bess so she could haul herself on the mare's back and flee.

But he must have seen her intentions for, despite his wounds, he came back and hit her with his fist, and she fell into blackness.

ॐ

Bill continued south, keeping the horse to a lope where it could, and going forward at a trot when it couldn't. He stopped at every farmhouse, every hacienda, every settlement, asking after a man dressed in fancy duds and a young woman riding a brown mare. He didn't get any news of them until after he'd left the Spanish settlement on the Cuchara. But while asking around in Leones, he had picked up the intriguing information that James Owen had up and got himself married, and might still be in the country.

*I can't stop to locate but one Owen,* he reminded himself, and pressed on south toward the Apishapa River.

At a farmhouse set back off the road in the midst of a field of wheat, he got the first encouraging report.

"I did see such a man yestiddy," said the woman of the household when Bill had roused her from pulling weeds in the kitchen garden. "I sold 'im a cut of beef and a few root vegetables." She wiped her hands on the apron covering the front of her drab dress. "It's handy to have a bit a dust in the house." She closed one eye against the sun and squinted down the lane. "I didn't see no girl." She pointed with her chin. "She may've waited down to the road."

Bill took his leave with thanks, his heart lighter for having the information that Thorne had gold. Then it skipped a beat. *Where is Marie?*

ॐ

Thorne had spent the day before alternating between railing at Marie and dismounting every other mile to open his pants and check the bandages he'd applied to his wounds. He swore mightily each time he reseated himself atop his saddle. She was glad she'd cut him there, although she would have preferred to have made a thrust into his black heart. At least he would not be coming at her anytime soon.

Today, their progress was as before. Thorne kept the horses at a slow, easy walk to prevent any jolting of his private parts. That suited Marie. The walking gait prevented any unnecessary jolt to her aching head.

Across a field of maturing corn, Marie glimpsed a couple of enclosures, rough corrals, with several horses divided among them. One small ring, where six or seven idlers lined the fence, detained a buckskin colt, kicking for all it was worth, desperately trying to rid itself of a puny human male who was sprawled halfway in the saddle and halfway out. His feet had no firm foundation, out of the stirrups as they were. The man gripped the colt's mane with one hand while the other grabbed naught but air. Yet he clearly endeavored to find a stable lodging upon the animal.

Bess continued her slow walk behind Thorne's mount. The distant colt spun ferociously, its hooves throwing dirt into the air, which then hung suspended in a half-obscuring cloud. Marie's detached observation turned to fascination with the age-old struggle between man and beast that was taking place in the corral.

*I need to do that,* Marie thought. *Get shed of this evil man trying to break my spirit.*

Just when it seemed the man would attain his desired seat, the horse leaped into the air and landed with its head down, all four legs closely bunched, then paused but a second, gathering strength for another burst of cyclonic activity. Jarred by the harshness of the landing, the wrangler lost his tenuous grip, left the animal entirely, and cartwheeled in the air a couple of times before he met the ground.

Marie drew in a sharp breath and peered through the murky cloud, watching for the figure to get up and try again, but he didn't rise. As the colt bucked and kicked, jumping closer to where the man had fallen, she bit her lip, her loyalty shifting in the moment to the human in mortal danger. The folks around the corral grew increasingly agitated, and she imagined there must be quite a noise being raised, although at this distance, she didn't hear much of it.

Then a figure wearing a dress and apron flew from the fence into the dust cloud, flapping her apron and swirling her skirt at the colt, driving it away from the horseman, who still lay prone in the ring.

She knelt alongside him, and for a moment, Marie thought the girl's skin was brown, but she discounted the idea, marking it up to imperfect vision through the opaque air swirling above the enclosure.

Although Bess's progress had slowed almost to a stop, Marie had just about passed the farm before the man got to his feet. As she looked back over her shoulder, Marie thought there was something familiar in the way he bent to pick up his hat, then used it to swat the dirt from his clothing. Her brothers used their hats in a similar fashion to beat dust off their shirts and trousers, but perhaps other men did the same thing.

Thorne growled something at her, and Marie reluctantly gave up watching the spectacle, turned toward him, and asked in a voice devoid of light, "What did you say?"

"I said we'll camp against that farthest hill." His face set in angry lines as he gestured ahead. "Pay attention. Those people can't help you."

"No one can help me," she agreed in an undertone. She gazed at her bound wrists as the raw umber cloud from the farm seemed to encompass her soul.

# Chapter 21

After traveling for several hours the next day, Thorne and Marie came upon a curious sight. A red buggy with gold fringe fluttering from the top occupied the road before them.

The vicious set of Thorne's face disappeared in an instant. He laughed heartily. "You don't see that every day. The rig belongs to a former colleague of mine." He turned his horse and circled it back toward Marie. "You behave properly, and I'll make it worth your while."

She nodded, wondering what Mr. Thorne's 'gift' would be. Anything was better than how she'd lived the last few days.

"Your nod better be as good as your word. I'll hold you to it," he said, released the rope binding her wrists, and slung the lead rope around Bess's neck. Then he put spurs to his horse's flanks, and Marie urged Bess into a trot to keep up.

As soon as they came alongside the buggy, Marie kept her head down to hide the bruises on her face. The one she got falling in the wagon was bad enough, although the color had faded to yellow. The newer ones from Thorne's mistreatment hadn't had time to heal. The best thing was to hope her bonnet cast enough shadow to conceal the worst of the color.

Mr. Thorne took Marie by the wrist and held it firmly. "Rallison!" he saluted the buggy as they trotted alongside. His cheerful voice gave little indication that he was aware that the male occupant of the rig had a pistol trained upon him. "Put that away. It's me."

The man reined in the buggy horse with one hand while he gave the gun to his female companion. Then he said, "I thought you were up north, Thornecroft. What are you doing in my neck of the woods?"

"The north is too hot for my taste, so I determined to have a bit of an adventure. I've acquired a new girl, name of Marie." He motioned with his head toward her, then inclined it in the opposite direction. "Here's my old friend, Guy Rallison. We worked together on the Mississippi riverboats."

Marie didn't dare look up, afraid disgust would show in her face, so she merely nodded. Here was proof that everything the man had told her was a lie, even down to his own name. She had been so blinded by fancy manners and cunning words that she'd believed the whole mess of falsehoods.

"Who is that with you, Rallison?"

The man chuckled. "I married, or didn't you hear? This is the wife, Madame Janette."

Clearly irritated, the woman spoke her name again, but she said it differently, and with great emphasis, "Jhah-net!"

Marie looked up briefly, only enough to catch sight of a beautiful brown-haired woman dressed in a deep yellow gown with a be-feathered hat to match.

"I beg your pardon, my sweet. Madame Jhah-net it is." He laughed. "Saucy, is she not?"

"The French often are. Are you stopping nearby?" Thorne asked. "I need to acquire proper duds for the girl."

*He's even changed the style of his words. There's no fanciness in his talk now.*

"You're in luck, Thornecroft. The little lady decided she doesn't care for blue anymore. I have her cast-offs in my trunk." He gestured toward the rear of the buggy, where a leather-bound wooden truck was affixed with ropes to the chassis. "Ten dollars, if you want the outfit." He climbed out of the rig, knocking off his hat against the buggy's top. He retrieved it from the floor of the buggy and put it on again, but not before the sun brightened the man's fair hair. He was quite tall, and strode on long legs toward the rear. He bent over to open the luggage and rummage inside.

Thorne dismounted and hauled Marie off Bess, whispering threats in a mild voice as he did so. They joined Rallison, and Thorne pawed through the clothes as well.

Rallison pulled out a short, dark blue dress. "Here it is." He held it up in front of Marie, pursing his lips. "It will fit. Ten dollars."

Thorne took the garment and fingered the material. "That's steep for used clothing. I'll give you three."

"Eight."

"Five."

"Six, and that's as low as I'll go."

Thorne raised his chin. "I'll bet you paid no more than five for new."

"All right. I'll take five-fifty. That's a fair price, mind you. The corset, petticoat, stockings, and hat go with it."

"Humph," Thorne snorted. "You drive a hard bargain. Five-fifty it is."

Mr. Thorne gathered up the outfit and turned to Marie.

Who was he? Thorne, or was he really named Thornecroft? Marie shook her aching head.

"Yes, you will wear it," he said, probably taking her headshake for refusal. "I didn't buy it to decorate my horse." He turned to Rallison. "Where are you bound?"

Mr. Rallison stopped in the act of climbing into the rig. "I have a place down the country a piece, near the Apishapa."

"What's that? A mountain?"

Rallison chuckled. "It's a stream. If you're looking for employment, Madame could use your girl. I already have one gambler working a table. If you want to set up another, you'll have to share your winnings with the house, seventy-five, twenty-five."

Thorne snorted. "Not too bad. I like seventy-five percent."

Rallison shook his head. "Seventy-five is my take."

"That's robbery!"

"It's my house. Take it or leave it." He gathered up the lines and prepared to slap the horse into action.

"Wait! I'll take it. Where is your establishment?"

Rallison furnished directions while Marie stood in the road, shivering. She was about to become a fallen woman.

౭౦

Bill rode into another farmstead just like the one before and the one before that. This one sat on the banks of a stream so sand-choked that he'd nearly been able to walk the horse over the top of the water when he crossed it.

He hailed the farmer in his field, left his horse ground tied, and waded his way down a crooked row through the crop.

"Good day," the man said, eying him suspiciously.

"Good day to you, sir," Bill said, taking off his hat and letting it dangle at his arm's length.

Evidently satisfied with what he saw, the farmer replied, "I'll have work for you next week."

Bill hurried into his question. "I'm not here about your harvest, sir. I'm inquirin' if you've seen a man and a young woman pass by. The man was outfitted in fancy clothes, vest, big hat, watch chain across his middle. The girl wore a plain stuff dress with a black coat, bonnet, and rode a brown mare. I don't recall the color of the bonnet, but her hair is dark colored."

The man considered for a time, then shook his head. "I might have been up to the house," he said. "I had chores thereabouts part of the day."

Disappointment tasted like moldy bread in Bill's mouth. "I thank you, sir, for your time." He turned away and started to traverse the field toward where he'd left the horse.

"Run away with him, did she?" the farmer called.

His words felt like an axe striking Bill between the shoulder blades, and he stopped and began to turn.

"I hope you do find her soon. He'll likely put her to work in that new house."

"House?" Bill swallowed at the lump building inside his craw.

"Tall fellow and his pretty wife built them a saloon down the country a piece in one of them Mexican towns. Plaza this or that. The wife runs the entertainment."

Bill waited until his voice might be steady, then asked, "Do you recall what name they put to the place?"

"Nah. Something furren-sounding, but not the Spanish." He paused. "If she's your gal, get 'er back afore she's soiled. Then whip 'er good for sloping off thataway."

Gall rising in his throat, Bill fled the man's presence.

The sun had almost slid behind one of the Spanish Peaks to the west. Thorne was still nursing his wounds and had exhibited his ill temper the afternoon long by threatening her over his shoulder in all manner of disrespectful language.

That behavior hadn't raised Marie's spirits. Her head still felt fuzzy from Thorne's blow that had made the world go dark. *I'm sure to have a black eye.* She wondered if they would arrive in the town before darkness fell.

The bristly end of a rope fiber dug into a raw welt in her flesh, and she moved her wrists slightly, trying to ease it out of its position. How could Thorne think the injuries from this mistreatment would be attractive? The man's mind had to be off plumb. She mourned the confiscation of her knife. If she'd had it in hand, Thorne would surely rue the day they'd met.

Presently, a town of the Spanish pattern appeared as they came in sight of a river valley. Thorne grunted and spurred his horse to a trot. The increased pace didn't seem to please him, as he soon reduced it to the previous placid walk. Even though Marie had no desire to get to their destination, her misused body told her that an end to the riding within a reasonable time would be well received.

Lights twinkled on ahead of them as inhabitants of the houses lit lamps against the coming night. A great many lights came on, one by one, in a building on the outskirts of town. Marie thought the structure would have been more suitably placed in Pueblo Town than here. *Or maybe Hell.* It was constructed of lumber, not mud-smoothed adobe blocks. Marie wondered how far the milled boards had traveled to be used there. *The shipping must have cost a pretty penny. Someone expects to make money.*

She shuddered, realizing it was Rallison's place of business. Once she passed through the doors, she would have little chance of exiting them whole.

Thorne took a path right through the center of the town, skirting the plaza. They passed a store whose proprietor bent to gather up goods that had likely sat in the sun in front of the shop all day. He straightened and gazed at them as they went by. Marie imagined his eyes drilling holes of disapproval into her back as he followed their progress.

At length they stopped in front of Rallison's saloon. While Thorne dismounted and came around his horse to remove her fetters, Marie looked at the gaudy sign hanging above the door. "Lay May-ee-sohn des Low-ee-sirs," she mouthed slowly as she worked out the foreign phrase. It had no meaning to her. But frothing mugs and bottles and face cards and wicked women in various states of undress decorated the margins around the words. They seemed to dance and sway, or maybe it was herself moving erratically as Thorne tugged on the fraying rope. She bit her lip to block out the other pain. Why had the inhabitants hereabouts let this monstrosity be erected? Didn't they know how it sullied their town? *It will surely sully me.*

She didn't know whether to sob or scream. Then Thorne untied the last knot around her ankle, and she hastened to dismount before he took a notion to topple her out of the saddle.

She stood beside Bess, shivering, unwilling to put her foot onto the steps leading to perdition. Thorne solved her inability to move with a jolting pull on her wrist, and she stumbled up the steps and through the doors in his wake.

What a picture she must make! Dirty, drooping bonnet sitting awry atop filthy locks of hair. Bruises of all colors marking her face and one eye. A welt on her neck. A sodden coat hanging limply from her shoulders. Missing bodice buttons that permitted her dress to gape open at the top. Raw welts about her wrists and bare ankles. Skirt and underclothing that reeked of urine.

What a bundle of shame she had brought upon herself! And Ma. And Pa. He would never forgive her for blackening the Owen name with her foolishness. All hope drained from her bosom as Thorne called out, "Here she is. The new girl."

Eyes turned toward her. Eyes from all corners of the room. Eyes of farmers. Eyes of drovers. Eyes of teamsters. Eyes of men with brown faces. She shuddered anew, sick with fear.

The brown-haired woman she had encountered on the road descended the last few treads of a stairway that clung to the far wall of the room and came toward her.

"What you doing to her? Why you make this spectacle?" she asked Thorne, her voice evincing strong disapproval. She approached Marie and laid her hand on her arm. In a more soothing tone she said, "Come with me, *ma cherie*. Madame Janette will take the *bon* care of you." Turning on Thorne, she raised her voice again. "Where is the dress, my fine azure dress?"

He produced the dress and its accompanying articles of clothing in a hurry. The woman turned away from him, scorn covering her countenance as she took Marie by the hand.

Madame Janette led her upstairs to a quiet suite of rooms, then left her in private to bathe herself and put on the unfamiliar clothing.

The woman returned just as Marie had figured out how to hold the stockings up.

"There," she said. "It is well. You are veree pretty girl. Eh, the bruises, the cuts, they heal soon. Then I will teach you the best ways to earn the money. More money than you think you see all your life."

Marie made a croaking sound, and the woman patted one of her barely covered shoulders.

"Come, come. It is not so bad as you think, *ma cherie*. You will see."

Marie crossed her arms over her chest, fists clenched, and bent over to hide her weeping soul.

"*Non non non, ma cherie*. Stand erect." She pushed back Marie's shoulders. "You sell more drinks if you smile big. Come, dry the eyes and we go down the stairs. You begin with get the men to buy the drinks. We save the rest for later, *non*?"

ജ

*Another little town*, Bill thought as he rode in, half dozing from fatigue. *Another box canyon.* He looked at the one o'clock sun and mentally ticked off the days since Marie had left with Thorne. *This is the tenth day.* Ten days she'd been gone! Four days ago Thorne bought food. He'd been alone. Bill's stomach twisted. Was Marie dead?

How could she be dead? His mind couldn't make the leap to thinking that. But if she was alive, was she whole? The encounter with the farmer had shaken him, more than he'd imagined was possible. He had to take several long breaths and let the air leave him slowly, slowly, before he could pull out that awful thought and take a look at it. Had that cold, dangerous man used her? He bowed his head in grief at the notion. Grief for Marie, for her suffering at Thorne's hands. Not grief on his own account.

His thoughts whirled. The corn farmer had spurned her, reasoning that the act had been done. He didn't know that with any speck of surety. *I don't know it.* He sucked in another lungful of air and held it until he grew faint before blowing it out. *I don't care. I don't care.* The thought echoed with such strength that his body vibrated. *If she's alive, it don't matter. I'll get her free from that filthy man and offer my name. If she'll have it. If she'll have me.*

His mind cleared with his resolve and he dismounted in front of an adobe store. Merchandise was laid out on blankets placed on the hard-packed earth. He shook his canteen, then took a sip of the brackish water. *Ten days.*

He entered the store and spoke to the proprietor in his border Spanish, stumbling over the descriptive words. *How the Sam Hill do you say 'sunbonnet' in Mex?* He decided to try 'hat against the sun.' *Sombrero contra el sol.*

The man's eyes grew wary and he took a step backward.

Bill put on an even more concerned expression and leaned his head forward slightly in encouragement.

The storekeeper finally decided to share his knowledge. "Ella pasó por aquí ayer con ese hombre." He motioned in the direction they had gone.

"They went by yesterday?" Bill confirmed in the same tongue.

"Sí, señor. Ayer por la tarde."

Bill cast his eyes upward and whispered, "Dear God, thank you. She's alive." At least she was yesterday afternoon.

The man crossed himself, then shook his head a bit. "Ella parece un poco maltratada." His voice held a sad note.

"Mistreated," Bill murmured, anger rising from his belly. He'd like to get his hands around Thorne's throat and mistreat him plenty. Batting down the emotion, he said, "Mil gracias, señor," and left the store, his heart seeming to throb in his throat.

*She's alive! Beaten down, but living still.*

He threw himself into the saddle and looked down the path

in the direction the man had indicated. A large building stood a ways apart from the town, aloof in its separateness. An American-style building, with a sign board beckoning him. That had to be the house with the foreign name, the new house the farmer had told him about. The house of entertainment.

Bill leaned forward and slapped the horse with his heels. *That's where Thorne took Marie.*

The horse responded to Bill's urging and lunged down the street. Moments later, he pulled it to a stop in front of the garish edifice. Yep. Those were foreign words splayed across the sign. Maybe French. He took a deep breath to steady himself. *If she's here, how do I get her out?*

A boy ran up and asked in passable English, "You want me to take care of your horse, sir?"

Bill pulled his mind around to the situation in front of him and asked the price, which the boy named. He dug in his pocket and paid the lad, then removed his saddlebags. But as the youngster led the horse off, he called out, "Where you takin' it?"

"To the stable in back."

Bill nodded. Good the horse was under care. He might be here for a spell, until he could figure out the dilemma that pounded through his brain. *If she's here, how do I get her out?*

He'd better make a start by entering the place, he decided, and took the steps to the porch. A deep breath before the flap doors, a shove against them, and he was inside. A quick look around and disappointment soured his stomach. *She ain't here.*

*Steady*, he thought. *Considered precisely, she ain't in this room.* He glanced upward, and hoped she wasn't above stairs. He walked on wooden legs to the bar and ordered a bottle and a glass to be brought to a table. *A table close to the door*, he told himself, then remembered his horse was not just beyond the veranda. He'd have to figure a plan for escape, as soon as he'd confirmed that she was in the place.

He choose an empty table, as near to the door as he could find, even if the horse was absent, dumped his gear on the floor and took a seat, pulling his hat low to mask his eyes. He scanned the interior, slower this time, taking in the details of the inhabitants. Three men standing easy at the bar. One barkeep.

Two girls working the men. Marie was not among them. Four other men, two to a table, on his left. A gambler engrossed in dealing faro, but he wasn't Thorne. A girl hovering over one of the players. Not Marie. Three more men, teamsters maybe, drinking at a table on his right. A table with a poker game in progress, but the man running it had his back to Bill. He couldn't tell if that was Thorne or not. The coat was different. No girls there. Light footsteps to his left, approaching. He stiffened, then swung his head to assess the danger, and looked up into the saloon girl's eyes.

# Chapter 22

Marie stretched her arms out in front of her as far as they would reach, reluctant to get close enough to place the bottle and glass on the table. The trail-worn cowboy seated there might take it into his head to grab at her. Then he looked up and she saw his face. She inhaled sharply. *Bill! He came for me!* Panic seized her as she realized the danger this place held for him, but she got a tight hold on her sense, lowered her eyes and whispered, "Your bottle, sir."

Her heart felt as though it had frozen in her bosom. *He's seen me, lookin' like this. Now he'll do something foolish and get killed.* She turned to skedaddle, but he grasped her hand. She turned back, shaking her head with tiny movements. "You want somethin' else, mister?" *Surely he can tell I don't want to acknowledge him.* He relaxed his grip. *He's puzzled. Please, God, he's got to play along.*

"Somethin' else for you, mister? I have to get back to my work."

He stared at her with such intensity that she thought her face would melt. *Please, please, Mr. Henry. Follow my lead.* "Enjoy your bottle," she said, and shook her hand free. She took two steps away and heard him clear his throat. *Don't call my name!*

"Miss," he said, instead.

She closed her eyes on a sigh, opened them, and turned back to his table. "Yes, sir?"

He nodded towards Thorne's back. "Does your dealer have an open seat at his table?"

She hesitated. Was he seeking information about Thorne? Of course he was. She took another moment to clear her own throat. "I believe Mr. Thorne, er, croft, Thornecroft will let you buy into the game." *No. Don't get close to him.*

"Thank you, miss."

She scurried back behind the bar and into the small room behind it, picked up her dishrag and resumed washing glasses, choking as black fear closed her throat. *Bill came to get me, but Thorne will kill him.*

℘

Bill watched her go, so relieved to see her, missing her already. He swore under his breath, cursing Thorne for putting her into such a state of injury and indignity. *That dress!* He wished he dared throw a tablecloth about her and quit the country. *Those bruises! He's been beatin' on her.*

He uncorked the bottle and poured a drink with a shaking hand. He took a sip. Frowned. Rotgut whiskey. Didn't matter. The whiskey was for show. *I dasn't get drunk.* He took the time between several slight sips to try to calm himself, but his anxiety persisted. *How do I get her out of here?*

He pushed back his chair as though he would rise, paused as though changing his mind, then drew it forward again, but turned a bit so he could watch the poker table.

*Thorne don't know me. Mayhap getting in the game is a good choice. I can read him better up close.* He scoffed at the thought. Thorne was a gambler. An unreadable face would be part of his stock in trade. *It's worth a try anyhow.*

Someone at the table raised his voice. The young man on the left. Farmer's clothing. Thorne replied, his voice cold. The young man rose to his feet and protested. Thorne brought a revolver out of his lap and shot him.

Bill inhaled sharply as the pistol boomed. The farm boy went over backwards and down onto the floor. Thorne didn't seem concerned. He'd pushed back his chair a bit, crossed his legs, pulled out a cigar and now leaned over a match, sucking air to light the cigar. The round was over.

Bill let out his breath and downed the whiskey. Maybe it wouldn't hurt to be a bit numb.

He let several minutes go by as the saloon sounds returned to normal. A new hand began. No one came to remove the boy's body. It lay crumpled, an empty shell made so by a callous hand, a twisted mind. Not right in the head, Rulon had said.

Thorne started gathering the cards, preparing to deal.

*Well,* Bill thought, *if there wasn't a seat at the table before, there surely is one now. I'd best get in the game.*

He steeled himself, got up and snatched the bags from the floor and slung them over his shoulder. He picked up the bottle and the glass, and made himself walk over to the table, keeping where Thorne could see him.

"What's your buy in?" he asked as he set the bottle and glass on the table.

Thorne looked up and squinted through his cigar smoke. "A hundred."

Bill swallowed and dug in his pocket for enough Federal coins to buy the chips. He unslung the bags and put them out of the way of the pool of blood. Then he sat, and pulled up the chair so lately pushed backwards by a callow youth with not enough experience to survive in Thorne's game. Did *he* have any better sense, willingly stepping to the brink of the man's dark pit?

Thorne dealt the cards, and Bill folded his first hand. Out of the action, he had a mite of time to study Thorne's bland face. The man was good at masking his thoughts, but Bill noticed that he puffed on his cigar twice after he drew new cards. Sign of a good or bad hand?

Thorne lost the hand. Two puffs. Poor cards.

Bill checked on the next hand, watching his opponent, who drew two cards after the betting round and shifted in his seat. Was that a telling action?

Thorne lost on a showdown. The cards hadn't been bad, but the man seated opposite Bill had a stronger hand and took the chips.

Third hand. Thorne leaned backwards ever so slightly when he looked at his dealt hand. Didn't draw cards. The hand must be good. Bill noted the movement in the part of his mind he'd set aside for listing any of the gambler's actions that might reveal what his face concealed. Thorne won.

Bill looked up when the barkeep came around and lit a lantern overhead with a long punk stick. The windows looked out onto a black night. How long had he been playing? Hours. He thought he knew one or two of Thorne's 'tells' now. Maybe three. Did the man even know he gave signs? Bill wondered what his own were.

The hand ended, and Bill won the pot. He stacked his chips, then rose and asked, "Privy out back?" At Thorne's confirming nod, he said, "I'll be back," and picked up his saddlebags. No sense leaving valuables about.

He borrowed a lantern from the barkeep and asked the way to the rear door. He might as well learn the layout of the place.

He stood in the outhouse, wondering once more how he could get Marie out of the place. Her work seemed to be confined to fetching drinks and whatever she did in the room behind the bar, but that could change at any time. Any of the men in the saloon might insist on a trip up the stairs. He knew he couldn't bear to see that happen. *How do I get her out?*

He couldn't stay much longer in the privy while he pondered on the matter. What advantage did he have? He buttoned up while he thought about the situation.

The man seated across from him had been winning steadily. Bill had amassed a pile of chips, and Thorne's piles were decreasing. Could he force bets higher and clean out the gambler? He'd heard of high stakes games where men risked personal property against a big win. He'd done a fair amount of gambling with a saddle or a pistol as stakes. Could he— He swallowed hard. Could he drive Thorne into wagering Marie?

The man seemed reckless enough. Marie might have been troublesome to him. He didn't know that. Did he dare take a risk on her spunky nature? Did he have enough luck and skill to pull off such a scheme?

He'd need an extra bit of luck. Could he get Marie to kiss the cards? He scoffed at that notion. He needed something real. A remembrance flashed through his mind. Chico had said something about Marie kissing his cards the night he'd tried out the card trick Bertie had used on him. The one and only time he'd tried it. It had worked, hadn't it? Could he give himself four of a kind?

He scrambled to fish out his old worn card deck from one of

the bags. His fingers touched the ranch deed. He hauled it out, too, and stuffed it into his coat pocket. Riffling the deck, he extracted all of the three cards and put them in his pocket, but he'd have to get them out of his pocket and into his lap as he sat down. Yes, he could do that. He put the rest of the deck back in the bag and abandoned the privy.

℘

Bill placed his hand of cards carefully on the table, face up, one by one, and grinned at Thorne in his best imitation of bleary-eyed drunkenness. Thorne huffed a stream of smoke around his new cigar and pushed the chips over to him.

So far, he hadn't used the trick, but his cards sat in his lap, awaiting need. Luck had been with him. The pattern on their back sides was the same as the cards used in Thorne's game. It was likely the only brand available hereabouts. His cards were a bit more worn, but he had to take the chance no one would notice if he was forced to use them.

The man opposite Bill had taken his winnings and departed two hands ago. The man on his left didn't have the sense to stop losing and go home. The seat between those two had been filled twice, but now sat empty. Thorne's chips had diminished significantly in the last hour. This was likely the time to start raising the bets.

Bill raised the bottle to his lips and took a swig. Then he managed to drop it to the floor, where it rolled until he heard it stop. Mayhap it fetched up against that poor boy's body.

"Barkeep, bring me a bottle," he roared, continuing the role of tipsy cowman.

The man sent Marie, and as she placed the bottle before him he grabbed her wrist to pull her down toward him. He planted a sloppy kiss as near as he could get to her lips, then whispered "Get your parcel," as he pretended to nibble on her ear.

Her eyes became aware, and she drew aside and slapped him. Then she dashed up the stairs. He watched her go through slitted eyes, enjoying the performance, hoping she had a clue what he was up to, hoping Thorne had none.

213

He raised a reckless amount on the next hand, driving the loser to quit the game. Thorne's eyes seemed like balls of ice as he gave Bill the chips. Those left in front of Thorne were a mere handful.

Behind Thorne, Marie came back down to the saloon. Bill took a gamble and slurred, "Whassa matter, dealer? Too rich for your blood?" He leaned forward and cupped his arms around his chips. "I've got all this to put in the next pot, an' the ranch, too." He blinked and looked around the room, then tried to focus on Thorne. "What you got to put up?" He leaned back. "How about a girl?" He leered lopsidedly.

"You're drunk," Thorne sneered.

"Yeah," Bill drawled, making his voice raspy and slow, "but I got all the chips." He clipped the last word and grinned again. "One more hand, dealer. One more." He pulled out the deed and put it on top of his stack.

A well-dressed tall man, who Bill took to be the proprietor, and a nice-looking, showy woman had come over to stand behind Thorne. She clung to the man's arm, and deigned to smile at Bill.

"This should be amusing," the owner said to the gambler. "Let him play one more hand." He arched an eyebrow. "What *will* you wager, Thornecroft?"

The gambler turned his head, searching, and when his eyes stopped on Marie, he beckoned to her. "Get over here! You've given me a lot of sass. It would serve you right if he won." He reseated himself facing Bill as Marie came to stand beside his chair. "Consider her among my assets."

Bill put a one dollar chip in the center of the table. Thorne put in his ante. He had a few chips left. Then he dealt.

Bill picked up his cards, and without looking at them, said to Marie, "Girl, come kiss 'em. I need a li'l more luck." Again, he clipped the last word.

Thorne had picked up his cards, looked at them, and leaned back in his chair.

Marie stared at Bill, her eyes fearful.

"Come on. I won't bite. Just put a li'l kiss on 'em." He held out the hand, grinning, despite his mouth having gone dry at seeing the gambler's tell.

She approached and bent to kiss the cards, her eyes holding his.

Even in that ridiculous get-up, she looked beautiful to him. He touched the kissed cards to his lips and finally looked at them.

He held a full house, eights on deuces. A strong hand. Thorne's tell said he also had good cards. Bill kept breathing as he had before, fighting to stay steady. He glanced down. His hands were shaking too much to substitute cards for any better hand. These would have to do.

"I bet two dollars," he said, putting the chips in the pot. "Two dollars," he repeated, remembering almost too late to slur his words.

"Call," responded Thorne, adding his two chips. "How many cards?"

Bill thought about his cards, not knowing if Thorne would draw new ones. How good was Thorne's hand?

*Lord,* he thought, *You know I ain't much of a prayin' man, but my mam taught me You're up there. You surely love Miss Marie. Lord God, for her sake, let me get her out of this mess.*

He reached for his glass and pretended to drink, playing for time to make his decision. He put the glass down with careful precision, although it quivered in a circle before it hit the table top. "None," he said, and inhaled gustily. "Not a single one." He weaved a little in his chair, sweat beginning to drip off the tip of his nose.

Thorne also declined to draw new cards.

Bill heard Marie's breath hiss out. She hadn't looked at his hand, but she knew what Thorne was holding, and she was scared. *I am too.*

Bill laid the cards on the table, backs up, and moved all his chips to the pot, stack by careful stack. Then he put the ranch deed on the top, allowing it to teeter and fall between two of the stacks.

"I bet a hunnert an' fifty-six dollars an' the ranch," he said, and weaved again.

Thorne looked at the proprietor.

He came forward and took the deed, unfolded the paper. "Texas, huh?" He looked a question at Thorne.

Thorne gave his assent to the property, then asked in a raspy voice, "Does the girl and six dollars equal his bet?"

The owner considered, quirking his eyebrow. Then he said, "A ranch is work. The girl is pleasure. That's equal."

Thorne said, "Call," and moved his chips to the pot. He narrowed his eyes and barked at Bill, "Do you want her atop the table?"

"No," Bill said, closing his eyes, and opening them with great effort. "S-she can sit in a chair." He pointed to one on his left between the other two vacant seats.

The tall man nodded, and Marie hurried around the table to sit.

"Show your hand, Thornecroft," said the proprietor.

The gambler laid down his cards. Three sevens. Two tens. A full house.

Bill stared at them. He wobbled as though he would fall face down onto the pot, then straightened and turned over his eights and twos.

He'd won.

# Chapter 23

When Thorne moved as though he would pull his gun, Bill was ready for him, his revolver already out of his pocket, and his left fist connecting with the man's chin. He went down without a sound, and Bill yelled to Marie, "Get the deed." He kept his pistol trained on the saloon's owner, who bore a curious expression, almost of satisfaction.

The woman said to Bill, "You have the luck," and tugged the man back away from Thorne.

"Hands high," Bill told the barkeeper, his eyes darting briefly to Marie to see what was holding her up. She held a sack in one hand and scooped chips into it with the other. "Worthless," he growled. "Leave 'em. Get my bags. Go out the back door. Now!" he barked.

She dropped the sack like it burned her fingers, hauled up his saddlebags and fled. Bill followed her, facing the saloon.

When he'd backed out the door and closed it, he jammed the bench beside the door under the latch. "That won't hold them long," he grunted, turning and relieving Marie of his saddlebags. She ran to a place along the back wall where she picked up a bundle. "Good girl," he said, and grabbed her free hand to run with her to the stable.

"Are you truly drunk?" she whispered as he slapped the saddle on Bess.

"Not so much," he replied, drawing the cinch tight and boosting Marie aboard.

He tacked up his own horse in a great hurry, and got into the saddle, then put his heels hard into the animal's sides.

They left at a run, the echo of the drum of their horses' hooves beating back at them as they fled past the town's adobe walls.

Bill pulled up a couple of miles outside the town to let the winded horses breathe. He swung down and went to assist Marie.

"He didn't follow us," Marie observed in a shaky voice as she dismounted. She look back the way they'd come. "It appears no one did."

"I put him out pretty solid," Bill said, shaking his hand. "Might have broke something." He flexed it with care, then asked, "How well liked was the man?"

She began to walk the mare. "Not at all. I reckon Miz Janette hated his lights and liver. For all Thorne's big talk of them bein' friends, I suspect Mr. Guy wasn't far behind that." She made a noise that appeared to be a muffled sob. "He'll come after us when he has revived."

"He'll come alone." He yearned to gather Marie up in his arms and make that haunted look in her eyes disappear. He didn't dare. Not yet. Not while they were still here on the road. "I passed a place up yonder. We can hide there for a spell. Leastwise until morning."

৪৩

The night was black as soot. Black as ink. Black as shoe blacking. A chill breeze scurried along the road from the direction of the town. Marie sat on Bess's back, wondering if it would rain again, as Bill led their horses forward, trying to locate the hiding place. She began to shiver violently.

After a long while, she heard a sustained sigh from Bill, then felt the direction of the wind change. They must be off the road. She tried to keep her teeth from chattering. Presently, she noticed a deeper blackness to the right, and he stopped the horses, speaking to them in a low tone. Then she heard his boots crunching on the earth, no, a gravelly surface, as he came to her side.

"Slip your feet free," he said. When she had removed her shoes from the stirrups, strong, careful hands grasped her on each side of her waist, lifted her from the saddle and placed her on the ground.

He must have felt her quaking. "We've got to risk a fire, get you warm," he said, and began to kick the ground.

"What are you doing?" She sat down and tried to make herself stop shaking.

"Clearing a spot."

She heard crackling. He grunted, then said, "Good. Here's a tree. Or a bush, perhaps." He must have kicked at it, from the increased sound of crackling branches. "This should serve."

He built a small fire close to her, using the old-fashioned method of flint and knife blade. By the flickering light, Marie watch him put a handful of coffee makings into his coffeepot, then empty his canteen into it and put it to heat.

"It's foolish—" He stumbled over the word and began again. "It's not canny to put the smell in the air, but I must be sober."

She nodded, pondering the word foolish.

"We'll drink it down before he comes."

She nodded again, feeling the weight of every action she'd taken lately. The heaping pile of her follies. She wanted to cry. She didn't dare make such noise, but put her face in her hands, just in case.

She heard him taking the tack off the horses outside the circle of firelight, the crunch of gravel when he brought his saddle to the fireside, and a small grunt when he sat down upon it. After a while, she heard him stir.

"I reckon I love you," Bill said.

His voice was low, and she thought she'd misheard him. She brought her hands down into her lap and looked towards him.

He began to talk again, fast, like his mouth was overflowing with words and he had to spill out the excess.

"I reckon my affection for you began to growin' that first day we met, with you all shocked and discombobulated, with leaves and dirt and such on your dress. Despite your disarray, I knew, I knew for sure, you were the most beautiful girl in the world."

She cringed. "Don't mock me!"

"I'd never do that."

Marie bent her shoulders forward and hugged herself. "I don't want your pity." Even in her distress, she couldn't take her eyes from his face.

He sat for a long time, looking down at the hatful of fire. Finally he lifted his head and gazed at her. He swallowed, then spoke, his voice steady, but holding a marked gentleness. "I bear you no pity. I have naught to give you but the devotion of a revived man." He paused for a moment, seeming to need courage to continue. "When your pa told me he was marryin' you off to the farmer, that bruised and battered my soul. When you left with Thorne, my heart shattered to pieces. I thought never to see you again."

She turned her head aside, unwilling to see the hurt in his eyes. "Going off with that wicked man was a terrible folly," she said, her voice bitter. "He bore me no love, as he had led me to believe."

"He's nothing but a confidence man, a very practiced, cruel confidence man."

Marie wanted so badly to cry, to give vent to her rage and her sorrow and her relief, but she simply couldn't show weakness in front of Bill. With all good intentions, he might smother her feelings, take charge, and reduce her to the state of vulnerability that she had lived in under Thorne's influence. She wanted never be that frail again.

He spoke again, his voice soft this time, and she had to lean forward to hear him.

"Havin' you here, my heart is whole again." He stopped talking.

She wished to goodness he was done talking about his heart when hers felt like a lead brick in her bosom.

When he commenced to speak again, his voice had changed. "The way I see it, we have two choices," he said in a more practical tone. "We could go to Texas. Life is mighty hard there with the carpetbaggers in control, but you would be spared any words of shame comin' from your folks." He stopped briefly. His next words came out forcefully. "We'd have to be wed. I won't take you that far without a ring on your finger."

She took a sharp breath and held it for two seconds. "What's your second notion?" She tried to keep her voice neutral, but failed. Bitterness crept into it again. A marriage based on Bill's pity would be worse than one built on Tom's lust.

"We could go back to your folks." He fell silent for a moment, and evidently, from the creaking sound the leather of his saddle made, he shifted around on his seat.

She glanced his way and noticed he held a much-wrinkled piece of paper that he was smoothing out with great care. Pink paper. Stationery. He had her letter.

He looked up, his eyes holding hers. "You told them the next time they saw you, you'd be a married woman. Thorne didn't live up to his word. I fancy replacing him. In your life." He swallowed hard. "In your heart."

She shook her head, breaking eye contact, and cut him off before he could say binding words. "There's another path." Her voice sounded to her ears hollow and beaten, as she motioned to her extravagant clothing. "I could become the wanton woman Thorne had in mind for me. I'm dressed for that life."

Her words brought Bill up from his seat and across the fire. "No! You can't consider that." He'd pulled her to her feet, and he gripped her arms, the pressure of his hands telling of his fury at the thought. "He tried to do you damage. Did he—"

"No. He never had his way with me. He tried, but I had a knife. He had to back down after I used it."

Bill relaxed his grip and sighed, a heavy exhalation. "It wouldn't matter to me if he had. It wouldn't matter one tad bit. Marry me, girl. I can't bear it one minute more." His hands tightened a fraction and his voice throbbed, as though he were losing control of it.

Marie meant to say, "I can't," but an explosion ripped the air, and turning loose of her arms, Bill fell over backward, onto the fire.

Struggling to move, he finally rolled off it, but the back of his coat glowed with tiny live embers. Another shot came from the darkness, and Marie grabbed the coffeepot and extinguished what was left of the fire. She fell upon Bill, beating the embers off with her bare hands, then dragged him away from the spot, inch by inch.

"I know I hit him," came a voice, the hated, disgusting voice of C. G. Thorne. "You get over here. I don't take kindly to uppity women."

Marie froze. Then she took a breath and held it. If she maintained silence, he couldn't know where she was. The darkness was too complete . . . except for one lone ember that she surreptitiously crushed with her foot.

Thorne swore. "Did you think you could get away from me?" He dismounted, his saddle leather creaking in the still air. "That cowboy can't shield you. He's worthless to you."

As Thorne kept up a string of demeaning invective, Marie's hands searched Bill's body for his gun. She found it at last in his coat pocket, and eased it out of confinement, fighting down panic and her rising conviction that Bill was dead or mortally wounded. *Not my Bill!*

From the sound of his voice, Thorne moved slowly, probably taking caution for his footing on the uneven ground. Marie got herself between Bill and Thorne, and hunched as low to the ground as she could.

"I don't know why I bother," Thorne spat. "You're a worthless piece of dogmeat, but you're wearing my investment."

*From Pa's gold.*

"I won't give that up. I'll take it from your dead body, once I'm through with you," he said, a step closer this time.

The menace in his voice nearly sent Marie into flight, but she resisted her impulse. *I can't leave Bill to his wrath.*

Thorne swore again, another step closer to where the fire had burned.

Bill moaned, and Marie's heart leapt in her bosom. *He's alive!* She put a hand behind her and found his face, his mouth, and patted his lips to urge him to silence.

"Ah, you're over there, cowboy," Thorne chortled. "This time I'll finish you."

Marie heard the click of the pistol being cocked as Thorne made ready for his killing shot. The sound was very close by. Another step. Gravel crunched. Another. He kicked a rock aside and it rolled a ways off. Another. He was standing not five feet off.

Marie thrust herself to her feet before he could advance any closer. "You won't do any of those things," she said softly, cocking her own pistol as she raised it, holding its weight in two hands before her as she stepped silently to her right.

Thorne's shot whizzed by her ear as he swore at her again. She angled the gun toward where the man must be and pulled the trigger, then kept cocking and pulling and cocking and pulling until all the bullets had been expended and only a dry click met her ears.

Thorne was down, lying with his weapon resting on her shoes, the heat of the barrel seeping through the thin leather. She tugged it out of his hand and stepped backward, almost stumbling when she fetched up against Bill.

He caught her in his arms. He was alive, and standing, and holding her . . . and she was melting.

"Give me his gun," he said, letting her go. "I have to check—"

"He must be dead." *You're alive!* Waves of emotion swept through her as she handed over the pistol. Relief. Revulsion. Disappointment at not being enwrapped in Bill's arms. Love. *Love?*

As Bill bent to his task, the moon peeked through the clouds, as though it came out especially to aid him. He lifted one lapel of Thorne's coat aside and felt for a heartbeat, then shook his head. Thorne was gone. But there was something about the way his coat had landed.

Marie flew at the man and dug in his coat pockets, inside and out. She came up with a small leather pouch and held it for Bill to see.

He snorted. "I didn't clean him out after all."

The high emotion that had sustained her through the past few minutes suddenly drained from her body, and Marie turned and retched on the ground. Bill was with her in an instant, holding her hair aside as vomit flooded through her mouth.

When she had finished, he gently wiped her lips with his handkerchief.

She spit out one last clot of bitterness, then whispered in a shaky voice, "I killed him." A cramp gripped her abdomen, but it wasn't the prelude to another bout of nausea. It was fear for her soul, cold and stark and threatening.

"Yes. You saved me."

She could see Bill's smile. The clouds seemed to be dissipating, and the moon cast a warm light over the earth. "I saved you?"

"He meant to kill us both. You prevented that happening."

The smile was gone, replaced by a soberness that calmed Marie a bit. "I did? I'm not bound for Hell?"

"No, no. Never." He shook his head and held her face in his hands. His left palm was sticky.

She lifted it off her face and examined it through eyes full of moisture. "That's blood." She saw a wet patch on the sleeve of his coat.

"Ball went through my arm. Don't hurt much." He raised his hand to his head. "This one put me out for a spell." He ran a finger through a groove in his scalp. "I match your pa."

"Hmm," came softly from her throat. *Indeed.* She blinked rapidly, surprised at the strong emotion welling in her heart, tightening her throat. Then she forced practicality to take control and said, "Shuck your coat. I'll bind up your wounds."

As he did so, she turned aside and lifted the hem of the horrid dress. She ripped a couple of strips off the fancy petticoat, and set to work dressing Bill's arm and head.

When she had finished, he motioned in the direction of Thorne's still form lying on the ground. "I'll bury him come sunup. Don't want critters to get a bad taste in their craws."

Marie nodded, now unable to speak.

"Whither are we bound?" he asked as he got to his feet. "Texas, or your place?" He didn't touch her, but stood apart, evidently waiting for her decision.

The tightness in her chest loosened a fraction so she could speak. "I want to go home."

"Where is home?" Bill's voice came out hushed, as though he were holding his breath and talking at the same time.

"Back."

He started to speak, but instead, hung his head and looked at the ground. She watched him struggle, something deep down causing him hesitation.

Presently, he raised his head and stared into her eyes. "Are you goin' to marry me?"

Marie stood still, rooted, it seemed, to the earth beneath her feet. All the dreams she'd had over the past weeks flashed through her mind, all the moments when she'd thought of no one but Bill

Henry. At once, she realized there was no one else she wanted for her husband, no one who could suit her better than the sturdy cowman who stood before her, his blue eyes cautious, hooded, going dark. She wished for nothing more than to brighten those eyes, bring gladness and light to them, and to feel his strong arms around her, sheltering her from harm, his touch turning her to liquid butter.

"Yes," she whispered. Then she said it louder. "Yes. Yes, I will." She heard her voice tremble. "I will be your wife."

Bill's eyes glowed, happiness shining through them, revealing the joy in his heart. His arms came around her. "We'll make a pretty pair before the priest," he murmured. "Me wrapped in bandages, and you in—" He broke off. "No. We'll get you clothes suitable for a lady before we seek him out."

She shook her head. "The ordinary clothes in my bundle will suit me fine," she said. "Once they're washed." She quivered in his arms. She knew that he loved her at least a little, knew that she cherished him. "You're a good man, never mind your head is bandaged." She touched his cheek and closed her eyes for a moment. When she opened them, she said in a rush, "Can you forgive my horrible folly?" She held her breath, anxious for his reply.

"With all my soul," Bill said. His blue eyes seemed to burn with light.

Marie swallowed hard, then she kissed him, not with maidenly reserve, but with a lover's passion and desire and fervor. It must have caught him off guard, all wooden in her arms for a moment, but he warmed to the notion of taking part in no time at all.

When they broke apart for air, she gasped, "Where does that priest dwell?" After she'd filled her lungs, she added, "I'll ride all night to get there. I do not fancy being a spinster one moment longer."

*The End*

Take a Sneak Peek at

# Ride to Raton

Book 4: The Owen Family Saga

# Excerpt from *Ride to Raton*

As soon as James Owen heard the Spanish priest's final amen, he stepped back from the makeshift altar in the Colorado meadow and made his legs carry him to the edge of the forest. Behind him he knew Ma, Pa, and the rest of the family and guests were crowding around to congratulate the bride and groom.

The bride was Ellen Bates—who'd been *his* fiancée.

And the groom was his brother, Carl.

His own brother...

James gagged.

When his stomach had emptied itself over the pine needles and columbines, he straightened up, chest heaving, and gripped a sapling until the quivering left his legs. He yanked his high, stiff collar loose and threw it on the ground, wiped his mouth with the back of his shirt sleeve, then threw a quick glance behind him.

Carl now sat down on the chair his brothers had used to bring him to the meadow. The bridegroom's gunshot wound was bleeding; a crimson stain spread across the hip of his trousers. Ellen fussed around, pointing at his brothers, Rulon and Clay. She shooed off the other cowboys, who seemed eager to put her on their shoulders for a shiveree.

Ma was looking toward James, her forehead furrowed with worry. She took two steps toward him, then stopped. He cleared his throat and spat, straightened his shoulders— which ached from the strain of keeping himself tightly under control—and took the path that led through the forest to the ranch headquarters.

He heard Ma call out, "James!" then "Rod, go see—"

"Leave Pa out of it," James grunted so low that she couldn't possibly hear him, and kept moving. He stamped through the trees, pounding his fist into his open hand and wishing it was Carl's face. He approached a holding pen, where a wild horse wheeled and snorted, upset by the noise James made.

James swore at his brother for getting injured. *When he gets well—* He pressed his lips tightly together, as though to restrain his vengeful thoughts.

The black horse watched every move James made, its wary eyes following him as he approached. It snorted, sniffed the air, then whirled around to track his progress along the fence line. James looked at the beast that Carl had caught as the Owen men returned from Texas with a herd of cattle and a crew of cowboys. When a gang of ruffians had kidnapped two young ladies, the Owen crew had confronted them in a gun battle. Carl had been sorely wounded.

A harsh sound escaped James's throat. It wasn't quite a laugh. *He took Miss Ellen. I'll take the mustang.*

James stalked into the shed, snatched a rope from where it hung on a peg pounded into the wall, and stalked out again. Entering the enclosure, he leaned against the gate and built a loop in his rope. *Let's see if the Texan's roping trick works.* He looked up.

The black snorted and moved off as far as it could get in the pen. James stepped toward the horse, holding the rope behind him. He crowded the animal to one side of the corral, then flipped the loop up from the ground and around the horse's neck.

Gripping the rope with one hand, he ran to the horse, grabbed a handful of mane, and hauled himself up. The horse tried to shake him off, but he got his right leg over its back just as the animal reared on its hind legs, bellowing. James stayed on, clamping his knees against the rough hair and bending low over the neck.

*You're not so easily rid of me.*

The black met the ground stiff legged, screaming, and James felt his stomach crowding his throat. He swallowed hard, digging his boots into the barrel of the animal as it whipped up its heels, tucking its head toward the earth. Then the two of them were airborne, and James braced for the shock of landing against the black's spine. His teeth jarred together, then again and again and again as, pitching, bucking, whirling, the beast tried to get James's weight off its back.

"Blasted devil horse," he muttered as he came down hard, a little off center, and grabbed for a new fistful of the stiff black mane hairs. But the horse was in the air again—head and heels together, back arched—and James lost his grasp on the mane and the rope. Flying off, he landed on his left shoulder in the center of the ring.

"You fool, you're like to be killed!"

James shook his head to clear away his father's strident voice, looked for the horse, then rolled clear when it dove at him with stiff front legs. Rising from the dust, he ran after the animal, grabbing for the trailing rope with his left hand as he kneaded his sore shoulder with his right.

"Don't you know when you've had enough?" yelled his father as he opened the gate. "Get out of there, you—"

James had the rope in his hands and wrapped it around his left arm. Then he dug in his heels to bring the horse under control.

"You're crazy," Roderick Owen shouted, shutting the gate and lending his weight to the end of the lariat whipping free behind his son.

"Get off my rope!"

"You're double dumb crazy." Rod held on, hauling backward.

"Get off! You're cutting my arm!"

Rod let go of the rope, and James was jerked forward, scrambling to keep his feet under him. Suddenly the animal quit fighting, its head drooping. It stood against the fence, quivering, its slick black sides heaving as it filled its lungs.

James flipped the noose off the animal's neck and dropped it in the dust, to the accompaniment of catcalls from a line of spectators along the fence. Doubled over, hands on his knees, his gasping matched the horse's. When he finally got his breath, he spat the grit from his mouth, surveyed the men peering through the fence, and waved his arms at them.

"This ain't a free show," he yelled. "All y'all get away from here!"

The crowd broke up, each man muttering his displeasure as he drifted back toward the meadow. James watched them go as he kneaded his shoulder again. He turned on his father.

"Why'd you butt in on my business?"

"You were next to getting killed, trying to ride that outlaw horse."

"I'm not talking about the horse. I'm talking about Miss Ellen. And Miss Jessica! You forced me to leave her behind in the Shenandoah and hatched a scheme to marry Miss Ellen to me. You got her pa to agree for a few sacks of provisions and a wagon!" James spat on the ground.

"It wasn't quite like that."

James ignored his father's response as his words rushed on. "You dragged me across the country, preaching duty every day. I obeyed you. I put off Miss Jessica to court Miss Ellen. I did my duty, Pa, and I even grew fond of her. I looked forward to settling down, having a little house, raising up young—"

"Stop it!" Rod's eyes narrowed. He squinted at James's left sleeve, watching a line of blood seep through the fabric. "You're hurt, boy."

James glanced at the sleeve, then shook his arm, wincing as pain lanced through the shoulder. He looked up, glaring. "Carl had no claim to Ellen, yet you let him take her from me. Did you think I wouldn't mind?"

Rod Owen's face resembled a limestone outcrop bristling with fire blackened buffalo grass stubble. His voice came out in a whisper. "It was Ellen's choice, James. She loves Carl."

"No!" James sucked in a ragged breath. "She wouldn't gainsay her pa's pledge."

"James, there's no telling what's in the mind of a woman. Maybe Miss Ellen didn't cotton to the idea of being traded for a wagon. I thought it was a good deal for both her and her folks. Somehow she didn't come to care for you."

"That didn't matter to me!" James shouted.

"She came to love your brother, and when he saved her life, that was good enough for her pa." Rod shifted his weight from one leg to the other. "Set your mind to keeping peace, now, and we'll get back to ranching."

James's breathing tore at his throat, and pain seared through his belly. "Peace?" He looked square at his father, then fury rose up and he jabbed the man's chest with his forefinger. "My pride and my affection for that girl is stomped into the ground, and now you call for peace?" He swore, his voice venomous, and his finger jabbed harder.

Rod knocked down James's hand. His voice was quiet, yet rumbled around the corral when he spoke. "Keep your place, son."

James reared back, gathered himself, then spat on the ground. "There is no place for me here."

Silence stretched like silver cobwebs between the peeled logs surrounding the two men. Even the horse was quiet. A bushy tailed squirrel rushed up a nearby pine tree, found a limb, and held its breath. Suddenly it chattered, scolding the frozen humans, then flicked its tail as it scuttled away up the tree trunk.

"Once you leave go of that anger, your place will be as large as your brother's. We got a big job of work ahead, son. Now settle down and let's get back to the party."

James stood still, his head thrown back. He was silent.

Rod scowled. "I've preached peace amongst my sons as long as I've had them. It makes the work go smoother." He rubbed his beard. "I need you here, James, but if you can't keep..." His voice trailed off to silence.

James squinted at his father.

Rod pulled in a breath and held it a long time before he let it go. His words came out soft as a breeze down the mountain. "Son, I reckon you're too prideful and angry right now to keep peace. Until you get free of that, the best thing is for you to light a shuck for someplace else."

Visit Marsha's website for more information on

# Ride to Raton

Website: http://marshaward.com

# About the Author

Marsha Ward writes authentic historical fiction set in 19th Century America, and contemporary romance. She was born in the sleepy little town of Phoenix, Arizona, in a simpler time. With plenty of room to roam among the chickens and citrus trees, Marsha enjoyed playing with neighborhood chums, but always had her imaginary friend, cowboy Johnny Rigger Prescott, at her side. Now she makes her home in a forest in the mountains of Arizona. She loves to hear from her readers.

Connect with her at:
Website: http://marshaward.com
Blog: http://marshaward.blogspot.com
Email: marshaw@marshaward.com
Facebook: https://www.facebook.com/authormarshaward
Twitter: https://twitter.com/MarshaWard

Do subscribe to Marsha's VMA Readers email list to receive advance notice of coming book releases. https://is.gd/rBXkA4

www.ingramcontent.com/pod-product-compliance
Lightning Source LLC
Chambersburg PA
CBHW050034180626
46810CB00002B/706